MORTICE
JUSTICE MORT STYLE

Mortice: Justice Mort Style © 2023 A J Wilton

All Rights Reserved. No part of this book may be reproduced in any form or by any electronic or mechanical means including information storage and retrieval systems, without permission in writing from the author. The only exception is by a reviewer, who may quote short excerpts in a review.

This book is a work of fiction. Names, characters, places, and incidents either are products of the author's imagination or are used fictitiously. Any resemblance to actual persons, living or dead, events, or locales is entirely coincidental.

Printed in Australia
Cover and internal design by Shawline Publishing Group Pty Ltd

First printing: September 2023

Shawline Publishing Group Pty Ltd
www.shawlinepublishing.com.au

Paperback ISBN 978-1-9229-9370-0
eBook ISBN 978-1-9229-9382-3

Distributed by Shawline Distribution and Lightningsource Global

A catalogue record for this work is available from the National Library of Australia

More great Shawline titles can be found by scanning the QR code below.
New titles also available through Books@Home Pty Ltd.
Subscribe today at www.booksathome.com.au or scan the QR code below.

MORTICE
JUSTICE MORT STYLE

BOOK TWO

A J WILTON

ALSO BY A J WILTON

You Killed My Wife

DEDICATIONS

I used to work with a bloke named Mort.

A Vietnam Vet, he was a hardworking, no nonsense bloke. Sadly, even with a loving and supportive family, Mort struggled with day to day life after his years serving his country.

This story is dedicated to him and all who have served their countries.

Thank you.

This is an act of fiction, so please forgive me if my imagination doesn't fit with reality, my aim is to entertain not write history!

All characters and events are figments of my imagination.

A special mention to our little mate 'Scout', who I wrote into the story on the day he passed.

ACKNOWLEDGEMENTS

My thanks to the following for their guidance and support.
- My two daughters Shannon and Courtney for their help and guidance
- My wife for her patience!
- To my editor Aidan – thanks - we got there!

1

Smoke on the Water seeps into my brain. *Shit, the phone's ringing!*

I grab it off the bedside table, and a voice I recognise says, 'Ireland?'

'Yes, sir.'

I'm wide awake now. For Major General Charles Rutherford – MGC for short, due to his initials and his love of cricket – to be wide awake and issuing orders at this time of night, something must be amiss.

'There's a plane landing at Archerfield Airport at 6:00 a.m. I need both of you on it. Full kits. Incoming briefing notes by email.'

'Understood, sir. I'll get Pig sorted.'

'Good. See you in a few hours.'

He hangs up. Of course, Suzie's wide awake beside me now. 'What's going on?' she asks.

'Not sure yet. They sent a plane for Pig and me. That's all I know,' I reply as I dial Pig. He answers his phone.

'Wakey wakey,' I say, and get a grunt in response. 'We're on. Full kits. They have a plane landing at 6:00 a.m. at Archerfield.' Archerfield is a small commercial airfield on Brisbane's south side, and the closest to me, either by accident or design. I pause to let Pig digest this, and when he grunts acknowledgement (that's two grunts from my favourite Pig already!), I continue, 'So why don't you pick me up?'

'Okay, I'll swing by around 5:00 a.m. That gives us heaps of time to make sure we aren't late.'

'Done.' I hang up.

Suzie's now sitting up, watching me with a little frown of concern, so I lean over and give her a quick kiss. 'Sorry, Lord and Master is calling.'

Of course, she wants to know way more than I know, and I tell her she knows as much as I do at present. Out of bed, I check my iPad. There's an official Section V email waiting for me, which I flick to Pig before glancing through it. There'll be time to read it once we're on our way, but it looks like we're heading via Canberra to Yass, where they're expecting a major incident from a far-right militia group set up on an isolated farm.

As Suzie has also signed the Official Secrets Act, I toss my iPad to her (gently, of course!) whilst I head to the bathroom. I need to have a good clean-up – I'm not sure when the next one will be. I know, I know, it's not exactly third-world around Yass, but you never know what time might permit!

After a quick shower, I pull out my 'go bag' from the back of the robe, which is always fully packed for occasions exactly like this. I keep a sealing tag in the locks so I know it hasn't been opened, just as a safeguard against 'borrowing' something from it and not replacing it. It has all the essentials – clothes, a spare set of boots, full wet weather gear, snack bars and water bottles. I carry it into the kitchen, where Suzie's making two coffees in travel mugs, one for me and the other for Pig. She's a darling, this one – even a keeper – so of course I tell her this as well. More brownie points, after all!

Then it's down to the gun safe. I pull out my and Pig's weapons of choice, our H&K USP handguns and EF88 assault rifles. Pig doesn't have a gun safe, and since we're now authorised to hold and carry weapons because of our involvement with Section V, we keep them all here. I grab Pig's latest (and new favourite) drone, Bernie. Yes, he names all his drones – however, I can't criticise, as I named my sniper rifle Betsy.

I go back up the stairs into the kitchen, where Suzie's having a coffee. She admits she's unlikely to get back to sleep, and briefs me on what the email said. It isn't a lot more than what I gleaned from my quick glance, simply that there's an anticipated domestic terrorist attack from this far-right paramilitary group, the Southern Cross Resistance, that needs to be snuffed out quickly. No mention of why the Glory Boys from the SAS aren't being called in, but we signed up to serve our country, so like all good soldiers, ours is not to reason why. It's a question I'll be asking when we arrive, though!

At 4:55 a.m., I hear the Camry pull up in the driveway. Suzie and I have a farewell kiss, and I'm told to be careful. 'I still have plans for you!' is her parting shot as I head off, silently closing the door behind me.

Pig has popped the boot open but remains sitting in the driver's seat with a smart-arse smirk on his face. I nearly leave his coffee on the roof, but hey, I'm not the nasty type. Fortunately, the Camry has a big boot, so two duffels, a drone case and two gun cases all squeeze in. I hop into the passenger seat and slip Pig's coffee into the cup holder. We fist bump before he backs out and we're on the road.

At this time of day, Archerfield Airport is only twenty minutes away, so we're nice and early. We lug our gear through the terminal, where there's only a night manager on duty. Thanks to our Section V passes, our security screening is waived, so we sit down and wait.

We're good at waiting. We both had fifteen years of practice whilst serving in the Australian Army at various battlefields around the globe, including two extended tours of duty in Afghanistan. At 5:45 a.m., I get up and wander through to the canteen, which is mainly for the use of pilots and staff, but at this time of the day, who cares?

Whilst waiting for the jug to boil, I text Maria, our part-time colleague, telling her 'You're it for a few days, as duty calls.'

Of course, I get an immediate response – she does have four young kids, so this isn't early for her – saying, 'Lucky shits. Be careful. So, I get to sit in the BIG chair!'

I reply, 'And don't make a mess in it!'

Maria is also ex-army, 1st New Zealand Regiment, and has done some fun tasks for us over time. We're training her in the finer points of our business, so this will be a further learning period for her.

I make four black coffees and go back to join Pig just as the duty manager comes out to say our flight has landed. Out with the duffels, gun cases and coffees we go. And there, coming to a stop in front of us, is a Falcon 7X of the RAAF VIP Squadron.

Pig and I look at each other with raised eyebrows. We sure are moving up the chain!

We head out onto the apron. The young copilot lowers the stairs, and once they're in position, I head up with my load, followed by Pig. Inside, the senior pilot stands at the door to the cockpit. I pass a coffee to him, and he says, 'We do have a full coffee machine on board, so you needn't have bothered.'

I smile. 'I guess we're used to old transports, not these fancy machines.'

'If it hadn't been such an early start, on such short notice, we would've had a steward on board to wait on you hand and foot.'

Wow, I think, *how the other half live!*

'So, you're the famed Mort and Pig,' he continues. 'I'm honoured to meet you both.' We shake all round. The young copilot is looking a bit puzzled, so he says, 'These two have won a few battles you and I would wet ourselves just thinking about, so they deserve the full treatment.' He nods to us. 'I'll get us underway. It's a one hour and forty-five minute flight time, so make yourselves comfy. After take-off, you're welcome to help yourselves to anything in the bar or kitchen.'

Pig and I settle into our seats, strap ourselves in, and await the start of another journey into the unknown.

2

As the plane takes off effortlessly into the awakening sky, I close my eyes. My mind drifts back over the four months since my and Pig's hunt for a bent cop. Suzie – my then-girlfriend, now partner – was kidnapped, and the Queensland State Government was crippled, but Pig and I brought the whole episode to a successful, if dramatic, conclusion. As a consequence, we'd been appointed as members of Section V under the control of Major General Charles Rutherford.

After the dust settled, all three of us took a break up on Fraser Island. When we arrived home, Suzie and I decided to move in together. As Pig was using the second bedroom at that time, a simple swap seemed the best solution. Well, except Suzie wasn't going into the second bedroom, I hasten to add, although it's fair to say she's taken it over with all her 'junk'. I made a bit of a ceremony scanning her thumbprints into our security system, ensuring she understood the significance of it, and making her promise never to roll her eyes about our security again!

Before Pig moved into her apartment, though, she insisted on doing a real tenant interview, which I thoroughly enjoyed sitting on the sidelines of. I guess he must've passed, because he's quite settled there now.

As Suzie and I have adapted to living together, we've had quite a few little battles – over bathrooms, hanging space, cooking, TV remotes, and so on – all of which have been fun. I certainly can't claim to have won many, although I have clung onto my wardrobe (well, a quarter of it!) and the ensuite. I told Suzie she has too much junk for the ensuite, so she's taken over the main bathroom as her own. Along with all the wardrobe space of the second bedroom. But you guys out there know what I mean!

Suzie and I had agreed to prioritise heading up to Bundaberg to spend a weekend with her parents. One public holiday weekend, we headed off just after 10:00 on the Friday morning, making it comfortably to lunch with my dad on Bribie Island on the way. Suzie hadn't met him yet, but they'd spoken a couple of times on the phone.

When we pulled into Dad's driveway, he was busy under the bonnet of his old Nissan Patrol. Here I was thinking he'd be inside getting lunch ready. He popped his head out, wiping his hands on an old oily rag (old habits die hard!).

Suzie jumped out of the car. Before I could introduce them, she gave him a hug, and asked, 'So, what's wrong with the Patrol?'

'Oh, nothing really. Just pottering.'

Suzie poked her head under the bonnet, and they were soon talking about carburettors, points, spark plugs – a foreign language to me! I left them to it and headed inside. Immediately, I smelled fresh fish cooking, and lo and behold, a lady came bustling out of Dad's kitchen. She stopped in her tracks upon seeing me, her hand going up to her mouth.

I smiled and put my hand out. 'Hi, I'm Mort.'

'Lovely to meet you. Chris is always talking about you. I'm Agnes.'

Just then, Dad rushed in behind me, a little rattled, I think, that Agnes and I had met without him introducing us. 'Ah, Mort, Agnes and I have sort of become friends lately, so I thought it would be nice for you to meet her. She offered to cook lunch, which is better than anything I could concoct.'

Of course, I couldn't resist. '*Friends*, ah?' I asked, giving Agnes a wink so she knew I was teasing. Dad was stammering again, so I quickly let him off the hook, reaching out to pull him into a hug. 'That's great, Dad! Hope she doesn't have to clean up after you all the time.' And I added, in a whisper, 'Mum will be pleased for you.'

Once things settled down again, Suzie and Dad were quickly back to chatting about engines, and Patrols in particular. Suzie's passion for the subject was clear for all to see, and Dad must've just been happy to have someone to talk cars with. They'd never been particularly interesting to Mum or me. The lunch of freshly grilled whiting Dad had caught that morning was a delight, but as we had another four-plus hours to get to Bundy, we didn't linger long.

As we exited Dad's home, Suzie piped up, 'I'll drive if you like,' holding her hand out for the keys. I passed them over – as if I had a choice!

Back on the Bruce Highway, I watched Suzie as she gave the Camry some gas and noticed it was pretty responsive. I tried to keep a straight face. To make this easier, I closed my eyes, but the surging of the car told me she was still puzzled. Eventually, she had to say something, and came out with, 'This goes much better than an ordinary Camry. How come?'

Still with my eyes closed, I replied, 'How many Camrys have you driven?'

'None like this. Why?'

I couldn't keep a straight face any longer, so I opened my eyes and, grinning, said, 'It's chipped. All three of my cars are chipped. You don't know when we might need to get somewhere quickly, or disappear quickly.'

'But you drive like a grandfather,' she replied, disgusted.

'Well, I don't like to attract attention and don't see the need to speed when I'm not in a hurry.'

Of course, this concept was totally foreign to Suzie, who had a few speeding tickets racked up. But that wasn't slowing her down – now she knew she had more power than she'd expected.

'Drive like a grandfather' – the cheek of her! I thought.

Only three and a half hours later, we pulled into her parents' driveway. Driving Suzie speed! They lived out of Bundy on a few acres, and her dad still pottered around in his mechanical repair workshop, even though he'd officially retired.

As we exited the car, I could sense the excitement emanating from Suzie. She was clearly thrilled to be home, and – so I liked to think, at least – keen to show me around. She grabbed my hand as her parents, Henry and Caroline, emerged from their veranda and came down the path to greet us. They were followed by the family hound, Rufus, an aging 'bitzer' and beloved member of the family, whose tail was wagging furiously. Suzie quickly ruffled his ears after hugging her parents.

After the greetings, we had an afternoon tea of homemade scones, fresh cream (yes, they have their own cow out back), and strawberry jam. Heaven for a sweet tooth like me! Suzie warned me that if I ate too many, I wouldn't be able to eat my dinner, to which I replied, 'Watch me!' (I almost said 'Yes, Mum' as well.)

Once we'd all had our fill, Suzie dragged me off to show me

the rest of the house. It was a typical country Queenslander, with most of the living upstairs and the laundry and garage downstairs, originally designed to improve air flow in the humid tropical seasons. The tour culminated in her old bedroom, which was still papered with posters of Madonna and Hanson and swimmer Suzie O'Neil – Madam Butterfly, as she was called in her heyday – a local world-class athlete and winner of eight Olympic medals. I pulled Suzie into my arms and whispered, 'So, what secrets could this bed tell me, ah?'

I got a quick peck and a push off. She hurried back out of the room, I suspect a little embarrassed. I reckoned I needed to revisit that question a little later!

In the hall, Caroline caught up with us. 'Mort, I've prepared Nat's old room for you. I hope you don't mind, but the rooms are quite small, so I don't think you could share Suzie's.'

I replied, 'That's fine, Mrs Dunn. I just hope Suzie can cope without me for a couple of nights.' This got me another dig in the ribs.

'Please, call me Caroline. Mrs Dunn sounds so old!'

We wandered outside, and I once again found I was holding Suzie's hand. I swear I didn't know how that happened, but hey, I wasn't fighting it. I was liking it!

Henry joined us as we headed towards the vegie patch, which he appeared to look after, whilst Caroline took care of the lovely shrubs and flower gardens. There were some dozen chooks scratching around, and Caroline said proudly that she hadn't had to buy eggs since the girls were little. So, they sourced their eggs and vegies from their garden, and with a couple of heifers and sheep also grazing in their paddocks, I reckoned their weekly shopping bill was rather light!

Once we'd finished the tour of the gardens, Suzie again grabbed my hand and we headed off towards her dad's workshop, which had a few old stock cars and other wrecks lying around. Suzie made a beeline to the one in best condition, which looked to me like an old-model Holden Commodore. She pulled the bonnet latch up and peered at the engine.

'Does it still go, Dad?' she asked.

'Did the other day when I fired it up,' he replied.

All of a sudden, Suzie was squeezing herself through the driver's window slot (the only way to enter those cars, I'm told). I commented, 'Very ladylike,' getting me a poked tongue once she'd righted herself in the driver's seat.

She strapped herself into the full racing harness, and fired up the engine with a mighty growl. As she dabbed the throttle, I watched the smile on her face. Clearly, she was enjoying herself. Then she engaged first gear and gave it a boot. Powered by the big Chevy 450, she was off with a loud roar. There was a clear path around the workshop, likely a practice track for testing the cars whilst they were being repaired.

Rufus came running down, barking at the loud noise, as Suzie slid sideways around the corner, making Henry and me step back as she buried her foot in the accelerator again. She made four or five laps before coming to a halt and telling me, 'Come on, in you get. I'll give you a ride.'

Of course, I couldn't say no – I wouldn't hear the end of it – so I squeezed my big frame through the window and tried to securely belt myself into the passenger seat. She didn't wait for me to finish. Off we went into the first corner, and she kept her foot down. Hard. I wasn't sure if she was trying to impress me by scaring me, but I wasn't letting anything show!

After another few laps, she slowed down, laughing. She turned the engine off, almost wistful when she said, 'Gee, that was great. Wish I could do that more often.'

I leaned over and gave her a kiss. 'It was great to see you have fun.'

'But I didn't manage to scare you, did I?'

'No,' I replied, 'you know what I've been through. A bit of fast tracking in dirt is exciting, not scary!'

In Afghanistan, I'd survived an IED explosion that tipped our Bushmaster over, crushing Pig's leg. Whilst we tried to save it, we'd then come under heavy enemy fire. I'd been in numerous other battles and firefights that kept me on my toes, most of which Suzie wasn't aware of. Those were a lot more challenging than holding on for dear life whilst Suzie had fun. But I didn't voice that and take her pleasure away.

All of a sudden, the day was ending, so we all wandered back up to the house, where Henry and I settled on the veranda for a beer whilst the girls busied themselves preparing dinner. The rest of the weekend passed quickly. Suzie showed me around her hometown, and we even met a couple of her former school classmates. When it was time to head home, back to Brisbane, Suzie quickly jumped into the driver's seat, so I warned her, 'Don't forget, any speeding tickets are your responsibility.'

Of course, she ignored me.

3

The Thursday morning after our trip to Bundaberg, Pig came into our office as usual and made himself a coffee. Then, unusually, he came and sat across from my desk.

I looked up, surprised, and he said, 'I'm leaving this afternoon – going to Melbourne for the weekend.'

I asked, 'Stacey?' and he nodded. With a big grin, I came around my desk and give him a hug. 'That's great, mate, but… you're sure?'

Almost as long as I'd known him – for fifteen years plus – Pig had been in one relationship. His former partner, George, is in prison, and will be for a few years. Pig and I put him there. It hurt Pig then, as I'm sure it still does.

I asked the obvious question. 'So, you're thinking of swapping teams?'

Pig smiled. 'Well, it won't be the first time. Before I met George, my childhood sweetheart – Tina – and I were inseparable. We grew up as neighbours. Same schools, same everything, really. Lost our virginity together. Everyone just assumed we'd be together for life.'

He stopped, but I couldn't leave it there. 'What happened?'

Pig pulled a face. 'I caught her sleeping with a mate. Apparently, it wasn't the first time. I was heartbroken. I thought we were tight, you know, no problems, but she was "restless", as she put it. So that put paid to that.'

Shaking his head, he took a sip of his coffee. 'I left home shortly after, and moved to the "big smoke". Didn't know a soul here. Went into a pub in the Valley one night. It was a gay bar – not that I knew what a gay bar was back then – and that was where I met George. I'd already signed on to join the army, so I was really just biding my time, waiting to be called up. Then, when I came back on breaks, George always showed me a good time. Our relationship just sort of evolved. No big declarations, or "coming out", or anything. It just quietly happened.'

He shrugged. 'Never said too much when in camp. I would've really copped it back then. Truth be told, I've had a couple of flings since, with both ladies and gents, so I think of myself as bisexual if anything. Not that I'm big on tags, as you well know!'

Damn, I thought, *you think you know someone, and* bang, *they hit you sideways!*

I grab him for another hug. 'Shit, man, I never realised. Always just accepted you as gay.'

He nodded. I remembered the surreptitious phone calls, the quick hang-ups when I entered the office, the dopey look Pig got on his face sometimes. I'd mentioned to Suzie on more than one occasion that he might have a new 'friend'. Suzie, come to think of it, had never said too much, so maybe she knew more than I did. *I need to have a chat with that girlie of mine*, I realised.

I went to get us both fresh coffees. 'So, you and Stacey?'

Stacey and her close friend Christi were 'escorts' who'd got caught up in a police sting. We'd rescued them, hidden them and set them up for a new life down in Melbourne. They both now go to TAFE (technical college) whilst working full time. Christi's doing a bookkeeping course and Stacey has enrolled in a community services course, with the aim of helping young kids from dysfunctional families and from the streets. Good on her too.

Pig nodded. As I sat back down, I asked, 'How do you think it will go?' (Subtlety isn't my strong suit!)

'Well, Stacey and I have discussed it at length, as you might imagine. She says if it's meant to be, it'll work. I'm in no doubt she wants it to work, and so do I.' Smiling, he adds, 'She even says she has the right experience to help me!'

Right then, Suzie came down the stairs. Seeing us sitting together at my desk, she raised an eyebrow.

'Pig's going to Melbourne for the weekend,' I said.

She smiled. 'Great. So, you're going to try it out!'

Clearly, I'd guessed correctly, and she and Pig had been discussing it, but I chose not to comment. It would be good if it worked out for Pig. He deserves someone caring and loving in his life. George could never have been accused of either. But then again, I'm biased, as George and I never got along.

Suzie and Pig chatted a bit more before Suzie headed off to work. Pig and I fist bumped, and I told him, 'Good luck. Go hard!'

I thought he got my double meaning, as he had a slight smile on his face as he headed back to his desk.

That night over dinner, it was my turn to be quizmaster and grill Suzie (after I grilled pork chops for dinner, of course). Suzie confirmed she and Julien, as she insists on calling him, had been talking for a few weeks. He'd been quite open with her about his feelings toward Stacey and had already told her that he was bisexual.

I suddenly remembered the first time Maria saw Pig. She'd come out and said she could get him to 'swap sides'. When I asked

Suzie if Maria knew as well, she confirmed Pig hadn't told her – but apparently, Maria had had a sixth sense about it, and hadn't been surprised when Stacey told her she and Pig were getting on like a house on fire.

It seemed big old muggins here had been the only one who didn't know the big secret of his best mate.

Shit.

*

The following Monday, I texted Pig early, suggesting a breakfast meeting at our favourite local café, Mickle Pickle, at 7:30 a.m. He responded, 'Your shout.'

You see, I was dead keen to know how his weekend went. I hadn't heard from him, even though I'd sent a couple of texts. One said, 'How's it going down there?' The second said, 'So, up or down?' Yes, a bit vulgar, but hey, we're blokes!

Whilst Suzie wouldn't come out and say whether she'd heard from him, I suspected not, as she seemed a bit peeved. I planned to catch up with him before he reached the office and she got hold of him.

Finally, 7:30 arrived, and so did Pig. We sat down with our coffees, and I said, 'So?'

He hummed. I could see he was teasing me by dragging it out, so I crossed my arms. He knows I'm losing patience when I do this.

After taking a sip of coffee, he said, 'You know, there are heaps of great coffee places in Melbourne – they brag about it.'

I sat there just looking at him, arms still folded.

His face broke out into a big smile, and he said, 'Mate, I had a great weekend. Possibly the best weekend of my life. Yes, the sex worked, right from the word go. Stacey helped, of course, but wow

– I couldn't get enough, and I think she was enjoying herself too. She wanted to do things I hadn't even heard about.'

My relief was tangible. I reached across the table to clap him on the back. 'You go, man!'

Right then, my phone buzzed with a text from Suzie. 'Where are you?'

I replied, 'Breakfast meeting.'

She came back, 'Where's Julien, then?'

'Breakfast meeting.'

'You shit!'

Grinning, I said to Pig, 'I suspect we'll see Suzie in a minute.'

I watched the road for the red Mini heading our way. Sure enough, I not only saw but heard it, tyres squealing as she did a U-turn and came roaring back to the car park.

Pig was still smiling. He knew what was going on – me outsmarting Suzie to find out how the weekend went first. Suzie marched into the café, gave me a glare, then said, 'So, how did it go, Julien? I didn't hear anything from you. I've been worried.'

Pig signalled he had a full mouth. His breakfast had been delivered just as Suzie was parking, and he'd stuffed a big forkful in before she entered, possibly suspecting he wouldn't get much time to eat once she arrived.

To add to the moment, I contributed, 'From the little I've learnt, I don't think he had time to send texts. By the way he's devouring his breakfast, maybe he couldn't even eat!'

Suzie just gave me another glare, but I could see Pig smiling. Once he'd eaten enough to take the edge off his hunger, or maybe just to allow the tension to build, he straightened and said, 'We really hit it off, Suz. Stacey was just so much fun to be with.'

'Oh, that's great. But what about… you know?'

'She means the sex, mate,' I said. 'She's just too shy to mention the word!'

I got yet another glare from Suzie. *Gee,* I thought, *I hope I've built up enough brownie points to offset all these glares!*

Pig reached out for Suzie's hand. 'It went well – no problems in that department. Quite the opposite, in fact.'

Again, I piped up. 'What *he* means is they couldn't keep their hands off each other. I remember when we were the same. Don't know where those days have gone now!'

I wasn't sure what reaction I would get, but she blushed a little, took my fingers in hers, and squeezed them. Not too painfully, so I took that as a plus. (Maybe even a good omen for that night!)

'I'm so pleased, and relieved,' she said. 'Having not heard from you, I was thinking the worst. Then when *this* shit' – she pointed a finger at me – 'grabbed you even before you got to the office, it just made everything worse. I'd been waiting for you to come in.' She shook her head. 'So, what else did you get up to?'

'She means other than the sex, mate.'

Another glare headed my way! *Fun.*

Pig explained they had done some sightseeing around the city, taking a few trams and a nice leisurely stroll along the Yarra from their room at the Luxton Hotel, which is right on the river. This was between rain showers and squalls – typical Melbourne weather, with all four seasons in one day!

'It didn't matter where we were,' he said, 'we just had fun together. Christi and her new partner joined us for dinner on Saturday night, at the Meat and Wine Co restaurant in Southbank, just a short walk from our hotel. That went well too. She and Dom seemed very happy.'

I nodded. Whilst we'd been instrumental in saving them from

the corrupt police force in Queensland, I'd never met Christi or Stacey. I'd spoken to them on the phone, but that was all.

'What's next?' I asked. 'When are you seeing each other again?'

'Stace is going to come up in a couple of weeks. She has a break after her upcoming exams, so she might take a sickie on the Friday and come up for a three-day weekend.'

'I'm guessing you'll be applying for a day's leave, then – or are you going to take a sickie too?' I said it with a smile, as Pig knows we don't keep track of his hours. Flexible accounting approach, I call it. (Just don't mention this to the 'dragon' accountant!)

Suzie found her voice again. 'I can't wait to meet Stacey when she comes up. We'll have to go out for dinner, or maybe just have you over for a barbecue. Whatever suits.'

'Might be better if we do the barbecue,' I said. 'That way, you won't be too far from a bed!'

This time, I not only got the glare but a 'Mort!'

However, I couldn't resist one last dig. 'So, mate, you think you can last the day, or will I find you snoozing at your desk – or worse, blushing as you talk to Stacey?'

Pig just smiled. And kept smiling most of the day. Numerous times, I told him to stop it and called him lovesick, but he just kept on smiling. Even Maria's constant teasing didn't faze him. They go at it constantly, which makes for an entertaining workplace. Of course, Maria had warned Pig that Stacey was her friend, so if he did anything wrong, he'd answer to her! She'd given me the same speech when we first met, warning me not to hurt Suzie. Maria – as a friend of Stacey's through her 'babysitting' duties a few months earlier, where she'd kept Stacey and Christi safe whilst the Queensland Police were looking for them – had got Stacey's side of the weekend. And she was happy to tease Pig about what she knew!

I suggested he invite Stacey along to the black-tie event by Paramount Wireless down in Sydney, where they'd be celebrating the three-way merger we'd helped initiate and implement. 'They did mention partners, and Suzie is certainly coming.'

Pig nodded, saying, 'Yeah, we talked about that. Stace even dragged me along dress shopping for a couple of hours *and* warned me I'd be paying for her outfit. It was hundreds of dollars, too.'

Poor Pig, yet to be exposed to the excesses of ladies when it comes to dressing up! I asked, 'Did that include shoe and handbag shopping as well?'

The face he pulled answered that question!

Maria also quietly mentioned to me that Stacey seemed just as excited by the new budding romance. 'She's all giggly and happy on the phone, so that's great. They both seem lovesick!'

There was little doubt we had a love-struck Pig in our midst.

Later that evening, as I finished up the kitchen duties – yes, it was my turn again – Suzie came up to me, gave me a lovely kiss, and whispered, 'You think we're getting stale, ah?'

'Not if you keep this up!'

She kissed me again, a long, lingering kiss, took me by the hand, and headed off to the bedroom. I followed as meekly as a lamb.

*

The next morning was one of our run mornings. Since moving in together, we've both changed our fitness regime, so we run five or ten kilometres three times a week. Suzie heads off to her regular gym on the other mornings, whilst I use the gym downstairs. It's not flash, but it has the basics I need – weights, a punching bag, a rowing machine – to keep in top shape. Fifteen years of army life has instilled the need for fitness in me, and my obsession with it has likely saved my life in many skirmishes. Suzie claims she likes her gym time to be a social occasion, as she chats with others whilst exercising. That's not going to happen training with me!

Pig also uses my gym. We have regular sparring sessions where we get stuck into each other, focusing on body shots to keep our cores strong. These have been known to get a little rugged at times. But hey, all in the name of fitness!

As we jogged along, Suzie and I settled into a comfortable pace that kept us moving along together and still enabled her to chatter. Not me – when I'm running, I need all the breath I can get, so she's used to getting the odd grunt as a reply. Doesn't deter her from talking, though!

We're both entered in the upcoming Gold Coast half-marathon, as is Pig. This will be his last public event before we head off to Canada so he can compete in the Invictus Games. So, I'm dead keen to beat him and have upped my training accordingly. That morning, I started stretching out with three kilometres to go on our ten k route, getting a few complaints from Suzie. But when I said, 'I'll see you at home, then,' she went silent, and bugger me, I couldn't shake her. With a kilometre to go, I stretched out a little more, and she did the same, surging ahead of me.

That won't do.

My turn to surge past her. I knew we were 500 metres from home, and I was really putting in the big strides (and bigger breaths!), hoping I could maintain this pace to the end.

I could sense Suzie just a pace behind me – I certainly wasn't shaking her – then with 200 metres to go, she stretched her long legs and strode past me, hitting our imaginary finish line a couple of metres ahead of me. Fist pump and all!

She turned, breathless, a big smile on her face, and pulled me in for a hug. We were both using each other to stay upright, whilst struggling to regain our breath. It was a few minutes before either of us could say anything, and of course it was Suzie who simply said, 'Ha, I beat you!'

Bugger.

Time to head upstairs for a stretch and shower before breakfast. We often eat out on the lovely big timber deck I'd built off the kitchen and lounge area, over the backyard. The barbecue is set up out there as well, of course, and thanks to the deck's retracting roof, it's an ideal spot for most of the year. When the bottlebrushes are in bloom, we even have colourful rainbow lorikeets chirping away as they busy themselves in the flowers. As beautiful as they are, they're bloody noisy!

Over breakfast, we discussed our times. Both of us achieved personal bests, so we were both a little pumped, and I told her I was already plotting to get her back. She'd already texted Pig to tell him she'd 'knocked the big plodder off this morning!'

Sure enough, before long, he messaged me: 'Beaten by a girl, ah!' My reply: 'Sexist Pig.'

At work, I reminded him that my times were closing in on his. Of course, he replied, 'You don't know what times I'm running.'

I smiled, pulled my phone out, and opened the Strava app. There were my times, Suzie's, and yes, Pig's – plus a few others I followed on Strava. Happily, I pointed out that both Suzie and I were gaining on him over the ten k's. I was pleased with that. He wasn't!

In addition to our exercise routine, Suzie was now back in netball training twice a week. With their season starting soon, this would take up much of her Saturdays as well. Not that I minded having the house to myself – as long as she didn't decree it to be housekeeping time!

Then the thought hit me. Maybe I could use Saturdays to get some secret training in and increase my running speed. I was, after all, in search of payback – and the best place for that would be the Gold Coast half-marathon.

Revenge will be sweet.

4

In need of a bathroom break, I get up and head back to the plane's toilet, then do a stretching routine before resuming my seat – and my daydreaming…

Joey Kovac, younger brother of the Jackals outlaw bikie gang president Anton Kovac, who was killed when we overran their stockade, had become increasingly vocal in vowing revenge for taking down his brother, using Facebook, Twitter, Instagram – you name it. Of course, he had no idea who'd done it, just vowing he and his crew would kill the pigs responsible.

Pig and I had discussed his rants a couple of times, as he seemed to gain strength from the silence of any opposition. After a few weeks of this growing to a crescendo, I said to Pig, 'I've had enough of this dickhead's shit. Shall we go and pay him a visit?'

I got a wicked grin in reply before he said, 'Was hoping you'd ask. I've already sorted his address, so we can go anytime you're ready. I reckon you're getting soft waiting this long!'

Nothing like the present. We were both working on assignments of ethical hacking, identifying companies' digital weak spots and recommending how to rectify them, but nothing as exciting as our other assignments of a few months back. Pig grabbed Bernie, his new drone, and we headed out to the van. He punched the address in Acacia Ridge into the GPS, and we were off, but only after grabbing a fresh coffee each!

We approached the address, an untidy place on a street of mixed homes, some neat, but most unkempt. Joey's house had a car body on the front lawn and a couple of Harleys in the drive, plus an old Holden Commodore parked on the footpath. We cruised down the street, not slowing as we passed, our dashcam capturing all we needed from the road.

Turning into the street behind his, we pulled up near a little park, leaving the van and heading to a nearby picnic table. There, Pig pulled Bernie from his satchel, then flew it off, using his iPad as the control panel. I watched on from mine. Pig and I are authorised drone pilots through Section V, and we can use drones anywhere with impunity – well, not officially, I guess, but that isn't going to stop us!

Pig skimmed Bernie over the rooftops until he recognised Joey's address, then hovered the drone about one metre above the roof. Silently, he placed 'invisible' raindrop glass microphones in the gutters, without anyone noticing. We immediately got some household noise, all male voices with a TV running in the background. Pig turned on the heat sensor, and we confirmed there were three 'bodies' in there. One was easily recognised as Joey by his voice. The other two we would need to check on.

We monitored the goings-on in the house over the next week, and it became clear there were three of them living there, Joey and two brothers, Liam and Brian O'Leary. A bit of background checking and we knew they were all members of the Jackals, who'd had minor run-ins with the law and didn't seem to work, but weren't short of cash. So, we made our own assumptions! We even heard Joey doing one of his rants late one night, which ended up on his Instagram feed. They didn't seem to venture out at night too often, and we suspected they had a billiard table in the lounge, as we frequently heard the clunk of the balls breaking.

After a week of listening, we decided it was time for a late-night visit. Pig joined Suzie and me for dinner, and we didn't head out until 11:30 p.m.

With Suzie and me still settling into living together, I'm sure it was a challenge for her to not ask where we were going and why so late at night. But she managed!

We didn't need much, going unarmed, as we were confident we could handle the three of them. Just as we arrived at our little park behind their address, we heard a fourth voice, one we knew to belong to Carl Goosen, another Jackals member. We looked at each other and shrugged. What was one more? (A bit cocky, aren't we!)

We took our time, and it was a little after 12:30 a.m. when we nodded to each other and exited the van. As always, the courtesy light was turned off, so it didn't light up as we exited. Dressed in black jeans and shirts and work boots, we wouldn't have looked out of place in the neighbourhood – if anyone even saw us!

Scaling the half-demolished wire fence at the back of Joey's house, we slipped around the left side of the house, having decided to enter via the front door. We didn't knock. The door wasn't even locked, so we silently worked our way towards the back lounge, where we could hear them talking and playing pool. We silently checked each room as we headed towards the back – all clear – and we paused in the hallway before entering the room, as we were only hearing three voices. Liam wasn't in the conversation, so with sign language, we guessed he must've been outside having a smoke or something. We looked at each other, shrugged, and nodded. *Let's do this.*

We slipped balaclavas over our heads and casually walked in. Carl had his back to us, poised over his pool cue, so Pig quickly gave him a neck chop, and he went facedown on the table with a *thunk*.

This got Joey and Brian's attention. Joey showed alarm, whereas Brian immediately charged towards me, head down, clearly expecting to tackle me somehow. I waited until he was close enough, sidestepped, and kicked him in the balls. I was wearing steel-capped boots for a reason!

This stopped him dead. He flopped to the ground, screaming and holding his prized possessions in both hands. Joey backed up against the far wall, clearly not so big as his words would convey. We're both large units, and whilst Pig isn't as tall as me, he's 'two pick handles wide', as the old saying goes. (And no lesser authority than Maria reckons he's even better looking than me! Go figure.)

As we spread out, going around the pool table from either end, I noticed a reflection in the rear glass door – Liam was charging me from behind with a baseball bat. At the same time, Pig said 'Six,' warning me of danger from the six o'clock position.

I paused, and Liam tried to bring the bat down on my head, hard. I swayed out of the way. With no impact, he lost his balance and stumbled forward. I grabbed the bat off him (like taking candy from a baby in his unbalanced state!), swivelled around, and cuffed him around the ear. Not lightly, either. He dropped like a stone. I flicked the bat to Pig, as Joey had found some courage and a knife. Pig caught the bat at the top of its arc and brought it down heavily on Joey's wrist, all in one fluid motion.

Bone cracked, followed by a scream. Pig gave Joey another

whack around the ear, and he collapsed to the ground, moaning and holding his broken wrist. Pig kicked the knife clear across the room as I came around the pool table.

I told Joey, 'Stand up.' I got no response, so I leaned down and hauled him up by his wife-beater top. When he still wouldn't stand on his own, I hung him from the pool cue hooks on the wall behind him. He looked rather feeble, hanging there, then I noticed he'd pissed himself as well. Big tough bikie now, ah!

'Joey,' I said, 'we've had a gutful of your whining about your dickhead brother. He got what he deserved. If we come back, so will you. Clear?'

He nodded, tears streaming down his face. I snatched his phone from the pool table, took a photo of him hanging there, wet patch on his jeans and all, and posted it to his Instagram page with the caption 'Actions speak louder than words'. We grabbed the other phones off the table, gave everyone one last glance, and went out the way we came in.

Once in the van, we fist bumped. Job done. In and out in less than five minutes. Didn't even raise a sweat. The benefit of good training and years of practice!

Pity it was a bit late for a beer – work tomorrow, after all.

5

A couple of days later, early in the morning, the office doorbell chimed. Pig and I glanced at the screen and saw it was Mel Black, Queensland Police Commissioner, standing on our doorstep.

I let her in. She was dressed rather casually. Certainly not, it would appear, for any formal occasion. We shook hands all round, and I congratulated her on her promotion, with Pig chiming in as well, and she demurely thanked us.

Pig and I had worked closely with Assistant Commissioner Black, as she was then, during the fiasco of a few months ago. But Mel's serious demeanour didn't bode well this morning. As we walked past Pig's desk, everything straight and particular, Mel studied it before turning to him. 'I assumed from your nickname you were sloppy and untidy. I now realise you're quite the opposite. Very meticulous, in fact.'

As she smiled at Pig, she took a seat in front of my desk. 'Mort, Julien, I won't beat about the bush. My major crime squad is tied up in a frivolous case, where someone unknown' – and she used air quote marks to note 'unknown' here – 'has assaulted Joey Kovac and a couple of his bikie mates.'

She paused here, waiting to see if we would say anything, but we knew better than to open our mouths unnecessarily, so she continued. 'Broke Joey's left wrist and left a few other bruises as well.'

Another pause. She must've been good in the interview room with all those pauses – careless crims would be opening their mouths just to fill the silence!

'Whilst my team may not know of any connection between these boys and you two,' she said, 'I certainly do.'

Again with the pause. Again, we sat there quietly looking at her.

She sighed. 'I understand why you two might've taken matters into your own hands to shut Joey up, but I do *not* want any vigilantes setting up and acting out on my patch.'

Another pause. Another silence. Another sigh. 'So, no more of these attacks, please, or I'll have to pull you two in for questioning. Clear?'

My turn: 'On what grounds would you be pulling us in, Mel?' I deliberately used her abbreviated Christian name, not her title. 'If I'm not mistaken, our names aren't in any documents, or recorded anywhere in relation to the Jackal clubhouse takedown. I could even argue you've breached the confidentiality of our agreement by being here.' This time, it was me leaning over the desk, giving Mel a bit of her own medicine.

She nodded, then opened her arms wide. 'Look at me. I'm dressed for a day of shopping. I walked to the bus stop and ordered my own Uber so no one would recognise me. None of my staff or family know where I am, and I've even turned my phone off so I can't be traced. I'm certainly not here in an official capacity. I took rather extreme lengths to make sure there's no connection between us. I just came to ask nicely – *please* do not do this again.'

Pig and I sat there, silent and motionless. She looked between us, then dug into her rather large handbag, bringing out a manila folder and handing it to me.

'The other reason I've been wanting to catch up with you is this. It was found taped to the bottom of DI Benson's drawer at police headquarters. We've verified the writing and the signature as his. We haven't spoken to the JP who signed it, but he's usually based at Orion Shopping Centre in Springfield.'

She fell silent as I read the document inside the folder. When I'd finished and pulled a face, I passed it over to Pig to read. He found a formal statutory declaration stating: 'If this document is being read, something has happened to me, so I wish to clear my name. I, Dillion John Benson, do formally declare I was not driving my Falcon police car, Registration No 747XZY, when it collided with and killed Liz Ireland. I was not even in the car at the time of the accident.' It was signed by Benson and the Justice of the Peace, with the little circular JP stamp and ID number.

Pig looked at me with raised eyebrows. Mel was watching me closely, trying to gauge my reaction.

'Shit,' I said. 'Never considered he wasn't driving it – all his statements and the others' pointed to him being the driver.'

Silence as they both waited for me to think through the implications of this. Eventually, I started vocalising my thoughts. 'Well, if he wasn't driving, who was? And why so much subterfuge to hide their identity? It can't have been Lancaster. He would've just bullied the coroner the same way he did for Benson, so what was going on back then?'

Mel said, 'Mort, I know investigating this accident is what started this unholy mess, so you deserve to know. I've put DS Chris Morris onto the case, but I will say it isn't a priority, so I don't expect any progress anytime soon.'

'I think you know the way I operate, Mel.' I gave a crooked smile.

'Can you give me Chris's contact details so we can work with him? We might even help him make a big name for himself, cracking this old case.'

She handed over a business card with Chris's contact details. 'I've briefed her, and she's expecting your call. She's reporting to me directly on this and will cooperate with you – within reason.' She gave me the eye.

'Thank you for sharing this with us,' I said. 'It's certainly a turn up. I thought I'd put this to bed. Now it's an even bigger mystery, and frankly, it's not so much about Liz's death anymore – I've buried her in my mind – but there was clearly something sinister going on back then. We need to find out what.'

'Keep Chris in the loop, and she'll keep me posted, but if you ever need to contact me directly, ring me on this number. It's for a new encrypted phone we all use these days.' She pointed to her business card sitting on my desk.

We stood and made our way to the front door. As Pig opened it for her, I handed over the four phones we'd confiscated off Joey and his mates. I didn't say a word, and neither did Mel, as they disappeared into her handbag.

'It's been a pleasure, boys. I only wish we could be open about our friendship, as I could certainly use your help from time to time. Good luck with this new investigation too. I'm intrigued, and concerned about where it might lead.'

Pig and I nodded. A smile slipped across her face. 'Loved the caption, by the way!'

As we both headed towards the coffee machine, Pig said, 'Shit, that's come out of left field. When you killed Benson, I thought that was *quid pro quo*.'

We made fresh coffees and both headed back to my desk to

ponder Mel's bombshell. We rehashed the details of who might've been driving and why there'd been so much subterfuge to hide it, then started making a list of objectives.

- Interview former DS Fleming, Lancaster's 2IC in the crooked cadre of police we'd exposed and taken down. (He and the other surviving members of the cadre, former DCs Josh Armitage and Byron Bruce, are all serving time in prison with no likelihood of parole anytime soon.)
- Interview the JP who witnessed the statutory declaration.
- Go back through Lancaster's bank accounts around the time of the accident, looking for large or unusual transactions.
- See if we could track where Benson and Lancaster's police cars were prior to and after the accident.

We discussed how we could do this final objective. We – well, I – had blown Lancaster's Falcon to smithereens (with a rocket, no less – yes, we did have some fun back then!), so we knew there'd be no tracing it back. Then Pig suggested it was highly probable that all police vehicles were tracked by IVMS (in-vehicle monitoring systems), so we agreed we needed to find their service provider and access this information from their database.

I then remembered I'd followed Benson to a meeting with a woman at an apartment on Regina Street, Stones Corner, in the early days. We decided we needed to find out her name and do some backgrounding on her before having a chat with her too.

That was enough to make a start, and I texted DS Chris Morris to set up a meet. Pig and I were still both shaking our heads at this left-field development. It simply didn't make any sense!

6

My reverie is interrupted by the sound of the Falcon RAAF VIP jet's wheels coming down as we approach Canberra Airport. I glance over to see that Pig is wide awake. He gives me a slight grin, letting me know he knows I've been dozing. There are no flies on this Pig!

The Falcon makes a silky-smooth landing, so I comment, 'Much better than the old Hercules transports,' and get a nod in reply.

The plane taxis away from the main terminal and comes to a halt near an old storage hanger. Once the stairs are down, we step down onto the apron, after thanking the pilots. Facing us are two white Toyota Land Cruiser 200 Series wagons, full-tint and dusty as, so clearly driven some distance to fetch us. Standing in front of them is MGC himself, along with another couple of soldiers, though none of them are in uniform. Interesting.

Instead of saluting, as we have done for the last fifteen years, we nod to MGC. 'Good morning, sir,' we say, and shake hands. He introduces us to Captain Robert Lowe, his adjutant, and his driver, Frank Pearson, whom I recognise from my visit to Canberra earlier in the year.

'Robert,' MGC says, 'you drive the second car back with their gear so I can brief them on the way to Yass.'

Clearly put out by being used as a driver, Robert reluctantly helps us stow our luggage in the back of the Cruiser. Pig jumps in the front with Frank, whilst MGC and I take the rear seats. MGC says, 'First stop coffee, I think, Frank,' to nods all round.

Frank finds a coffee shop at the servo on the exit road from the airport, and Pig and I snaffle a couple of muffins as well. We need sustenance, and we can't be sure when the next opportunity will present itself. We're just pigs, really (excuse the pun!).

Once we're underway, MGC unfolds an ordnance map, laying it out as best he can in the confines of the Cruiser. 'This outfit is hardly worthy of the name,' he says. 'They call themselves the Southern Cross Resistance. They're a motley crew of misfits, but we know them to be armed, trained, and supposedly planning a domestic terrorist event right here in Canberra, according to intel being gathered through the Australian Cyber Security Centre.'

'How many of them?' I ask.

'We've counted about fifteen of them, but their homestead's surrounded by five hundred metres of cleared earth, and they've shot down the drone we put up, so we can't really say for certain.'

'What about arms?'

'Again, we aren't sure, but they have regular shooting sessions. In fact, that's how we heard of them. One of the neighbouring farmers contacted police to tell them there was a lot of shooting going on in the property. It's called Kirkcaldy after the original settlers' hometown in Scotland. It was bought by a trustee company, set up by accountants, so we don't really know who the beneficial owner is yet. We suspect it's one Joseph Smith, who was quite loud in his anti-establishment criticism a few years back. We're still trying to track all this down, as it's only come to light in the last few weeks.'

MGC shakes his head. 'Rather a coincidence,' he continues, 'getting a message from the local Yass police about the same time as the Cyber Security Centre started hearing propaganda and threats being transmitted by phone. We've accessed their WhatsApp, so we're privy to what they think they're saying in secret. This is where we've learnt of their plans.'

Pig beats me to it. 'What *are* their plans?'

MGC is silent for a few moments. 'In a couple of weeks, it's Remembrance Day. As always, there's going to be a commemoration service at the war memorial. They're planning an open raid on the service, gunning down as many people as they can, before barricading themselves inside to claim the memorial as their own. Their belief being that Remembrance Day has been desecrated by all the "woke nonsense" and that it's up to them to restore it to its rightful place of honour. Not sure how killing innocents respects Remembrance Day, but that's their plan.'

'Okay, but why us and not the SAS Glory Boys?' This time, it's me asking the question.

'We need to be more subtle than the brigade. Small force, quiet infiltration. Stop them in their tracks before they gather any further momentum.'

I turn to Pig. 'Good to know we're more subtle than the SAS, ah!' This gets smiles from Pig, MGC, and Frank, who's clearly listening intently as well.

MGC continues. 'We have live surveillance of their property – well, at least their driveway. The farm is some three thousand acres, and it's still a working sheep station, so some of these people do know their way around the land. We believe they've installed electric fences and surveillance approximately one kilometre out from the homestead. Some areas even have tripwires. The country around Yass is, if you're not familiar, rather hilly but not mountainous, and we suspect they've set up surveillance from some of the higher points on their farm. All in all, we're unsure how we can gain access for a surprise attack.'

Pig pipes up. 'Just send in the air force on a training run. Boom, problem gone!' Of course, he's smiling as he says it, but MGC doesn't respond.

We travel in silence for a little while, before MGC tells us, 'We're all staying at the Yass Motel. That'll be our first stop, so you can drop your gear. Then we'll proceed to what I think is our best observation point, as I'm keen for your input on how we can access the property and shut this down quietly.'

An hour or so later, Frank pulls the Cruiser to a stop. We're on a gravel road, having turned off the bitumen some ten kilometres earlier. He's stopped in the middle of a wooded area, mainly gum trees, with dense smaller scrubby bushes at ground level. Robert parks the second Cruiser behind us as MGC pulls the map out and spreads it out on the bonnet. We all stand around whilst he points out our position. 'We're approximately one kilometre from the homestead. This stand of bush continues for nearly five hundred metres in that direction,' he says, gesturing to the left, 'then it's open paddocks right around the homestead, which sits on a slight rise, so it has good 360-degree views. Easy to monitor and difficult to attack or sneak up on.'

Robert takes up the narrative. 'On the far side of these trees, they have CCTV set up. They've done a thorough job, without blind spots, and have likely placed tripwires as well. It isn't possible to access the property undetected, and all other directions are even more difficult.'

Pig and I share a look. 'What else can you tell us?' I ask.

MGC says, 'Not much. We're a bit stuck. No sense sending in another drone – they can monitor them, and as Robert says, they seem to have set up an impenetrable barrier to prevent anyone getting too close.'

'Okay, we' – I indicate Pig and myself – 'will go and have a look at their setup ourselves.'

Robert is immediately defensive. 'I told you it can't be bypassed. You're just wasting time here.'

I shrug, and MGC adds, 'Well, that's why I called you boys in, so we'll wait here for you.'

Robert flushes and looks angry at having his assessment questioned. Too bad.

'We won't take any comms with us,' I say. 'If they have CCTV coverage, it's possible they have audio as well.' I gather from the look on Robert's face he hadn't thought of that.

Pig and I head off back along the road, checking the verge for any sign of car or motorbike tracks through the scrub and trees. There are a couple of stock or wildlife trails, but no sign of vehicle usage. Once satisfied of this, we head in slowly along one of the animal trails, checking for tripwires and cameras mounted in the trees. I'm in front, checking for tripwires with a small but powerful magnet I hold out in front of me, pointing to the ground. Whilst not foolproof, as they could use plastic wire, it's certainly better than nothing and has proved useful in the past. Pig, behind me, is looking for hidden cameras with his excellent eyesight.

After following the trail for nearly two hundred metres, I stop as the magnet starts tugging towards the ground. There, about a metre in front of me, is a tripwire set thirty centimetres off the ground. Then I see another just after it, higher, this one about fifty centimetres. They're both coated with brown plastic and nearly invisible. But we have them. I point them out to Pig, who nods. We stay where we are, suspecting this will be the start of their barrier.

A couple of minutes later, Pig taps me on the shoulder and points to a camera mounted in a big gum tree off to our left. We move off the track to have a closer look at the camera and its range of vision. It's slow going, as we're trying to force our way through the scrub without leaving any impression, in case this mob comes out and does routine checks on their equipment. I'm thinking, *The setting and terrain could hardly be any more different from Afghanistan!*

Once we arrive behind the camera, Pig indicates he's going to climb up the closest tree behind it, as he wants to see its field of vision, and hopefully spot the next camera in each direction. I point to myself and raise an eyebrow, implying I should go instead. But, as always, he declines my offer. Truth be told, with his superior eyesight, he is the best option, and his false leg has never been an issue. He can even run faster than me with his special curved running 'blade' – yes, just like the Blade Runner!

But I digress. Pig is now comfortably sitting on a branch at a similar height to the camera. I watch as he moves his phone around, taking photos at different angles. Once happy with that, he stands up and indicates to the left, so I know he can see the next camera that way as well. After taking a few more photos, he clambers down. We continue moving through the undergrowth, keeping it slow as to not leave a trail of broken branches that would show our passing.

When we reach the next camera, 250 metres away, Pig once again clambers up an adjoining tree and replicates his pattern, taking plenty of photos and identifying the next camera to the left.

This goes on for a couple of hours, as it's a long and thick area of scrub. When finished, we're over five hundred metres to the right of the Cruisers, where MGC and the others are still waiting. Before we head back to them, we stop, clear of the bush on the road verge, so Pig can brief me on what he found.

'I reckon that second camera has a blind spot of about ten metres,' he says. 'It's a big tree, and they've mounted the camera slightly to the left, so the trunk will hide the far right of its coverage area. I can't be certain until I check the range of the camera, though. I have the name and model from the photos, so I'll do that at the cars, or back in Yass. If I'm right and we stay in that blind spot, say for a hundred metres, we'll be clear of the bush and past their primary barrier – assuming we don't miss any more tripwires, of course!'

'Okay, let's go back and let MGC know. You happy to put your drone up to have a look-see?'

'Yeah, no way these hillbillies will find it. It's designed as a stealth drone, with the same anti-radar coatings they use on the most sophisticated stealth bombers these days. We should also be able to place some of our raindrop mics near the doors and windows.'

We head back down the road towards MGC and his small team. As soon as we arrive, he asks us if we've finished, and I nod and say, 'For now.'

He replies, 'Good. We've been out here too long. Let's head back the long way, so we aren't seen going back past their driveway. I'm sure they're monitoring that. We'll reconvene at 8 p.m. for dinner and to discuss your thoughts.'

'Sounds like a plan, sir,' I reply. 'That'll give us time to research a couple of things, which should make our discussion more meaningful.'

7

When 8 p.m. comes, we're all seated at a large table in the dining room. Pig comments, 'No one else around?'

MGC replies, 'No, I had them book the whole motel, so we won't be disturbed or interrupted.'

'I hope none of the staff are friendly with those out at Kirkcaldy,' I say, getting me a look from MGC!

Once we have our drinks (four beers, so a simple order), MGC is straight down to business. 'Okay, what have you discovered?'

I take the lead. 'We found their CCTV cameras are roughly two hundred and fifty metres apart, well inside the timber line. They're using SPRO cameras, a good solid infrared unit, which works in both day and night and has a normal range of four hundred metres. However, in most of their positioning, this is dramatically reduced by the scrub and trees in the immediate vicinity.'

Robert interrupts. 'How do you know what brand the cameras are?'

'I climbed a tree and had a look,' Pig says, with a look of contempt. Robert's attitude is starting to annoy us both. Seemingly, he sees himself as the senior officer, who should therefore be in charge. That's not going to happen! As far as I'm concerned, he's a greenhorn, and I'll treat him as such. Frankly, I thought MGC would've wised him up by now.

I continue, 'But what's most important is that the positioning of one camera in particular leaves a blind spot that we should be able to squeeze through.'

Pig says, 'Yeah, the second camera from the left is attached to a large gum about fifty centimetres in diameter. They have it mounted slightly to the left, so with this camera model's narrow angle, all they'll be seeing in the right half is the tree trunk. Therefore, as long as we stay within this three to four metre line and keep the tree trunk between us and the camera, we should be good to go.'

Robert speaks again. 'Should be or will be?'

This time, it's MGC who shuts him down with a look.

'We also found two tripwires, but didn't explore past the cameras for obvious reasons,' I say. 'Pig and I will go back early in the morning, leaving here around 1:30. We want to see what sort of routine they have for overnight security – what sentries or patrols are about. We'll also launch a drone to check the homestead and outbuildings.'

'I told you,' Robert again butts in, 'they shot down the last drone, so sending in another one will only alert them that we're still looking.'

Pig beats me to it, giving Robert a glare. 'My drones are built from the same materials as the latest stealth bombers – they're invisible and totally silent. They carry infrared and heat-seeking sensors, so we'll get a true body count, and we also plan on placing some mics near the doors and windows.'

'We don't buy our drones at Harvey Norman, Robert,' I add. 'These are the latest high-tech units, direct from the manufacturer overseas and not usually available for sale, but we have a few friends in high places who owe us big time for past works.' Taking a sip of my beer, I pause, then look to MGC. 'Instead of going back out in a Cruiser, though, can you organise a Telstra van, or something? Something no one will take any notice of, even at 2:00 in the morning.'

MGC gives a nod to Frank, who grabs his phone and leaves to make arrangements. Our main courses arrive – steak for Pig and me, lamb chops for MGC and Frank, whilst Robert has gone for some salad thing. Frank is quickly back at the table, confirming that a Telstra van will be dropped off before 10 p.m. tonight.

Good support and logistics, I think.

'I'd like you to take Robert with you,' MGC says, turning back to us. 'He's new to the field, and has a lot to learn. He'll benefit greatly from seeing your detailed planning in progress.'

Robert looks far from impressed.

'With due respect, sir,' I quickly respond, 'a third is unnecessary for this type of surveillance. You can all watch the video feed from here. In fact, we have our drones all set up so their feed automatically uploads to our cloud-based server. We'll set up a link so you can access it in real time, or on delay if you need your beauty sleep.'

This time, it's me getting the eye from MGC, but I look directly back at him, not giving an inch.

'Hmm,' he says. 'Okay, let's proceed on that basis. You two head out. What time will you get back?'

'We'll likely stay and watch their early morning routine, so we should be back for breakfast,' I say.

'So, this drone of yours will last three to four hours, will it?' he asks.

'No,' I reply. 'Two hours max, but we have spare batteries, and once all the mics are in place, we'll hear everything that's being said anyway.'

He nods as our coffee is served to complete the meal. Pig and I excuse ourselves, taking extra coffees for the morning and heading for a little shuteye before our early start. As we leave, Frank says he'll slip the Telstra van keys under our door.

I make a quick call to Suzie, and of course, she asks a hundred questions that I don't answer. She's going to have to learn to live with that! When I come back into the room, I notice Pig quickly putting his phone away. I ask, 'Stacey?' and he smiles.

Good, I think!

*

At 2:00 the next morning, we're off with coffees in hand. The road is deserted. We decide to take the long way so we don't need to go past the entrance to Kirkcaldy. An hour later, we coast to a stop not far from where we parked last night.

Pig and I have worked together as a team for many years, often in difficult and dangerous environments, so we don't need to say much. We both know what the other is thinking. This morning is no different – Pig grabs his drone case out of the van, and whilst he prepares to launch it, I do a quick reconnoitre of the surrounds to ensure we don't have any guests.

Pig flies the drone in ever-increasing circles, starting at our location with the infrared and heat sensors on, checking just to make sure no one is hiding away. All clear. He takes it up higher and heads towards the homestead. We both have high-definition headsets on and are watching our separate iPad screens. As the drone approaches the homestead, we notice a lone guard patrolling (make that wandering!) around. Pig halts the drone where it is so we can time and track each circuit. It takes him just under six minutes for each circuit, meaning we'll have less than three minutes to rise from cover and sprint the 500 metres to the homestead when the time comes. Just as well we're both keen runners!

Once we know his pattern, Pig takes the drone over the top of the homestead. The heat sensors tell us there are only three bodies in the house itself, so Pig moves it over the top of the shearers' quarters. Sure enough, this is where the bulk of the bodies are (shouldn't call them 'bodies' just yet, should I?), as we can count twelve heat signatures, with ten guys in what looks like one large dormitory room and another two in an adjoining room.

After checking to see where the sentry is and waiting a minute until he's passed, Pig lowers the drone over the gutter above the entrance to the shearers' quarters. He positions a raindrop mic there, then does the same above the window of the dormitory.

We immediately know the mics are working, as we get assailed by snoring and heavy breathing and the occasional fart. But no voices, and we haven't sensed any movement either. Good to know there aren't any insomniacs.

Pig brings the drone slowly back to us at low level, activating the magnet mounted on the unit so we can search for tripwires or other traps. Nothing stands out, but we only focus on the open country, as we won't have time to be too cautious as we sprint across it. We'll search for tripwires hidden in the undergrowth as part of our access, which will be slow anyway as we avoid the cameras.

Pig quickly loads two more mics onto the drone and replaces the battery just to be safe. Off it zooms again. This time, the first mic goes over the window to the main living room – we have the house layout, as MGC had obtained it from the local real estate agent. Pig places the other mic over the kitchen window. Our well-proven theory is that we'll hear more through open windows than we will from doorways. The drone can only carry two mics at a time, so as soon as these two are deployed, it's back to base to collect the last pair. They go above both doors to the house.

Job done, Pig moves the drone in a grid pattern across the open ground, looking for any hidey-holes where we can take refuge if our stealthy approach comes unstuck. Other than a dam off to our right, we find nothing useful, but it's good to know we have this backstop if need be.

We continue to monitor the sentry (though I may be doing the term *sentry* a disservice by calling this bloke that) as he wanders around. He doesn't look anywhere but where his feet are heading, so he'll be any easy target. We're confident he'll be on duty this time tomorrow morning, as duties are usually set weekly from a Sunday.

Whilst we wait for them to wake and rise, Pig takes the drone up and checks out the two highest points closest to the homestead to see if there are any signs of protection up there, such as long-range cameras. But there's nothing out of the ordinary, so he moves it back to the homestead.

The first stirrings are at 5:30 a.m., with a couple coming out of the shearers' quarters and one from the house. They all congregate at the side of the homestead for a smoke, before heading back in at 6:00 when the whole camp is waking.

We decide that's enough for now and Pig brings the drone home. As he busies himself repacking it, I climb a large wattle tree and secure an aerial as high as I can. This will act as a repeater for the audio from the mics, which will automatically upload to our cloud base and then on to whoever we authorise.

All done. We fist bump and head back to town, just as the first glimmer of dawn lightens the horizon. On the way in, we discuss a basic plan, agreeing that a team of three is a minimum. Thus, to use Pig's words, we'll have to 'hold Robert's hand', as we're both sure MGC will expect Robert to be the third team member.

*

As planned, we reconvene in the dining room at 8:00 a.m. for breakfast. Before coming in, Pig and I listened to the morning routine out at Kirkcaldy, but didn't learn too much more.

'I gather everything worked okay,' MGC says. 'I've heard some of the chatter from the homestead, so clearly your mics are in place.'

By the time they've ordered their breakfasts, Pig and I have finished ours, so we're now on our second coffees. I give them a full debrief, at the end of which MGC says, 'So, your plan?'

'We'll be ready to go in tonight, around midnight,' I say. 'We want to give ourselves two hours to get through the tripwires whilst avoiding the cameras. It's likely to be belly crawling to avoid too much bush movement, and we want to rest up before making our dash across the open space. The sentry takes roughly six minutes to walk around, so we need to cover those five hundred metres in under three minutes.' I gesture to Pig. 'We're in training, so don't see a problem with that.'

MGC turns to Robert. 'What about you? Can you get up from the crawl position and cover five hundred metres in under three minutes?'

'I average five kilometres in twenty-five minutes, so reckon I'm good.' I give him a thumbs up as encouragement.

'Okay, proceed with your plan,' MGC says.

'Once behind the wall, Pig and, we assume, Robert' – I raise an eyebrow at MGC, who nods – 'will take positions outside the shearers' quarters. I'll wait on the sentry to come around the corner and take him out. I'll then move to the main homestead entrance and, hopefully quietly and quickly, incapacitate the three in the house, who are likely Joseph Smith, the leader of Southern Cross Resistance, and his two lieutenants, Bryce Howard and Jeremy Cathcourt-Smythe.'

I run my finger along the table, tracing out paths on an imaginary map. 'Once that's done, Pig and Robert will enter the shearers' quarters and take the others prisoner. I'll be able to come in as backup if needed. As a safeguard, we'll have the drone overhead with a small explosive device that we can detonate as a distraction. If we start our run around 2:00 a.m., it should be all settled and under control within the hour. We'll be back here for breakfast.'

MGC gives a snort (see, not only Pig gets to snort!), knowing full well that something is likely to go wrong, making the outcome no less certain, but more complicated. He sits there sipping his coffee, obviously thinking through the plan, before firing off his questions.

'Is three of you enough?'

'Yes, sir, we believe so,' I answer.

'Weapons?'

'Our EF88 assault rifles and sidearms should be sufficient.'

'You don't need more time to prepare or do further reconnaissance?'

'It's a simple assault and seizure, sir. Not saying something can't go wrong, but it should be fairly routine.'

'Risks?'

'One, being spotted by the cameras. Two, being spotted crossing the open ground. Three, failing to secure the sentry. Four, someone being awake in either the house or the shearers' quarters and raising the alarm.'

I lean back in my chair. 'We've identified a dam two hundred metres to the right, where we'll get protection if it becomes necessary. Also, Pig and I will be in full bulletproof outfits, so we're not likely to stop until we finish the mission. It'll be different for Robert; he'll need to desist if it turns into a clusterfuck. Worst case, it's a diabolical failure, and you have to call in the Glory Boys after all.'

Another pause as MGC contemplates it all, then, 'Very well, let's put this into action tonight. Robert, what's the weather forecast?'

Robert is clearly taken aback by this request, so I reply, 'According to the ABC, tonight's going to be clear with an overnight low of six degrees, no rain or fog forecast. Moon will be bright, so we're good to go. Pig and I will give our weapons and equipment the once-over this morning, then have a quick nap before popping back out to the access point. We want to inspect our planned route through the bush in daylight and tag it so we can easily identify it in the dark. Then we'll head back to bed for a bit more sleep until 10 p.m., to hit the road around 11. That suit you, sir? And Robert?'

MGC nods. 'Robert, whilst I acknowledge you are the senior officer, the team leader is Mort, followed by Julien. You are to follow their instructions immediately and without question. Are we clear?'

'Yes, sir,' says Robert, who seemed to have come to that conclusion himself.

I say, 'Welcome aboard. You'll be in the number two spot. I'll be leading, with Pig "tail-end Charlie". Bear in mind, since Pig and I have full bulletproof clothing, in any action we're likely to take rather aggressive manoeuvres, whilst you'll need to be more circumspect. Understood?'

'Yes.' You can almost hear the 'sir,' but Robert restrains himself. 'How did you get full bulletproof outfits? I didn't know they were available.'

I reply, 'They aren't. Ours were provided by the Yanks a few years ago, when we did a couple of little jobs for them, but still work pretty well. We gave them quite a test out in Brisbane a few months ago.'

MGC is watching this little interplay closely. He, of course, knows about our suits, but still hasn't heard the full story of how we got them. I claimed I was bound by the Official Secrets Act when he quizzed me last time!

'Robert, you coming back out with us this afternoon?' I ask.

He looks at MGC. 'Sir?'

'Yes, it'll be a further learning experience for you.'

'Good,' Pig says. 'You can drive.'

*

We reassemble at 1:00 p.m. for a quick lunch before Robert, Pig and I head off for one last reconnaissance. We arrive at our planned entry point and Pig quickly puts his drone up to ensure we have no one sniffing around. All clear.

I climb the tree and sit astride the branch just above the camera, so I can guide Pig into the channels where we'll remain hidden from it. Pig puts little dabs of iridescent green paint on the leaves, which we'll easily be able to spot with our night vison goggles, but will remain difficult to see in daylight. Robert stays back at the starting point, watching and learning.

It doesn't take long. We're soon back in the Cruiser, heading to town. Pig and I discuss our plans in a little more detail on the drive back, but there's not much more to do, other than prepare interjoined zip ties as ready-made handcuffs – and, in my case, four strips of tape to cover the mouths of the sentry and my hopefully sleeping targets.

8

As planned, we arrive back at our designated start point at midnight. Pig launches the drone. We find the iridescent markers we'd painted earlier and follow them, being careful to avoid the two tripwires we'd already identified.

Afterwards, the going gets a little tougher. The undergrowth becomes quite dense, and we belly crawl through some sections. Only when we're getting close to the cleared land can we stand up and walk, though we still go slow, half-crouching. I identify a third tripwire, but Robert isn't paying attention, obviously, as it's only Pig firmly grabbing his shoulder mid-stride that stops him from bringing his foot down on it. I sense the disturbance behind me, so you can imagine the filthy look he gets from both directions.

Once we reach the clearing, we again settle down on our bellies and remain inside the line of the scrub, surveying the ground ahead of us. We're ahead of our timeline, as we're in position by 1:45 a.m. We allow the sentry to do five circuits whilst we lie waiting to see if there are any changes to his routine. Other than stopping once to light a cigarette, his routine remains unchanged.

Once we're all ready, and the sentry is heading towards the corner that'll take him out of our sight for three minutes, we stand

and start moving cautiously forward, still checking for any further tripwires. Never hurts to be too cautious, after all.

The sentry hits the corner, and we're off – three silent, menacing figures armed to the teeth at a full run across the open ground. We know this is one of our biggest risks. If someone is awake and looking out the window, our movement may be noticed.

We hit the corner under our three-minute time and all slip down into a crouch. I peer back around the corner, down almost at ground level, and see our sentry sauntering along, smoking another cigarette. I wave the other two on to their posts as I settle behind the bushy plants running beside the building, which give me a semblance of cover. I bring my breathing down to a bare minimum, similar to what's needed to take a sniper shot, which makes it a lot harder to hear.

I hear the sentry's footsteps before he turns the corner, taking another puff on his cigarette. He walks straight past me. I rise up silently behind him, and my hands close around his neck, shutting off his windpipe so quickly he can't make a sound before he slips into unconsciousness. A strip of tape over his mouth and a pair of zip-tie handcuffs around his wrists, and it's one down, fifteen to go!

I give a soft bird whistle, so Pig and Robert know step one is over. Rapidly and silently, I move through the kitchen door, which is right next to where I disabled the sentry, and down the hallway, into the first bedroom on the right. As expected, there's one body inside. I follow the same procedure, digging my hands around his throat and squeezing the pressure points, and he too is in la-la land. Tape placed, zip ties tightened, move on. The next two bedrooms are just as straightforward.

After I give another low whistle, I hear Pig saying, 'Righty-o, boys, rise and shine,' at the same time as he and Robert arm their guns, which always sounds ominous in the dark and quiet!

I quickly head their way, back through the kitchen, knowing there's every chance someone will want to be a hero. As I exit the house, I see a figure sneaking up on the main entrance to the shearers' quarters from the back. He's armed.

I don't hesitate, firing a single round into his left knee. Down he goes – I don't miss.

I kick his gun away as he lies there, screaming. I do him and everyone else a favour and give him a clip around the ear with the butt of my assault rifle. Silence returns.

Stepping into the shearers' quarters, I say, 'Anyone else fancy their chances?'

Pig and Robert are standing alert. I nod to them both, so Pig tells one of the captives, 'Carry on. Remember, we'll be checking to make sure their cuffs are on properly. You might meet the same fate as your mate outside if they aren't.'

As we'd agreed, instead of increasing the risks by putting all the handcuffs on ourselves, we get one of them to do it. This man, chosen at random, once again busies himself cuffing his mates. They'd all been forced to turn around and face the rear wall, so they have their backs to us. Robert goes along behind to check that each set of handcuffs are nice and tight.

Once he's finished, I go outside and call MGC to report that all's in order and under control. He confirms the NSW and federal joint police force are on standby, then says, 'I heard one shot. Is anyone injured?'

'Yes,' I reply. 'One down with a bullet to the knee. He's unconscious.'

'All right, I'll send in medics as well.'

I go back into the shearers' quarters. Pig orders all the prisoners to sit on the floor with their legs crossed, thus making it much harder for them to escape. As they move, I recognise Lenny Leggs, a one-time member of our Army unit, who says to Pig, 'Shit, I thought you two had retired.'

Pig answers, 'You must've heard wrong, Lenny. What the hell are you doing tied up with this mob of losers?'

He smiles and shrugs. 'Seemed like a good idea at the time – three good feeds a day and a roof over my head.'

All three of us stand guard until MGC comes over the radio, saying he and the police convoy are entering the gates, with an ETA of five minutes. Pig and I prepare to leave the way we came, as we don't want to be recognised as having been part of the action. Robert moves back further, giving him a better view of the whole group, and we step out the door, striding back to our starting point. Pig might have a prosthetic leg, but he's still quicker than me – bugger it!

We make it comfortably, then stay hidden in the scrub to make sure there are no break outs. When we see the police convoy approaching the homestead, we move back through the scrub, again avoiding the tripwires and staying in the camera's blind spot. Within minutes, we're in the Cruiser and headed back to Yass – after a fist bump, of course – job done.

9

After a big breakfast, Pig and I hit the sack for a few hours' sleep, before MGC wakes me on the phone to suggest a meet and debrief in the dining room for lunch. Pig, of course, rose with the sound of the phone ringing. The cheeky shit jumped in the shower ahead of me, too.

When we enter the dining room just before 1:00 p.m., MGC, Robert, and Frank are already in there. MGC gets up and comes around the table to shake our hands. 'Good job, nice tidy outcome, so thank you both.'

'Thanks, sir,' Pig and I chorus.

We also shake hands with Robert. I tell him, 'Well done – but you nearly blew it.'

He looks sheepish and explains to MGC and Frank, 'I nearly stood on a tripwire, but Pig stopped me.'

MGC's response is, 'Well, I hope you learn from it, because you won't always have a team as good as these two to save you.'

We take our seats. With the waitress hovering, we study our menus whilst the others order. I decide on an Angus beef burger, but Pig goes the whole hog (get it?), ordering a rare T-bone.

MGC then recaps what's happened since we left the scene. The joint police task force took over and have just held a press conference where they claimed the credit for breaking up a 'domestic terror group'. There were questions from the police commanders about the raid, but MGC stared them down, and they tidied up the story to suit. Apparently, the man I shot will recover okay, but will always have a limp. Fine by me.

MGC then asks for a full debrief, which takes most of lunchtime to complete, including all his questions. As we near the end of our meal, MGC advises he's ordered the VIP Falcon to take us back to Brisbane for 4:00 p.m., so we'll be back home for dinner tonight.

Good deal, I think.

As we break up, MGC once again thanks us for our efforts, and I reply with a smile, 'Our pleasure, sir. We'll send you our bill.' A friendly reminder we get paid for this shit now, and not on army pay rates, either!

He nods. 'Frank will be ready to leave around 2:45 p.m. to take you back to Canberra Airport, as Robert and I will be staying on here a bit longer yet.'

Pig and I fist bump as we head back to our room to pack – after grabbing a coffee to go, of course. I text Suzie to let her know I'll be home for dinner and that it's her turn to cook. I get a heart as a reply, followed by, 'Should I watch the news?', which I ignore!

The flight back from Canberra is uneventful. We have different pilots, along with a steward this time to look after our needs. It's all very relaxed and comfortable.

On the drive home, I remind Pig he only has four months to up his training before the Invictus Games. Now, he's been formally included in the Australian team for the 400-metre, 1500-metre, and 10,000-metre events. He in turn reminds me that he's been running four to five days a week for months. But we do agree we'll start training together at Murarrie Recreational Ground next week. I promise to have no mercy on him!

A little after 6:30 p.m., Pig drops me and all our gear off, then leaves to go to his apartment. I pack the guns away in the safe and head up the stairs, where I get a nice welcome kiss. Heaven behold, Suzie has cooked a lovely meal, even placing candlesticks on the dinner table. I'm looking forward to a lovely romantic evening already!

10

Next morning, it's back to work. First up, I reply to a text received whilst we were in Yass from DS Chris Morris. I send another message saying I'm back in town and keen to connect. A short time later, a reply comes in suggesting a meet that afternoon at MadCuppa Coffee House in Milton. I quickly accept and let Pig know.

At 2:00 p.m., Pig and I wander into the MadCuppa café. I note a smartly dressed woman sitting on her own at an outside table, seemingly watching us as I scan the rest of the clientele. No one else looks remotely police material, so I turn back to her, saying, 'Chris?'

She smiles, appearing amused. 'You were looking for a male Chris, weren't you?'

As we shake hands, I reply, 'Yes, being honest, I was. I apologise for being so sexist!'

As Chris laughs it off, Pig says, 'Mel even said *she*, if you'd been listening.'

Clearly a smack for me!

Introductions out of the way and coffees ordered, we start chatting. Pig comments on the location of the meet, to which Chris replies, 'It's a bit hard to meet discreetly anywhere near police HQ, so I enjoy wandering down here. Good coffee and good location to watch the world go by.'

Fair enough.

Once coffees are served, I ask Chris what she understands about the case. 'I know it was your wife who was killed in that accident,' she says, 'and I know the basics of the events that followed. I was in City Hall when you took down the assassin, and was part of the team arresting the politicians and senior public servants. But I missed the action over at Darra.'

Pig and I remain impassive. We'd been very clear at the highest level that our involvement was never to be mentioned, so I'm not sure if Chris is testing us, or if she simply doesn't see an issue with discussing it face to face.

'Can you give us some inside background on Lancaster and his crew?' I ask.

'Happily,' she replies. 'Lancaster was an arsehole. An out-and-out prick. Treated everyone like cretins. No one liked him, and we all wondered why he always seemed to have free rein. The standing inside joke was that he must've had a photo of the commissioner and a donkey to get away with what he did.'

She stared down at her steaming coffee.

'I worked with Flem a few years ago. Before he went to the dark side, he was a good copper, a good detective. I never could understand how he got enmeshed in Lancaster's group.' Her face hardened. 'Benson was a sexist pig. Another arsehole. Thought all women were there for him and him alone. You couldn't go past him without copping a slap or a grope.'

'You don't seem the type to accept that.'

I get a grin in reply. 'Well, he did it to me once too often, so I turned and gave him a knee to the balls, which had him howling in pain. Lancaster even came out of his office to see what was going on. Before Benson could say anything, I told Lancaster, "He accidentally ran into my knee, sir," staring him defiantly in the eye. Lancaster just looked at me for what seemed an eternity, whilst I was thinking, *Shit, there goes my career.* Then he simply nodded and headed back into his office with Benson hobbling in after him.

'Benson left me and all of my friends alone after that. But a few policewomen have left the force because of him and others like him who never got brought into line. Besides, Benson was a lazy bastard. Never went the extra step, simply took the quickest and easiest route to an outcome – or no outcome. It made no difference to him.

'I don't really know Armitage or Bruce. They're a little younger, and I've never had any direct dealings with them. Never heard anything particularly good about either of them, but never heard anything bad, either.'

Silence ensues for a couple of minutes as we digest this information, before Pig asks if she'd like another coffee. 'Sure, another skinny cappuccino, please,' she replies.

Pig knows better than to ask me what I want. He heads inside to order three coffees, ours straight black – he's weaned himself off sugar again. Back to 'true soldier's coffee', as I often tease him!

Chris asks, 'What's with you two? Mel's told me you run Digital Data Solutions, but I'm not quite sure how that helped you crack Lancaster and co.'

'Pig and I are both army vets, special forces, but not SAS.' With the recent tainting of the SAS's record, I need to make that clear! 'Still, we have specialised skills, plus plenty of far-reaching contacts.'

'Yes, I've seen and heard of some of those,' she says, with a smile hovering around her mouth.

Once Pig is back and seated, I ask, 'What do you think should be the first step in moving forward to either prove or disprove Benson's statutory declaration? Firstly, do you believe it's legitimate?'

'In my view, there's no doubt it's the real deal. I've had the signature and the writing verified as his by our handwriting expert.' She continues, 'I'm going out to Palen Creek Prison to interview Fleming, Armitage and Bruce individually next Wednesday. I'll be ensuring there's no contact between them before or during these interviews. I've also requested the prison not even tell them I'm coming.'

Pig asks, 'If you're satisfied the stat dec is real, it would seem sort of out of character for Benson.'

Chris takes a long sip of coffee before responding. 'Yes, it is at odds with the Benson I knew, and that's hard for me to say, considering how I detested the man. The only conclusion I've come to is that maybe he didn't want his kids to think he killed the lady – sorry, your wife,' she adds, looking at me. 'Okay, that's what I know. What can you tell me that might help?'

'Not much, I'm afraid,' I say. 'I never saw anything that caused me to question whether Benson was the driver at the time of the accident. Clearly, the coroner had no doubts about who was driving – but he had other concerns, being pressured as he was by Lancaster to sign off on the report. It's unlikely that Benson was covering for Lancaster. If Lancaster had been the driver, he wouldn't have tried to switch the driver's identity, but would've simply pressured the coroner, the same as he did for Benson. Frankly, this whole thing has come out of left field. Any thought that whilst the stat dec is legit, he was actually lying?'

Chris purses her lips. 'Well, yes, I've wondered about that. A lot. But again, for what benefit? Sure, he has us going round in circles, but believe me, he wasn't a deep thinker. "Deep as a puddle", as they say. I wouldn't expect him to even consider making the declaration just to set us off on a tangent. That wasn't his style. The here and now was all Benson thought about. Then again, I was dumbfounded when we found the stat dec. Never would've expected he would think to do that, either. But that sort of makes it seem more real, if you know what I mean.'

I ask, 'Have you tracked down the Justice of the Peace who witnessed and signed the stat dec?'

'Yes, we've identified him.' She pulls her notebook out of her jacket pocket. 'Jack Ryan. He's a JP based in Orion Shopping Centre in Springfield Lakes – close to where Benson lived. But he's away overseas for another month or so, taking an around-the-world cruise with his wife, I believe.'

Pig has diligently written the name down, so we can do our own research. He asks, 'Do you know if all the police cars are IVMS tracked?'

'Yes,' is the immediate reply.

Pig says, 'You wouldn't know who handles it, would you?'

'Why? Or is this where you say, "Ask me no questions and I will tell you no lies?"' Chris smiles, so we both smile back. She ponders for a couple of moments, then says, 'It's a local Queensland company, Big Brother or something like that. I remember thinking I'd never heard of them when the contract was awarded a few years ago.'

She finishes her coffee, pushing the mug away, then looks me directly in the eye. 'You said earlier that Lancaster was pressuring the coroner to sign off on his report. How do you know that?

It certainly isn't public knowledge. I didn't even know it.'

I say, 'Now you know where Digital Data Solutions comes in. Request a copy of the coroner's original report and read his notes.'

Chris doesn't break eye contact with me, her stare rather steely now. She says, using her detective voice, 'Are you saying you've hacked the coroner's office?'

'No. We don't use the word *hack*. That's for the baddies. I will say we're members of Section V, if you've heard of it. We're also contractors to the ACSC – the Australian Cyber Security Centre – so we do have certain skills.'

We continue to stare at each other until a slight smile breaks out on Chris's face, and she declares, 'Well, doesn't look like I'm going to win this staring competition, so I'll quit whilst I'm ahead.'

Pig and I both laugh with her. As she stands up, she tells us she'll be in touch after she's interviewed the three cadre members next week. 'The commissioner has told me to keep you informed of all developments, considering your assistance in the past, and considering it is your wife's death we're talking about.'

We nod and shake hands, before she heads off back up McDougall Street, toward police HQ. Pig and I go in the other direction to where we'd parked the van. We agree she seems dedicated and professional, a no-nonsense sort of copper. The afternoon has got away from us, so on the drive back, now in peak-hour traffic, we plan our next moves.

11

Next morning, I head over to the address on Regina Street, Stones Corner, that I'd followed Benson to many months ago. Clipboard in hand, I head up the stairs of the old-fashioned apartment building. Benson had gone to the door of the second-storey unit on the left, so it's easy to put a number to it: Unit Three.

Once back in the office, I do a property search in a couple of highly restricted databases we have access to and identify a Marissa Polonsky as the tenant of Unit Three. I pull up her driver's license and confirm she certainly isn't Benson's mother, being only 44. A further search finds she's a single mother with an eight-year-old daughter and works at a local men's barber shop. I dig further and see she's been arrested for a 'drunk and disorderly' and has a few speeding fines. Her financial position doesn't look great, with a few overdue bills, but she gets by week to week.

I turn my attention to the IVMS company and quickly find a local business called Big Brother Fleet Monitoring. On their website, they claim Queensland Police Force and a couple of other state government departments as clients. Using the 'special skills' I was taught by the army when seconded to the Light Electronic Warfare Team, and then by the United States CIA and other shadowy organisations – official and otherwise – I gain access to Big Brother's database, easily identifying the police force file. Once in, I input the registration number of the two cars I'm interested in, add the dates I'm looking for, and wait to see what data it spits out.

It doesn't take too long. I upload the data to our secure cloud server, then check to see where both cars were thirty minutes prior to the accident, so around 6:30 p.m. They were both parked at the same location, which Google tells me is the Fairfield Gardens Shopping Centre. Both cars were there for some forty-five minutes. Strange.

Working backwards, I see they came from different locations, so the shopping centre was where they'd rendezvoused. Then, both headed off, travelling south on Ipswich Road in convoy. Just before the corner of Ipswich and Beaudesert Roads, the site of Liz's accident, both cars came to a halt. After five minutes, Benson's Falcon suddenly accelerated, leaving Lancaster sitting where he was.

Bang!

The accident is obvious, as Benson's car came to an instant halt, a red star next to it representing a 'hazard' on the report. Lancaster's car hadn't moved, still sitting where it had been just before the intersection. It remained there for fifteen minutes after the accident before heading off at pace. *Likely with lights and sirens,* I surmise.

After only six minutes, it stopped at a location I identify as the Rocklea International Motel, where it stayed put for the night. I'm on a roll, so I access the Rocklea Motel's database (we don't *hack*, remember!), pull up the date in question and search for records of anyone checking in between 7:15 and 7:45 that night. There are two. A Mr Smith and a Mr Jones. Very clever!

I go one step further to see what phone numbers and contact details they left, and find the number for Mr Jones is one we know Lancaster used. I put the other number into Telstra's database, then Optus's and Vodafone's, but each says it isn't a valid number.

Bugger! I wonder if it was cancelled after the accident. But I'll need help to access the phone companies' old logs. I do have my limitations, so I flick the number to Pig, who's more adept at this sort of accessing than I am, and leave him to work his magic.

I then pull up the records for the three phones we know Lancaster used, to see if there were any calls to the other number shown. Yes, there were a few, particularly in the two weeks leading up to the accident, and one just before both cars arrived at the Fairfield Shopping Centre. So, the owner is a proven long-term contact of Lancaster's. I don't know what was said, of course, but I do now know it was a legitimate phone number given to the motel.

We just have to find out whose it was.

12

I'm sitting at my desk, working away, when I hear Suzie's little Mini Cooper S idle into the garage next door. Pig comments, 'She's early,' and I acknowledge this with a grunt. (See, not only Pigs get to grunt!)

Suzie comes in, giving me a kiss, as is her wont when arriving home whilst I'm still working. She then pauses dramatically, before saying, 'I resigned today!'

I raise an eyebrow, whilst Pig raises his head. Suzie has previously said she's likely to resign when it's time to head off to watch Pig compete in the Invictus Games, but that's still months away.

She continues, 'That arsehole Paul, my boss, had one too many long lunches and came back half-sozzled. When I walked past him in the hallway, he slapped my butt! Bloody prick. So I slapped his face, hard. My hand hurt for five minutes, I swear. Jenny and the girls all saw and heard it.'

Leaning her hip on my desk, she folds her arms. 'I went back to my office to try and decide what to do, and thought, *Stuff it, I've had a gutful.* Jen came in and I told her that was it, so she helped me write up a statement, with all the girls as witnesses. I also wrote an official complaint against him addressed to the Law Society. Not that those old coots would do anything except have a laugh at Paul being in such a predicament, but I had a plan.

'Once I was ready, I marched into his office, slammed the door behind me, and slid out all the statements and my letter of complaint. Then, once he came to terms with the embarrassment of being known as a sexist pig – no pun intended, Pig! – I told him I wouldn't send the letter if he agreed to the terms of my resignation.'

She stops there, clearly quite proud of herself, so I bite. 'And what terms did you offer him?'

'I resign effectively immediately, he pays me six months' salary, *and* I get to keep all my clients. So, from tomorrow, I'm in business for myself, already with a good client base. Nearly worth getting my bum slapped!'

She has a big smile on her face. I get up to give her a kiss, saying, 'Wow, that's certainly flipping a difficult situation to your advantage!'

Pig also comes over and gives her a hug. 'So, where are you setting up office?' he asks.

Suzie looks sheepish. 'I was hoping we could share with you here. Not for too long – just until I have a chance to find something suitable.'

'*We?*' I ask.

She winces, maybe a little embarrassed. 'Well, Jenny walked out too, and I'll need a good PA. I told her to come here in the morning whilst we work something out.'

I look at Pig. 'What do you reckon? And before you answer, bear in mind how quiet and peaceful we have it, and how that'll change with two windbags in here with us.'

Suzie pokes her tongue out at me.

'Pig,' I continue, 'maybe I'll let you handle the rental negotiation, so you can get your own back for the apartment interview.'

They both have a laugh, then Pig shrugs and says, 'It's okay with me. You two are the ones who'll have to work *and* live together!'

'I'd love to help you get started in your own practice, Suz,' I say, 'but what about your clients' privacy? You can't just discuss their business whilst Pig and I are working here.'

Suzie pulls a face. 'Yes, that's a bit of an issue. Most is done by phone and email these days, but we'd need to work something out when I'm going to have a client visit.'

'Sounds like we're going to get kicked out of our own office at the drop of a hat, Pig.'

I'm smiling, though, and Suzie gives me a hug. 'It won't be very often,' she says.

I reply, 'Well, try and make your appointments around midday, so Pig and I can go out and have lunch on you.'

This has us all laughing, with Suzie seeming somewhat relieved.

'What rent are you willing to pay?' Pig asks, looking like he's relishing the chance for payback.

'Before you two get at loggerheads,' I say, 'this calls for a celebration.' Going over to our fridge, I pull out a couple of beers for Pig and me, along with a bottle of sav blanc I keep in there for whenever Suzie joins us for a drink after work. I pour us all glasses and hand them out. 'Congrats – I'm proud of you.'

We clink glasses and take a drink. I let Suzie and Pig go to and fro about 'fair and reasonable rent'. Suzie wants to know how many square metres she'll have to pay for, so they get up to pace out the office, whilst I sit on my desk enjoying the camaraderie. It'll be cool having Suzie around more, and of course, I can always go out of the office 'on assignment' if it gets too noisy!

Later, after we've had dinner and Pig has taken an Uber home, I say to Suzie, 'Okay, onto the bed with you. I need to inspect your bum to ensure there's no damage!'

'It's fine,' she says.

'Maybe, but this isn't just any arse we're talking about. It's a *great* arse, a work of art in my view.'

This gets me a smile and a kiss, and I think, *I want to see that smile for the rest of my life.*

As the kiss lingers (or is that it heats up?), somehow, the bum inspection gets forgotten.

13

Next morning, Pig and I are at our desks when Suzie comes down just before 8:30. I say to Pig, 'Lawyer hours – maybe we can adopt them too, ah?'

Suzie chooses to ignore me. Instead, she goes to the front door to let Jenny in. Whilst I've met Jenny a couple of times, having had dinner with her and her husband Maurice, Pig hasn't. Suzie introduces them, and Jenny says, 'Nice to finally met you, Julien,' getting a snort out of me (get it?). 'I've heard so much about you.' She looks at me with a half-smile. 'You both, actually.'

'Should I be blushing?' I ask.

Jenny laughs. 'If I'm honest, yes, you probably should!'

Suzie says, 'Okay, that's enough. I don't want to hear any whispers or sniggers. Jenny, our conversations are bound by client confidentiality, and as you know, Mort is a client. Besides, I don't want to be made to blush.'

'Ah, where's the fun in that?' I ask, getting a grin out of Jenny. 'Okay, grab a coffee and let's work this out. It wouldn't take much to expand the office over here.' I gesture to the right. 'We could easily get Bob the Builder back in to remove this wall and replace it, say, three metres into the garage. We'll still have plenty of room for four cars, and if we push the rear wall back a couple of metres as well, you two can have a private office and work area for Jenny. The existing waiting area' – which is really just a coffee table and two chairs! – 'is enough for us. That way, you don't have to worry about looking for another office, and, well… working from home might come in handy one day.'

I know when Suzie gets my meaning, as she colours slightly. She recovers well, though, coming back with, 'That depends on the terms. What rent do you want?'

Pig shrugs, so I say, 'We'll work out how many square metres you'll get, and we'll charge a commercial rate – but only after six months, when you've established yourself.'

Suzie's clearly pretty pleased with this, as she heads towards me, hopefully to plant a kiss. I add, 'As long as my ironing gets done each week.'

This is, of course, met with loud laughter from all three, and I still get my quick kiss, along with a whispered 'Thank you.'

All worth it!

Pig asks, 'So, what name are you going to be using?'

Suzie pulls a yellow legal pad from her satchel (every lawyer seems to use these, as if it makes them special!), she starts reading out some of the names she and Jenny have been toying with: Suzanne Dunn Lawyer, Dunn Legal, Suzanne Dunn Legal, Dunn and Associates.

Pig pipes up, saying, 'Dunnie's Law.'

Jenny and I crack up. 'Yes,' I say, 'Dunnie's Law, where we don't take shit!' This gets another round of laughter, with even Suzie joining in.

In the end, she decides on SDA Law (Suzie Dunn & Associates), and we all agree it has a good ring to it. Of course, Pig can't resist having a brass plaque made up, which we put on Suzie's office door, reading 'Dunnie's Law – we don't take shit!'

To her credit, she simply rolls her eyes and allows us to have our fun.

*

The following Thursday, I get a text from DI Chris Morris, saying, 'Interviewed the three yesterday. Want to catch a coffee?'

'Yep, can do anytime today or tomorrow,' I reply.

'10:30 tomorrow, same place?'

'Done.'

The next day finds Pig and me back at MadCuppa in Milton. This time, we beat Chris, but knowing what she drinks, we go ahead and order. She wanders in just as the coffees are delivered.

As we've come to expect from her, she takes her time, enjoying the first sips of her coffee, chatting about the weather and the Broncos' ongoing poor form, touching on the media's talk about dumping their coach. 'They can't keep blaming the coach,' she complains. 'He's not out on the field doing all those dumb things. Useless twits!'

She's more passionate about the Broncos than either Pig or I – but eventually, she pulls her notebook out.

'Well, I guess you guys are keen to know how it went yesterday?'

You think!

After taking another swig of her coffee, she starts. 'The interviews went about how I expected. Both Armitage and Bruce claimed they knew nothing about the accident, other than what had been reported on the news. They both separately claimed that my questions were the first they'd heard of anything fishy. They were astounded when I showed them Benson's stat dec. Frankly, I believed them both.'

She sets her mug down on the table. 'When it came time to interview Flem, at first, he also denied having any knowledge. I sensed he wasn't being entirely truthful, so I told him, "Flem, you taught me better than that. Don't bullshit me." He went coy. Even wanted to know if he might get some leniency if he spilled. So, I said if he was helpful, I'd talk to the commissioner.'

Rolling her eyes, she says, 'He then admitted he didn't know anything much. He'd overheard a few titbits of conversation between Lancaster and Benson, really just enough to raise his suspicions that the accident wasn't what it seemed. I quizzed him about what he'd heard, but he remained vague.'

I ponder this, before I reply, 'Does he know more than he told you?'

'I'm not sure. Flem knows what I'm like – I'll beaver away until I get to the truth – so one side of me thinks he's aware it's a waste of time to delay telling me what he knows, but the other wonders if there's someone out there pulling strings who he's more frightened of.'

Pig and I share a look. I ask, 'Who?'

'I have no idea. There might not be anyone.'

'Do you think there'll be any benefit to me going and visiting him? Maybe I can take a different angle, encourage him to tell the whole truth.'

Chris bristles. 'You don't like my interview technique? I do this for a living, and I'm very good at it.'

I quickly reply, 'I have no doubt you are, but I've done a few "interviews" myself, and I'm also pretty good at getting to the truth. I just use different tactics.'

Pig butts in, 'Not sure you'll get away with your tactics in a Queensland prison, though!'

Chris looks between us, clearly trying to gauge how serious we are. I smile and reply, 'True. We might have to break him out before we can really interview him.'

This makes Pig laugh, which, in turn, makes Chris realise we're joking. (Or are we?)

*

Since tracking Benson and Lancaster's cars through the Big Brother database, I've been pondering why Benson's suddenly sped away from the verge before hitting Liz's car only seconds later. It just doesn't make sense.

The next morning, in the office, I voice my thoughts to Pig. After a lengthy pause, Pig raps his knuckles on his desk and says, 'The only way that makes any sense is if it was deliberate. If they actually targeted Liz.'

Another long pause.

'Shit, that would make it murder,' I say. 'Why? Who the hell would target Liz? She was a schoolteacher, for Christ's sake. She wouldn't hurt a fly.'

'Maybe she witnessed someone doing something illegal. I'm guessing she didn't even know she had, as there's no evidence that she'd reported anything to the police, and Kevin didn't flag any concerns when you met him, did he?'

I shake my head. 'That means they must've had someone following Liz, or a tracker on her car. They knew where she was and when, down to the fact she'd be passing through the intersection of Beaudesert and Ipswich Road. They were sitting there waiting.'

This idea turns our thinking on its head. But it does make all the pieces of the puzzle fit.

Following this theory, we decide that if Liz had seen something, it would've taken time to put something like this into place – to identify Liz, track her down, learn her habits, and set up the hit. Even a month would've been hard work. We decide we need to push our search pattern back to cover the six weeks prior to the accident.

We start making a to-do list – after making fresh coffees, of course! We'll need to check the photos on Liz's phone, along with her credit card receipts, to see where she'd been for the six weeks prior to the accident. I'll likely need to revisit Kevin, her 'almost-partner', and ask if she'd mentioned anything that concerned her or seemed odd. I'll also pay a visit to the woman Benson had called on in Stones Corner – see what she knows as well.

Then it hits me. 'If Benson was taking the fall for a murder, he would've been paid very well, wouldn't he?'

Pig nods. 'Bloody oath he would.' He pauses. 'We need to go further back through Lancaster's bank accounts, look for any big payments to Benson, and hopefully find some equal or bigger deposits in the six weeks prior to the accident. If we find anything, we'll need to talk to Benson's wife to see what she knows about it too. It's a bloody big gamble he took, risking being charged with murder when he wasn't even in the car. No wonder Lancaster was putting pressure on the coroner!'

*

At 2:25 the next morning, I get a text from Police Commissioner Mel Black saying, 'Chris assaulted. Badly injured in an attack in her own home.'

Suzie pulls the pillow over her head to block out the light disturbing her, so I turn it off and go out to the kitchen to text

Mel back. 'Shit. Where is she?'

'This is police business. I'm telling you as a courtesy only.'

'WHERE?'

The reply is a little slow, but it does come. 'ICU, PA hospital. Immediate family only.'

I'm quickly dressed and out the door, coffee in hand, leaving a note on the kitchen bench for Suzie. A short time later, I enter the ICU – having changed into scrubs, hair net and all – to find the Commissioner scowling at me from a bedside chair. She whispers angrily, 'How did you get in here?'

I shrug. 'Told them I was her partner. How's she doing?'

Just then, a doctor comes bustling in. Seeing me there, he stops short, and Mel introduces me as Chris's partner whilst giving me a filthy look. Playing the part fully, I go to the other side of the bed and take Chris's hand in mine, watched closely by both Mel and the doctor. He then glances at his clipboard and declares, 'She should make a full recovery. There's no sign of brain damage, although her head wounds are serious. We'll keep her in an induced coma for another twelve hours so we can monitor her closely.'

I ask, 'How long will she be in the ICU?'

'She'll likely to go to the ward tomorrow, all being well, once she comes out of the coma.'

With a nod to us both, he departs. I take a closer look at Chris, but I can't see too much, as she's extensively bandaged. 'So, what happened?'

Of course, Mel can't resist starting with a lecture. 'You have no right to be here. You hardly know Chris.'

I look straight back at her and say, 'This is personal now. I'm fully engaged.'

She knows she isn't going to intimidate me, so whilst still glaring, she starts, 'Chris called 000 around 8:30 last night and identified herself, requesting both ambulance and police before collapsing whilst still on the phone. Paramedics were there within seven minutes, and a patrol car wasn't far behind. She was quickly sedated due to her wounds but gave the responding officers a brief run-down. Apparently, two men were inside her unit when she got home just after 8 p.m. They attacked her, and as you can see for yourself, she took a right beating. She also reported they told her to "leave it alone", but couldn't give any descriptions before she lapsed back into unconsciousness.

'I still have officers at her home, talking to neighbours, checking for CCTV footage and fingerprinting. Of course, it's early days, but both immediate neighbours claim to not have seen or heard anything out of the norm.

'Mort, I know how you operate and admire what you get done, but this is a police investigation. One of our own has been seriously injured. We will take care of who did this. Do *not* get involved.'

Whilst Mel has been talking, I've been studying Chris, still holding her hand. I now look closely at her fingernails. Whilst she has a worker's fingernails (no long flash nails for her), I can see strips of what looks like skin stuck under a couple of them.

Mel, sensing something, comes over to take a closer look. Without a word, I show her Chris's hand with the skin fragments showing.

'Shit,' she says, heading to the door. She returns within a minute. 'They'll be here soon with the necessary equipment to extract those bits of skin. Hopefully we'll get DNA from them.'

'Mel, I'm already involved. That's not going to change,' I start. Already, the glare is back. 'This shows you still have one or more rogue officers within your force.' I hold up my hand to stop her immediate denial. 'Who knows she interviewed Lancaster's cadre? It was only on Wednesday, so the attackers moved very quickly and decisively. Someone on your force has turned traitor, and they must be in a senior role to have access to Chris's movements. You have to assume her investigation into the accident is now compromised.'

Mel deflates in front of my eyes as reality rams home. 'Damn. I've tried to clean out some of the older officers – the plodders, you know, the ones just punching the clock to get paid. I was confident I had a clean force. Mind you, the leak might've come from the prison.'

'Yes, it may have. I'm not going to tell you how to run your force, or how to run an investigation. Still, we'll be investigating too, in our way. I'm happy to cooperate, but only when I'm confident our involvement will remain confidential.'

A nurse comes in, pushing a trolley with some surgical instruments. She asks us to leave so she has privacy whilst cleaning Chris's fingernails and checking her vitals. I lean back over Chris, giving her hand a squeeze and pecking her cheek – playing my part to the end!

Mel and I say our goodbyes. I ask for Chris's address, expecting another argument, but she just stops and works her phone for a minute before saying, 'I've texted it to you.'

Once in my car, I look at the time. It's a little after 5:00 a.m., so I ring Pig and bring him up to speed. We agree that he'll head straight over to Chris's address in Toowong, an inner Brisbane suburb, and check what CCTV cameras he can find in the area. We'll likely put a drone up. It's easier to find cameras from the air than by walking the streets and checking manually.

Unlike the coppers, who have to approach each system's owner to get permission to access a copy – and sometimes, they even need to obtain a court order – we have our own, quicker way. We simply access each system directly ourselves.

Pig, too, is now out for vengeance. Chris is one of the good guys and didn't deserve a horrible beating.

14

I hit the office and quickly order flowers be delivered to Chris in the ICU. Then, with Pig busy over in Toowong, I get started on another list:
- Check who knew Chris interviewed Fleming and co.
- Check outgoing phone calls from the prison.
- Check whether emails sent from the prison can be tracked.
- Check Chris's police and personal phone and email.
- Check to see if Chris is a member of any private groups.
- Check who's accessed Chris's case notes.

When Maria comes in, I give her a brief run-down, and ask her to check Chris's social media. She'll be quicker at tracking and accessing them – we consider her our social media guru.

Mid-morning, Pig returns. He found a few CCTV cameras, so he's keen to access them and download what he can. He also chatted to a Detective Sergeant Brian Cooper, who's in charge of investigating the assault on Chris.

'He seemed pretty keen to catch the "bastards who did this", so that's a good sign,' Pig says. 'We just have to make sure he backs up his words with action. I told him we'd been "assisting" Chris and offered to assist him as well, but he didn't seem interested – even gave the impression he didn't need amateurs' help!

Clearly, Mel hadn't had a word with him yet.'

'So be it,' I say. 'We'll carry out our own independent investigation.'

Pig gets busy tracking and accessing the relevant CCTV footage. I go out to the storage area and retrieve Liz's old phone. Digging into the file box, I find her accounts folder, which includes her credit card statements for the twelve months or so prior to her death. Starting from the date of her accident and working backwards, I highlight any significant amounts that may be of interest, nothing over the preceding six weeks.

It doesn't amount to much. Five entries, with two at fancy city restaurants, one at Marriott Gold Coast, which looks like a weekend away, and another for a concert. When I check, I note the date of the concert was after her death, so I rule that out. Another is from Rick Shores, the renowned restaurant at Burleigh Heads on the Gold Coast, on the same date as the Marriott Hotel charge. Clearly, she enjoyed herself down there!

Having put her phone on charge when I dug it out, I then go to check her photos, but there's none. *That's odd*, I think. *Everyone has photos on their phones!*

I give a techie I know a call, asking if he might be able to identify any photos that have been deleted from an old phone. He says, 'It depends on too many factors, but send it in and I'll see what I can do.' I agree to express post the phone down to him – he's based in the Gold Coast.

Maria reports that Chris's Facebook and Instagram are locked, so she's unable to access them. Pig says, 'I've found something, or somebody, I guess.'

I get up and look over his shoulder, as does Maria. He pulls up an image showing two heavily built guys, caps pulled down hard over the faces, walking directly towards the camera. It's like they knew it was there, as both are hunched forward and looking down, making it difficult to get a good view of them.

Pig adds, 'This shows these two coming out of the Royal Exchange Hotel car park just around the corner and heading up Benson Street towards Chris's apartment just after 7:00 p.m.'

He pulls up another image, which shows them walking away from a camera. 'This is the same two heading back at 8:20, after Chris's assault. Neither looked in a hurry, so they were obviously confident, and they blended in well with the pub crowd.'

We silently watch a video of them walking back into the Royal Exchange Hotel. Even though we watch for another fifteen minutes, no cars leave the car park. And there doesn't seem to be a camera showing the taxi pick up point, which does seem odd, considering they're a common location of conflict.

So, whilst we can confirm the likely culprits, the images are of no use in trying to identify them. Yet.

Pig uploads the videos to our secure server in the cloud, then takes copies of the best face-on shots and adds them to our 'Chris's assault' folder. 'No harm sending these clips to Midge. His gait-matching software might come through.'

I nod. We stay in touch with some of our contacts from the CIA still, and Midge, who helped us tremendously over the last few months, is a hacker extraordinaire. We still don't know which department he works for, and we will never ask! He's vowed to always help us, as we – well, Pig, mainly – saved his life a few years ago. And so far, he's been true to his word. We hope to catch up with him when we head off to the Invictus Games in a few months, and share a few beers again!

Chris being assaulted has given our investigation a jolt of

adrenaline, so to speak, so next I decide to identify Benson's wife.

This isn't hard. Their home in Springfield Lakes was in their joint names, so I now know hers is Beth. A little bit of further digging and I find she and their two kids still live there, but it's currently for sale. It's listed as a mortgagee sale, meaning the bank is selling it, likely due to Beth being in arrears on the mortgage. I also find she works part-time as a barista at Zarraffa's Coffee in Augustine Heights, adjacent to Springfield Lakes.

Her actual financial situation doesn't look pretty. She owes $436,000 on the home, which is currently estimated to be worth around $500,000. No doubt, once the bank and lawyers gouge all the fees they can think of, Beth is unlikely to see much at all from the sale. Of course, as a part-time barista, she doesn't earn anywhere near enough to make reasonable mortgage payments.

Whilst I've been digging into Beth Benson, Pig's been going back through Lancaster's bank accounts. He's flagged two payments of $250,000, each shown as going to Benson, but to a different account at a different bank. The timing of these payments is too close to be coincidental, the first being five days before Liz's accident, the second ten days after.

Dillion and Beth Benson's joint bank account and mortgage are both with NAB, but these two payments had gone to an account set up in Dillion Benson's name only at the Bank of Queensland. Pig checks it, with me leaning over his shoulder, and we see the account has $686,000 in it. Pig finds regular cash deposits into the account as well. Two of these payments came in the weeks after we witnessed Lancaster sharing the crooked cadre's 'quarterly bonus'. Benson had obviously been saving for a rainy day, and with the family home currently being in a forced sale, it's likely his wife has no idea. Pig takes a screen shot of the bank statement, so we have proof of its existence.

Somewhat surprisingly, Pig can't identify any significant receipts to Lancaster that coincide with the payments to Benson. 'So, how did he get paid, if there's no financial record?' Pig asks.

'That certainly is the sixty-four-dollar question.'

We continue to debate it, listing other options. Lancaster might've had other bank accounts, or a cryptocurrency wallet, though we've seen no evidence of one – a question for Midge, maybe? He could've also been paid in cash, though where would this be?

Pig jokingly says, 'Buried in his backyard.'

We share a look, and I say, 'Not such a silly answer. Maybe we should run a metal detector over the property.'

Of course, this leads to a debate about what use this would be if he'd used bags or nonmetal containers. I acquiesce to Pig's suggestion of an infrared probe, which will quickly show any items hidden in the ground. He brags that he can do this from a drone, ideally at night, so the property's current occupants wouldn't even know.

When I bring him up to date on Beth Benson, we decide we should do a quick recce of the Benson home, then also decide a quick trip past Lancaster's house in Chelmer wouldn't hurt, either. Needless to say, we grab fresh coffees before we go!

With Pig driving the van, I do a search on Lancaster's property. It's been sold to a younger couple – a banker and a kindergarten teacher. I also reactivate the CCTV cameras we installed in the street outside the house when we had Lancaster under surveillance.

When we get to Summit Drive, Springfield Lakes, we drive slowly past the Benson house. It's not hard to miss, with the *For Sale* signs large as life on the front lawn. We agree to visit

Beth at work tomorrow morning, thinking she might feel safer meeting two unknown men there than at her home. Big, imposing men at that.

Pig decides there's no time like the present, so we head back to the office and he loads up his drone for the search of Lancaster's backyard. I decide on an early mark as well and wander upstairs.

At the end of her day, Suzie finds me in the kitchen, resplendent in my apron – but don't worry, I do have shorts and a tee-shirt on as well! Once she's changed and set the table, we toast, and I start the conversation with: 'I kissed another woman today.'

I don't get the reaction I wanted, as she simply keeps eating whilst raising one eyebrow. So, I tell her how I became Chris's partner to get into the ICU, and, once there, had to act the part. I also explain in detail how it now appears Benson wasn't driving the police car that killed Liz and describe what we'd subsequently discovered.

When I finish, Suzie asks the obvious question. 'What does it matter who was driving?'

I reply, 'I need to understand why they, whoever *they* are, wanted Liz dead.'

Later in the evening, Suzie says to me, 'You know, I'd be more worried about any women you kiss who you *don't* tell me about than the ones you do!'

*

The next morning, Pig gives me a run-down on his infrared search. He believes that there's something buried on the edge of what looks like an old vegie garden, but it seems too small to hold any large amount of cash. We conclude that it probably isn't a significant find, so we won't worry about it for now, though we do agree to keep an eye on the new owners. If we see them packing up to go on holiday, we might sneak in for a quick dig.

I also get an update from the PA hospital advising Chris is out of her coma and has been transferred to the critical care ward (another benefit of being her 'partner'). I send her a text wishing her a speedy recovery. She replies quickly, saying she has aches and pains all over but is feeling lucky. I tell her I'll buy her a lottery ticket, then!

15

On arrival at the Zarraffa's a few hours later, it's easy to recognise Beth, as the other baristas are all younger. We order coffees (and a toasted banana bread each – just don't tell anyone!). Then, when the place is quiet, I go over to her and introduce myself, telling her we're investigating the accident where her husband killed a woman. I ask if we could talk privately for a few minutes, so she gets another of the servers to take over.

She's obviously a little nervous, but we keep it cool, chatting about how things are going with her kids. She has two daughters aged nine and seven. She tears up when she says they both miss their dad. 'So do I,' she adds wistfully.

'How did Dillion seem after the accident?' I ask.

'Well, it was a little strange, because he was stone-cold sober when he got home. That wasn't usual on a Thursday night. He and his team always had a session after work on Thursdays. Sometimes, he'd be late home afterwards, and I'm pretty sure he was having an affair.'

We just nod, wanting her to keep talking.

'Honestly, he'd always been unfaithful. Even the week before we got married, I caught him out. But by then, I was pregnant, and I had no desire to be a single parent. I did love him. Still do, in fact, even after all he put us through.'

Sighing, she clasps her hands together. 'We met at university. I was studying nursing, and he was trying to do law. But after the first year, he knew he wasn't going to make it, so he applied to join the police force. He had all the right intentions back then.'

She gives a melancholy smile. 'Then, as he got hardened by life as a policeman – the abuse and blatant hypocrisy of the law, the police, and the justice system – he changed. Changed a lot. But he was always a good dad and husband, just not a faithful one.'

I nudge the conversation back towards the accident. 'So, he was sober when he got home that night. Did he talk about what happened?'

'It was late when he got home. After 1:00 in the morning, I think. He woke me, which was unusual, and sat on the bed to tell me he'd been in an accident. He quickly assured me he wasn't injured but the other driver had died. So, of course, I was all worried and upset for him. He explained there would be enquiries, both from the coroner and internally from the police, but he claimed he was in the right, that the other car had run a red light.'

Pig and I share a look. Liz hadn't been one to speed, let alone run red lights. She'd never even gotten a ticket.

'In retrospect,' Beth says, 'he seemed very keen to assure me he didn't do anything wrong. I even asked if he'd been drinking. He quickly said no, that he was on assignment with DI Lancaster when it happened, so he hadn't been to the usual Thursday night session.'

After a pause, she carries on. 'That DI Lancaster was a bad influence on Dillion. Joining Lancaster's squad seemed to make him lose a lot of his zeal for being a cop. He became quite indifferent, rarely working in the evenings, and more content to sit and watch TV. It meant we had more time together, so I didn't mind it.'

Time to try a different tack. I ask, 'I'm sorry to have to bring this up, but since he's died, how have things been?'

Beth immediately becomes upset, angry even. 'After all the years he put into the force, he wasn't accorded an official funeral, as they claimed he was acting as a criminal when he was shot. I haven't even got his superannuation or life insurance!'

Tears well in her eyes. 'The bank's foreclosed on the house. I don't earn much here, and I had to give up on my uni degree once I got pregnant, so I don't know what I'm going to do for the kids.' She's openly sobbing now, and a couple of her colleagues are glancing over, their concern obvious. 'Dillion always promised if anything happened, we'd be taken care of. I always believed him, so I never considered we'd end up like this. Being married to a cop, you know they see and do ugly things, but he'd tell me, "You'll be fine, babe, always."'

I pass her my hanky (don't worry, it's clean!), and she blows her nose and wipes her eyes. 'The auction is in a couple of weeks. I have to be out beforehand, and I still don't know where I can move to. I never got on with his parents. My mum has remarried, but they only live in a two-bed apartment. And Dad... well, I don't want to go there.'

I let her finish before I say, 'Well, Dillion may have done the right thing for you.' Unfolding the copy of his Bank of Queensland account statement, I show it to her.

She's slow to comprehend what she's seeing. Eventually, she finds her voice, after picking her jaw up off the floor, and manages, 'You mean he has a separate account, and it has six hundred and eighty-six thousand dollars in it?'

Pig and I nod in unison. She bursts out crying again. This time, there's laughter mixed in as well, as she waves the page in the air. A barista comes over, likely to ask if everything's okay, and Beth gets up and hugs her. 'Annie, he had a separate account hidden away for me. He didn't let us down after all!'

Pig and I sit there letting her come to terms with this life-changing moment, and it takes a while for her to compose herself. Her relief is obvious. Multiple times, she starts crying, then it turns into laughter. Once she's settled down, she asks, 'So, how do I claim this money as mine?'

I reply, 'I assume you're the beneficiary of his will.' She nods. 'It should be a simple matter of fronting up to the bank, then. You may have to take a copy of his will, and they might even need proof he's dead. Thinking about it, it may be best if you take a lawyer with you, to ensure there are no issues.'

I pull one of Suzie's cards out. 'If you want any legal advice or assistance, I can highly recommend Suzie. She'll be happy to help you. In fact, whether you use her or someone else, I'd urge you to question why you aren't getting Dillion's super or life insurance. As far as I'm aware, he's never been charged with any criminal act, so I suspect they have no valid reason to not pay out. A good lawyer should win that battle for you as well.'

This brings another bout of tears, and I can sense Pig is getting restless. I decide to bring the meeting to a close, saying, 'Beth, we'll leave you now, but do you mind if I give you a call in a couple of weeks to continue our chat?'

'Sure,' she replies. 'And thanks for this good news – you don't know what it means to me and the girls!'

When we get in the van, Pig says, 'So, you just gave Suzie's card to the wife of the man who was holding her at gunpoint when you shot him, and told Beth that Suzie would be happy to help her. You sure of that?'

'Damn,' I say, 'I didn't think of it like that.' I ponder this for a moment. 'Nah, Suzie will see a woman in distress and go into full support mode.'

'I hope so, for your sake,' is all Pig says.

Shit, I think, *so do I!*

'So, now you're an item with Stacey, you think like a girl too?' I ask.

'It's called empathy,' Pig replies.

*

That evening, when we sit down to dinner – Suzie actually cooked for a change, so I'm looking forward to it – I tell her, 'I handed your card to a lady who seems to need a good lawyer. You might get a call from a Beth Benson.'

Suzie surprises me by saying, 'I already have.'

'Don't forget my commission, then.'

She smiles. 'You're eating it.'

Bugger. Women!

With Pig's comment still ringing in my ears, I continue. 'Did you recognise the name?'

I get a puzzled look. 'No? I haven't rung her back yet, so I'm not sure what it's about.'

Ah well, in at the deep end: 'You remember Dillion Benson?' Suzie's fork stops halfway to her mouth, so I hurry on. 'Beth is his wife. We met her today, and both the police superannuation and Benson's life insurers are refusing to pay up. I thought you'd be able to help.'

Suzie has recovered enough to resume eating, but still has a half-frown on her face. When she finishes her mouthful, she says, 'So, you think I'd want to help the wife of the man who held a gun to my head then covered me in his blood when you shot him?'

Hmm, I think. *Maybe Pig was right.*

'Well, yes. Beth is being royally screwed because of Benson's actions, not through any fault of her own.'

Being honest, I'm not getting a positive vibe here!

'How much is at stake? How much is she entitled to?'

'No idea,' I reply. 'I didn't ask, but the bank is selling the family home from under her, and she has nowhere to go. No family that can help. She and her two daughters are really up against it. We showed her Benson had a secret bank account with over six hundred grand, but she'll need to prove she's entitled to it – which she'll likely need help with too.'

Suzie continues eating until she's finished her meal, her face not giving much away. 'Mort, I can't believe how insensitive you've been, making me relive that horrible episode again. I'd done a good job burying my memory of it. Now you offer that arsehole's wife my card?'

I can see she's getting very upset. *Wow, boy,* I think, *you've buggered up big time here.*

I take her hand in mine, gently rubbing it. Fortunately, she doesn't snatch it back, so I say, 'Suzie, I'm sorry. I didn't think of the consequences. All I could see was a woman being screwed over by others, and I simply thought you were the best person to look after her. But I should've thought of the history. It was truly dumb and thoughtless of me.'

She leans over, putting her head on my shoulder, but remains quiet. I stroke her hair, letting her make the next move. Wiping a couple of tears from her eyes, she lifts her head and gives me a light kiss.

'You're forgiven, but there will be consequences. I'll help Beth. Does she know you killed her husband?'

'No, I certainly didn't tell her. Nor did I mention he was holding you hostage when he died. I would be surprised if she knew any of the details of his death.'

'Okay, let's keep it that way.' With this, she pushes her plate towards me. 'First item of punishment: you're on cooking and clean-up duty for a week. And don't think that's the end of it, mister.'

I pull her in tight and kiss her. She joins in, then pushes me away. I say, 'Don't deprive yourself of one of life's pleasures just to punish me!'

'Ha,' is her only response, as she grabs the TV remote.

16

Next morning, Pig accesses Palen Creek Prison's system, commenting, 'Shit, that was easy. It's a government department – you'd expect them to use tighter protocols.'

He checks what time Chris logged in and out, then accesses their email server, seeing what was sent in the hour after she left. Nothing suspicious in there. Then into their phone log. Of course, the calls aren't recorded, so we have no idea what was said, but we can identify which phone extension they used – and, thereby, whose office they were made from. We record the numbers called and run them through our database to see if any match numbers we've come across previously.

Using a software package Midge provided us with recently, we can retrospectively identify phones that accessed a certain mobile phone tower and the numbers they called. By pulling up a map covering the prison, we identify the nearest tower, then download all the numbers that accessed it for the three hours of Chris's visit and the hour after.

There were a surprising number of calls. Looks like many of the prisoners have access to mobile phones, or maybe there were plenty of visitors! Once again, we upload all these numbers into our database and leave it to do its thing.

Pig checks internal CCTV, tracking Chris from her arrival until she enters the interview room. We can't see any prison officer taking any undue notice of Chris. There's no sign of any footage or audio from the interview room – and there shouldn't be, so that's at least reassuring.

Because we share a kitchen with Suzie and Jenny, the four of us often mix whilst making coffee or having lunch. Today is no different. After our difficult conversation last night, Suzie and I hadn't seen each other this morning, as I'd headed off for my usual early morning run and today was one of Suzie's gym days.

Now, we find ourselves in the kitchen together. I do get a smile as I enter, but it isn't the usual wholehearted effort. With Jenny also there, watching intently, I reach out and giving her hand a little squeeze. And a smile, of course. A high-wattage one too. I can't help it.

Not much else is said. I don't think it appropriate to ask if she had talked to Beth yet.

See, I can learn – though slowly, sometimes!

Pig's computer gives off a little ping and an alert comes up saying 'Number recognised'. The cross-checking has brought up a number already in our database. It's the same one Lancaster called the night of Liz's accident (or is that murder?), the one we can't trace. It isn't in the databases of any Australian communications company. So how can it be used?

We discuss calling it, but decide not to risk raising suspicion. I send an email to both Midge and Robert, who's now our Section V controller, flagging the number and requesting any further information they can provide. In this case, we aren't hopeful Midge will come through, as his databases don't have much Australian content. But he had helped identify some crims in our previous battles for law and order.

The easy part is identifying who contacted this number. Deputy Warden Carl Thomas used his own phone to make the call. To whom? We need to ask him, but not just yet. Tipping our hand before we know enough may have far-reaching consequences.

We do need to bug his phone, though. And soon.

Whilst inside the prison's server, we check his personal details and note he lives in the closest town (make that village), Rathdowney, with his wife and two teenage kids. We also check his roster for the next week. He's back on the morning shift from next Sunday.

I suggest, 'Might be a chance to catch him at the local pub Sunday or Monday night?'

We decide that as I'm likely to still be in the bad books with Suzie come the weekend, it would be prudent to plan our visit for the Monday evening. Wimp, aren't I!

Pig's phone starts ringing with the tune of Keith Urban's *Blue Ain't Your Colour*. We look at each other, saying in unison, 'Midge.'

Sure enough, when Pig answers, there's Midge, large as life on the screen. Before getting down to business, we have a quick chat. We're planning on catching up with him when we get to the States in about two months, after Pig competes in the Invictus Games, and he says he can't wait to share a few beers! He has no update for us yet, but assures us we'll know if the number has been identified previously.

'How could a number be used if it isn't carried by any of the national phone providers?' I ask.

Midge scratches his chin. 'There are hidden carriers available on the dark web that piggyback off the majors. They provide total anonymity to their users.'

'This number might well be one of those, then,' Pig says.

'Interesting,' Midge says. 'I'll dig into it a bit more, but understand that those hidden carriers are costly. They're usually only used by heavy hitters. You need to know what you're doing, or know the right – make that the *wrong* – people to access them. Watch your backs.'

'Yes, Midge,' Pig and I chorus, getting a strange look from Jenny as she walks across to the kitchen.

The response from Robert at Section V, which comes a little later, is as expected. Nothing on file, but the number has now been registered.

*

The next Monday afternoon finds Pig and me leaning on the bar of the Rathy Pub in Rathdowney. We're dressed in hi-vis workwear, so we fit right in, a couple of workers stopping for a quick feed and cold bevvies.

We recognise Deputy Warden Carl Thomas sitting at a table over to our left with a couple of other regulars, or so we guess. We order a feed each, Pig going for the rare T-bone steak and I for the medium rump. Both solid choices in any country pub, and as usual, the steaks are as big as the plates. Worth the hour drive for the feed alone!

We keep to ourselves whilst being friendly to those around us. When Carl gets up to go for a leak, Pig waits a couple of moments and follows him into the toilet.

A few minutes later, Pig returns. He successfully scanned Carl's phone through the flimsy cubicle walls, giving us his contacts and call history, and activated the mic within his phone after 'accidentally' knocking it out of his hand.

Once Pig's back on his bar stool, he quickly AirDrops a bugging app to Carl's phone. We don't need to get permission from Carl, as our special phones force the app through the standard AirDrop option. This means we'll receive hourly updates on his calls, texts, and any conversations held within earshot of the phone. There'll be heaps of rubbish, but maybe, just maybe, we'll glean something important.

First step is to see if our secret phone number is listed in his contacts. As I'm done with my food, I grab Pig's phone to check whilst he finishes his rare T-bone. (Yes, rare as in *blue*, blood congealing on his plate. Yuck!)

Sure enough, the number is recorded against the name Joe. Bugger, not much help there. But we'll no doubt be seeing our friend Carl again one day – or dark night – soon.

On the drive back, we ponder whether the name Joe somehow relates back to our old nemesis Joe Lancaster. Seems unlikely, but stranger things have happened. We know Lancaster is dead – he swallowed his gun in front of me after a battle inside the Jackals' stockade. He is dead, no question.

Later, once I'm home and settled on the couch watching TV, Suzie comes in from netball training. Whilst she has a shower, I fire up the microwave and heat a meal for her. I wouldn't say things are frosty between us, but they're cooler than I'd like, so I'm trying to worm my way back into her good books.

Suzie comes in, wet hair still wrapped in a towel, and flops down beside me on the couch. She picks up her dinner, and yes, she does mumble, 'Thanks.'

After she's eaten maybe half of it, she puts the plate back on the coffee table. 'I've been meaning to tell you, I was able to help Beth. She now has that six hundred thousand plus from the other account, with the police super and life insurance payout both now being processed.' Whilst saying this, she's curled her feet under her and turned to face me.

'That's great,' I say. 'So she kept the house?'

'No. She decided a clean break would be best, and as she was nearly packed anyway, she decided to buy another place. She's pretty excited about moving on with her life.'

'Good outcome, then.'

'Yes, more of your "Mortice" – justice, Mort style, ah?' She gives me a sweet smile and a kiss. I like where this is headed!

Suzie pulls back. 'Not that I've fully forgiven you, but Beth really did need help. Now it's all sorted, I've decided on the rest of your punishment.' She stops, looking at me with an intent, determinedly serious face, before saying, 'Mort, I can't stay mad at you. I've been trying, but it doesn't last. Must be love, I guess!'

She smiles wryly. I lean in for a kiss, but she avoids it. 'That doesn't mean there won't be a punishment. I've decided you'll be paying for all my shopping when we go to Canada and the States. You know I can't wait to buy a couple of new handbags and some nice shoes, and it'll all be on you.'

As I lean in again, I say, 'Ouch, you drive a hard bargain, but I accept.'

She laughs. 'I should hope so.'

We kiss. I pull back. 'Your dinner is going cold.'

'Maybe dinner isn't what I want.'

I don't need a second invitation, so I wrap her in my arms and stand up without breaking our kiss. You know where we're headed!

17

On the Thursday that Stacey's coming up for the weekend, Maria does a countdown of the hours for Pig, teasing him about how long he can wait. Of course, he gives it back tenfold. He asks her how she coped when Ronnie, her husband, was away at the mines three weeks out of four. Even makes a couple of suggestions I won't record here! Then he claims Ronnie gave up on working away because Maria 'couldn't go without'.

Me, I just smile and get on with my work.

Pig starts getting edgy as it nears one o'clock, when he'll have to leave to get Stacey from the airport. At about 12:50, Maria picks up a file and walks over to him, saying, 'Can you give me a hand with this? Won't take long.'

Of course, Pig just looks at her and says, 'Piss off, I'm leaving now,' clearly realising she's just winding him up.

He packs up and leaves, with a further reminder from Maria to 'come up for air occasionally', and from Suzie about the barbecue we're having on Saturday evening.

*

The day of the barbecue comes around. It's the first time Suzie and I have met Stacey, although I feel as though we've known each other for a long time.

During the dinner, Suzie's chatting away, talking about going shopping in Sydney last time we went there, when Stacey quietly adds, 'As you do.'

This brings Suzie to a sudden halt. She goes around, gives Stacey a hug and apologises for being insensitive, considering Stacey's background.

All of a sudden, Pig is thrown aside for tomorrow, as Suzie and Stacey decide to go dress shopping for the Paramount Wireless black-tie function next weekend. Suzie tells Pig to hand over his credit card to Stacey. He does it, though not without grumbling!

*

Next Friday evening finds us all in Sydney. We head off to the Four Seasons Hotel, where we're again booked into high-floor 'harbour view' rooms.

When I open our room's door for Suzie, I'm hoping for the same response that I got last time. And I'm not disappointed!

We spend Saturday morning sightseeing in Sydney Harbour, much like we did last year when Suzie came down. Then the girls say they need to get themselves ready, and I'm barred from our room, having to take my gear over to Pig's.

It's worth it. We're both gobsmacked when our girls present themselves downstairs in the bar where we're waiting. Many a head is turned when they walk in. Of course, I've seen Suzie done up to the nines previously – if only once – but this is a new experience for Pig.

Needless to say, we have a wonderful evening, with only one moment of seriousness. Margaret, Paramount's CFO and my primary contact with them whilst we helped with their data theft last year, takes me aside and asks for my help.

'My nephew, Hoang, is being bullied,' she says. 'He's a big kid, a real nerd, and all the "in" kids tease him mercilessly both at school and on social media. My sister Rosemary and her husband Bao, who have a small supermarket up in Cairns, are worried sick that he might self-harm, or worse.' Her voice cracks and she pauses, choking back a sob. 'They work so hard. They barely stayed afloat through COVID, and business hasn't improved much up there, as it's so dependent on international tourism.'

Suzie joined me in the middle of this, taking my arm a little possessively, but she now places a gentle hand on Margaret's. Margaret goes on, 'Rosemary's been to see the principal, but he claims there's nothing he can do. No teachers have raised any issues, and of course, he has no control over what's being said and done on social media. I was hoping you might be able to help, knowing what you can do with computers. They can't afford to pay anything, but I can. I want to make sure Hoang's okay, that he can have a bright future. What do you think?'

This last sentence is said with a healthy dose of hope. I'm never one to sit on the sidelines when someone's being bullied (that's even how I met Suzie, come to think of it), so I tell Margaret, 'I'm not sure what I can achieve, but email through your sister's details and I'll shoot up there next week.'

'Oh, Mort, thank you!' she exclaims, pulling me in for a hug. (I give Suzie a smile as she watches this!) 'How large of a deposit do you need?'

'Don't worry about it. I'm happy to do this for you if you cover my flights, hotel and meals. I did all right from the Paramount deal, after all.'

Again, Margaret hugs me, saying, 'Thank you!'

I reply, 'I haven't achieved anything yet, so save the thanks until I do.'

Margaret reaches out to Suzie. 'You're a lucky lady.'

Suzie smiles. 'Yes, we both are. He'll always have your back as well, it seems.'

Later, back in our room, Suzie takes me in her arms and says, 'Margaret's the lady you said no to, isn't she?'

I manage to get a 'yes' out before my lips are otherwise engaged.

Next morning, we have no plans. As the rain has set in over Sydney, Suzie comes back to bed, after opening the curtains to the grey clouds. 'Looks like you got your wish this time, mister!' she says.

We have a very late lunch.

18

Monday morning finds Maria and me at Brisbane Airport. I'd texted her on Sunday, asking if she was available to come to Cairns with me for a few days on a new case. Her answer was 'Sure, Boss', so I had her book flights, getting us into Cairns early afternoon.

Cairns is a city in the Northern Tropics of Queensland, famous for being a gateway to the Great Barrier Reef, one of the seven wonders of the world. On arrival, we pick up our rental car and head off to meet Margaret's sister at her home. It's clear Rosemary is a little intimidated when she opens the door to find Maria and me standing there. Maria has a full sleeve of tattoos on her left arm (and others I don't need to know about!). She's six feet tall, lean and athletic, so handy when needed to bang a couple of heads together. I guess we are an imposing couple, which gives me another idea.

Nevertheless, Rosemary invites us in. As expected, Margaret had spoken to her and told her I'd be coming. Once we're settled, I ask her to start at the beginning and walk us through their concerns. She explains the challenges they face in a little more detail than Margaret did. During the COVID lockdowns, she and Bao had to double their own shifts at the shop just to stay afloat, meaning less parental time with both Hoang and their younger daughter Maggie (so named after her aunt).

She admits the bullying has been going on a long time. Hoang is a large boy who doesn't enjoy exercise and is happiest when at his computer, playing games and 'doing whatever else he does', as she explains it.

'What school does he attend?' asks Maria.

'Sacred Heart. It's Prep to Year Twelve, so both Hoang and Maggie go there.'

I ask, 'Do you know who the main culprits of the bullying are? And are they the same on social media?'

'It's the "cool group", mainly boys, but a couple of girls as well,' she answers. 'I don't use social media myself, so I'm not sure what they do on there, and Hoang won't talk about it.'

Maria has her phone out to check Hoang's Facebook, but confirms it's locked, not open to outsiders. 'That's a good thing!' she comments.

I ask, 'What time does school finish, and how does Hoang get home?'

Rosemary looks at the wall clock. 'Quarter past three. He and Maggie usually walk together.'

'Okay, so if we leave now, we could meet them at the gate?'

'I suppose,' she replies, with a hint of uncertainty.

'Can you identify the culprits as they come out?'

'Yes, I know them all by sight. I've even tried talking to some of their parents, but they just think their kids are perfect and won't consider anything that suggests otherwise. The main instigator, Justin Heeps, is the football and swimming captain, so the principal won't hear a word against him. On top of this, his mother is chairman of the P & C committee. This, of course, makes him think he's untouchable.'

'Okay, let's go,' I say. 'You can come with us, if you like. We can all fit into the rental.'

We arrive a little before 3:15. As we get out of the car, I tell Maria to roll her sleeves up. She gives me a questioning look, then smiles as she realises we're going to give these kids a little of their own medicine. Her rolled-up sleeve shows her full arm tatt, done in the traditional Māori fashion. She and I position ourselves close to the main gate, and I suggest that Rosemary stay apart from us but close enough to let us know when any of the culprits appear.

As the kids start trickling out, Maria and I get plenty of attention from them, and from some of the parents, with the teacher on duty also keeping an apprehensive eye on us. I make a point of talking to Rosemary, so he knows we have a right to be there.

Maggie comes skipping out with a couple of friends. She halts when she sees her mum there, a look of concern immediately showing on her face, but Rosemary quickly tells her everything is okay. She introduces us as friends of Aunt Maggie, which seems to put us straight into the good books!

Then Rosemary says, 'That's Justin and Holly coming out now. She's one of his cronies.'

Maria and I immediately stride through the main entrance, forcing kids to go around us, and stop directly in front of Justin. He goes to my left whilst Holly goes to Maria's right. As they do, we walk backwards, keeping pace with them, and I'm staring at him intently. But I don't speak.

Clearly getting a little nervous, Justin looks around to see where the teacher is, but he's deep in conversation with a parent. Justin quickens his stride, so I swivel around and walk with him. Holly has the sense to stop and keep out of the way. Maria stands beside her, intimidating her without saying a word.

Now I have Justin almost running, turning every couple of paces to see what I'm doing. There's growing apprehension, even fear, in his eyes. Good. I'm achieving what I wanted.

I stop. As I return to the school gate, I realise I've created quite a stir, with many parents no longer talking, just standing and watching – and more than a few students are smiling. I'm guessing Justin may not be as popular as he thinks.

Hoang has come out and is standing with his mum and sister. I retake my position, Maria joining me, but we stay silent. Rosemary says, just loud enough for me to hear, 'That's Simon Wallace and Joe Banks coming now – more of Justin's groupies.'

Maria and I again impose ourselves on their course. We don't follow them, but we keep close eye contact, and I suspect they'd been warned, as they quickly get on their way. They're hearing my message.

The teacher comes over rather apprehensively, saying hello to Rosemary and asking if everything is all right. I make a point of going over and joining the conversation, introducing myself as a friend of the family. I ask, 'I understand you have a culture of bullying in this school?'

I'm speaking loud enough for others to hear, and I can sense other parents stopping to listen. The teacher, who introduced himself as Bob, is immediately on the defensive. 'Any concerns of that nature need to be taken up with the school principal.'

Rosemary quietly says, 'I've done that. It's a waste of time.'

Bob shrugs. 'Sorry, it's out of my control.'

I say, 'We'll see you again tomorrow, then.'

19

Back at their home, I ask if we can chat to Hoang on his own. When he's ready, we head out onto their rear patio to talk in private.

Maria takes the lead. 'Would you like to talk through the bullying?' she asks softly. 'We're here to help you, and we *can* help.' This last sentence is spoken with a lot of authority and conviction.

Hoang is slump-shouldered, staring down at the ground, so Maria and I sit quietly. Patience is a virtue and we, through our respective years of army service, have had plenty of practice!

After about ten minutes of silence, he seems to realise we can wait him out. He lifts his head, looks at us and says, 'They're so mean. Just because I have a Vietnamese name and look Asian, I've been teased all my life. Most kids enjoy sport and camping and fishing and stuff like that, but none of my family likes it, let alone has time to do it. Mum and Dad both work seven days a week – I even work in the shop three nights too now. We don't have a choice. Mum and Dad need all the help they can get. It just gets to me sometimes.'

Tears well in his eyes, and Maria lightly places her hand on his arm. Another moment of silence, and he straightens and says, rather proudly, 'I've captured them all, too. All their sly and nasty posts.'

'You go, boy!' is Maria's empathetic response.

I give him a nod. 'How do you mean?'

He smiles for the first time, saying, 'I'm pretty good on the computer. Don't tell Mum, but I can sort of hack into things. I've even accessed the school's records, so I can see what they've done about other bullying complaints. Which isn't much other than filing them. But I've also made my own app, which searches out any phrase you put into it, highlights the time and day the phrase has been used, and records the user's IP address. Trouble is, I can't find out who owns the addresses.'

'We can,' I quickly respond.

'How? How can you do that?'

This time, it's my turn to smile. 'You're not the only one with hacking skills, Hoang. We just don't call it hacking. It sends the wrong message, don't you think?'

His face lights up. 'So, if I give you the IP addresses I've traced, you can tell who they belong to?'

'Yep,' I say.

'Wow! I'll go get them now.'

He hurries inside to grab his laptop, and Rosemary sticks her head out, asking, 'Was Hoang smiling?'

'Yes,' I say, 'we've made a few good first steps.'

She quickly goes back inside before Hoang returns. He fires up his laptop, fingers flying over the keys, and opens a file that has quite a number of nasty and offensive expressions. His name is even used in a few of them. Under each phrase is the day, time and IP address associated with it.

'Can you extract the IP address list?' I ask.

'Sure,' he says. I give him Pig's email (which is under the name Julien, not 'Pig'), and ask him to send it through. Whilst he's doing that, I get up and move away, ringing Pig to explain what we've found. He tells me he may not get all the names until tomorrow, as he'll get Matteo to help. Matteo is another man of mystery Midge has introduced us to. He's more on the 'commercial' side, as Midge explained, and has a top reputation for tracking digital trolls across social media platforms.

Once I've finished talking to Pig, I tell Hoang, 'We should have all the culprits' names and details in the morning. We'll review them, make a plan, and meet you after school at the gate, like today. That sound good?'

He nods. 'You can really identify them from those IP addresses?'

'Yes, we certainly can.' I go on to explain we're contracted to the Australian Cyber Security Centre, which he knows all about. I tease him by asking, 'When you accessed the school's files, you didn't improve your grades, did you?'

He answers me seriously, though. 'No, I wouldn't do that. My grades are pretty good, so I don't need to.'

Serious kid, all right!

He's looking much more composed now, and I ask him to show us how his app works. Opening Facebook, he activates his app, 'CatchEm', typing the word 'fat' into the search bar. He adds today's date into the parameters and presses go, then switches to Instagram and does the same thing.

By the time he returns to Facebook, the screen is showing two captured messages, both referring to him. We check their IP addresses, and yes, they're on the list Hoang has sent to Pig. He flicks back across to Instagram, but there's nothing there today – so far, he adds.

Maria says, 'That's a pretty cool app, Hoang. You must be proud of it!'

He smiles. I add, 'I'd be interested in helping you develop it further. We could certainly use it for some of our research – it might even help trace people through their messages. Would you be interested in becoming partners? I can fund any costs you'd have as well.'

'Cool!' is his immediate response. 'What would it be worth? How much money can I earn? Maybe I can help Mum and Dad keep the shop.'

I laugh. 'It's a bit early for any of that, Hoang, but it'll be worth something, no doubt. Tell me, does it only check public posts, or private ones as well?'

'Only public. I could include private messages if I wanted to, but that would be illegal.'

'Any other apps you're working on?'

He blushes slightly. 'Well, yes, there's one, but I'm not telling anyone about it yet.'

'Okay,' I reply. 'When you're ready, we can talk about it too. We might have to give you a job when you leave school!'

'I'm hoping to go down to Queensland University of Technology and study computer science, but I'm not sure we can afford it.'

'I reckon you can with CatchEm! Does your mum know you've developed this app?' He colours a little further and shakes his head, so I say, 'Well, I think she should – it's something to be proud of, not ashamed of.'

Maria gets up, opens the door, and asks Rosemary to join us. Maggie comes out too, clearly not wanting to miss out on what's going on.

'Rosemary,' I start, 'we expect to have proof in the morning of who specifically is behind the online bullying.' She gasps and covers her mouth. I nod. 'Yes, it's going to be very easy, as Hoang here has written his own app that can search both Facebook and Instagram for any words you want to see. It's pretty amazing, and will make him quite a bit of money, I suspect, but only if handled appropriately. We'll help him patent the idea as well.'

This brings another gasp from Rosemary and a look of surprise from Hoang, who obviously hadn't thought of that possibility, but likely couldn't afford it anyway.

Rosemary gives Hoang a loving hug, and Maggie joins in. With tears in her eyes, Rosemary asks, 'Once you identify who the culprits are, how will you deal with them?'

'Our first stop should be to meet with the principal, but I have a few other ideas as well,' I say, with a small smile. I get a meaningful look from Maria. Again, I sense she's thinking along the same lines as I am about making examples of these digital thugs. Gutless wonders, in my book.

It's getting late, but I ask Rosemary for a quiet word before we leave. When Hoang and Maggie have gone inside, I say, 'Hoang's a clever kid. You and your husband should be very proud of him. He's coped with this bullying most of his life, yet he's turned it around and found a way to identify the culprits, and likely make some good money as well. So don't be too hard on him whilst he's shut in his room doing who knows what – some good is going to come of it!'

Rosemary's slightly overcome from all of this, so I tell her we'll touch base with her in the morning. As she needs to work at the shop most of the day tomorrow, I assure her we're happy to meet her and her husband there, and Maria takes down the address.

We get into the rental. Maria smiles at me, and we bump fists. Yeah, I know, Pig and I do it all the time, and I'm sure Maria was sort of teasing me by offering her fist, but hey, we're all equals, right?

20

The next morning, I take the opportunity for a good long run around the Cairns Esplanade and small port. It's a hive of activity, as all the dive and tourist boats are preparing for another day on the Great Barrier Reef. Maria and I adjourn after breakfast to read through the names Pig has sent through. We compare the messages to the names, and it's very clear the two main culprits are Justin Heeps and Simon Wallace. Others, including Holly, are more followers than instigators. No less guilty, in my book!

Plan made – or at least a draft plan, as we agree we need to act only on Hoang's or his parents' behalf, not wanting to start something they aren't comfortable with – we head to the Cairns CBD to meet with Rosemary and her husband Bao. At their supermarket, which is really more a minimarket, we find Rosemary at the checkout. As she's busy serving a few customers, we wander around until we find a man who must be Bao unpacking fruit and vegies. On seeing us, he asks, 'Mort and Maria?'

We both nod, and the three of us make small talk whilst waiting for Rosemary to finish serving. However, customers keep coming in in dribs and drabs, until finally Bao excuses himself. He pops out of the store and returns in a couple of minutes with a lady in tow. She steps in for Rosemary on the cash register, and we head back to the storeroom for some privacy. Bao explains that the lady and her husband own the Chinese restaurant next door and they often help each other out.

Once the door is shut, I pull out our list of names, showing all the specific comments each of these kids has made. Rosemary bursts into tears on reading it. It's quite extensive, and some of the comments are downright offensive.

Bao comforts Rosemary as best he can. Maria and I wait for her to compose herself before making a couple of suggestions on the best way forward. It's clear they're both very upset at the extent of the cyberbullying, which has been perpetrated by a total of eight students – six boys and two girls. After some debate, it's agreed Rosemary will make an appointment with the principal to formally demand action be taken, now that there's proof of what has been said and by whom.

'But what if he wipes his hands of it and isn't willing to do anything?' asks Rosemary.

I reply, 'Then we'll play dirty.'

*

Come 2:00 p.m., the three of us are sitting outside the principal's office. I tease Maria, saying, 'I'm sure this brings back memories for you.' Her response is her middle finger! Rude, isn't she?

Roger Dean, the principal, comes bustling out. He comes to a quick halt upon seeing Maria and me. 'Sorry, I can only talk to parents.'

I reply, 'Not this time,' and usher him back into his office. I've told you I can be intimidating, and he certainly thought so.

Rosemary takes the floor, introducing Maria and me as family friends, before saying she now has proof of longstanding and ongoing cyberbullying by at least eight of his students. He naturally wants to see this proof, and she hands over the list, which shows the content of each message, its date, its sender and their IP address, as well as who 'liked' it. The list runs to over two pages.

He quietly looks through it. Finally, putting it down on his desk, he says, 'It's a comprehensive list, but where's the proof they actually said any of those things? Might I add, if it's true, this is a horrible, horrible situation. I need to be absolutely certain it's real.'

We leave the silence to lengthen until it becomes a little embarrassing, letting him stew. I'd told the girls I would handle the discussion if he didn't immediately support our position, so they know not to say anything.

'Mr Dean,' I say, eventually, 'that list is clear evidence. You can ask each of the individuals what their IP address is, and if they refuse, I'm sure your IT tech could gather it from their phone, tablet or laptop. To use your own words, this is a horrible, horrible situation, and you need to address it immediately. We've provided proof of an ugly situation *you* have allowed to develop within your school. Now it's time for you to grow a pair, stand up to these bullies and bring it to a stop.'

More silence. Finally, Dean says, 'I'm sorry – I cannot accept this as proof of anything. I need to take some advice.'

'Call your IT tech in,' I say. 'He'll confirm that you can easily verify the individuals' IP addresses.'

'No.' He stands. 'I need to talk to Head Office before proceeding.'

Whilst Rosemary rises like the polite lady she is, Maria follows my lead and remains seated. I calmly say, 'Mr Dean, you are no doubt aware of the saying "Every action has a consequence". Well, you won't like the consequences of this inaction.'

I let the silence linger before I stand, politely shake his hand,

and head out the door without saying another word.

Once outside, I smile and say, 'I was sort of hoping he'd take that stance. Now we can spice it up and give Hoang some real revenge.' Maria is, of course, smiling with me, knowing what I'm planning.

It's not quite 3:00 p.m., so it's too early to take our station at the main gates for a repeat of yesterday's intimidation. I text Colleen Hill, our friendly journalist at Brisbane's *Courier Mail*, asking her, 'Hi, who's a good contact at the *Cairns Post*?'

Not surprisingly, my phone rings immediately, so I wander away from the girls. I'm greeted by Colleen saying, 'You're *my* contact, and I'm not sharing you with anyone!'

Like she owns me! She calms down a little when I tell her it's a situation of school bullying in Cairns. 'So, you're up north now, are you?' she asks.

'Yep,' I reply. 'Who do I need to talk to?'

'If it's only a local issue, I suppose that's okay. I'll text you Barry McLeod's phone number. Tell him he owes me one, and make sure you call me next time you have anything juicy.' She pauses, then adds, '*Please!*'

'Will do, and thanks,' I reply.

Sure enough, I receive a text with Barry's details shortly before the school bell rings. Maria and I head to the front gate to have a little fun. She's wearing a sleeveless top, and whilst it's suited to the warm and balmy weather up here, it also serves the purpose of showing off her tatts. I'm not a fan of tattoos, but hers do look the part.

Once again, it's Maggie who comes out first, followed by Hoang. They go over to stand with their mum. Holly appears, accompanied by a couple of girls this time. I watch her intently and see her saying something to her friends as they edge further away from Maria and me. We let her go.

Then it's Justin, Simon and Joe, all walking together. We move into the centre of the gateway as they approach. Whether by coincidence or fate, they arrive at the entrance when no other kids are there. Our positioning forces them into single file to go around us. I keep my eyes on Justin the whole time, and he's clearly uneasy.

He is going to have a very eventful day tomorrow.

We drop Rosemary, Maggie and Hoang back to their home. I ask for the final time if they still want us to proceed as planned. Both Hoang and Rosemary nod, so as Maria drives us back to the hotel, I dig out Barry McLeod's phone number.

After I'm done, I touch base with Pig. He confirms all's ready for tomorrow morning's plan. Whilst I'm up in Cairns, he's been continuing our regular data audits and monitoring our favourite prison warden. Nothing too exciting has happened there, but apparently, Midge's gait recognition system has just come through with two names from Chris's bashing: Louie and Nico Giovani. These two brothers are members of the notorious Melbourne Redskins bikie gang. Midge had also warned Pig that they're reputed to be enforcers for multiple mafias, so they're not to be taken lightly. Pig and I agree he'll dig up what he can so we can make a plan upon my return.

Of course, I also give Suzie a call – but I do that a little later from the privacy of my hotel room.

21

The following morning, Maria and I are up early to check if our plan has been implemented at 6:00 a.m., as scheduled.

Yes, it has been.

We've set up a post on all our culprits' Facebook and Instagram pages, which reads: 'I'm a cyberbully. Here are some of the things I've been saying about fellow students in the last six months.' This is accompanied by a reel of their previous posts, showing what they said and when. So, Justin, Simon and Joe, along with a few others, should be highly embarrassed right about now. Hopefully, they're being subjected to some hard questioning from their parents.

Barry McLeod has, as agreed, published a story on the *Cairns Post's* website, highlighting the details and extent of the bullying that's been going on unchecked. It names the school, and even includes a photo of it. It concludes with the statement: 'We have sought comment from the school principal, Roger Dean, but have not yet received a reply.'

I say to Maria, 'Looks like Roger's had an early start!'

We decide we deserve a big breakfast and head down to a local café to so indulge. We're still there when Rosemary calls, sounding a little overwhelmed, to tell me the principal has contacted her and asked if we could attend a meeting at school as soon as possible.

'Sure,' I say, 'we're just finishing our breakfast, so we can there by 8:30 if that suits you and the kids.'

'Yes, all I want is to get it over and done with. But before you go, Hoang wants to speak with you.'

She hands the phone over to Hoang, who says, 'Hi, I've had lots of messages from other kids who've been bullied, so I set CatchEm up with a few different words. It seems Justin and Simon have been saying nasty things about a lot of people.'

'Good job, Hoang,' I tell him. 'Please bring this latest list with you to school this morning.'

'Okay, will do. See you there.'

He hangs up. I had my phone on speaker, sitting on the table between Maria and me, and she notes, 'He seems pretty upbeat about what's going down. Good for him.'

I nod.

*

We're sitting outside the principal's office a little before 8:30 when Rosemary, Bao, Hoang and Maggie all come in. On seeing us, Rosemary comes over and hugs us both.

'Thank you so much,' she says. 'If the school finally takes action, it'll take a lot of stress out of our lives.'

Bao, having thanked us both as he shook our hands, adds, 'They bloody better. What more proof do they need?'

We're kept waiting for quite a while. Finally, the door to the principal's office opens and out comes Justin Heeps, followed by who I assume are his parents. The mother is in tears, the father looking rather angry. They see us all sitting there, and their focus is drawn to Hoang. I immediately stand up to my full height.

After a slight pause, the father pushes his wife and son outside.

Would've been the ideal opportunity for the parents to get Justin to apologise, I think, *but then again, his racial and social attitudes are most likely a reflection of theirs.*

Roger Dean comes out. He asks if both Hoang and Maggie can stay outside, but Rosemary says, 'No. Hoang has borne the brunt of this bullying, so he's entitled to hear the outcome.'

Roger nods, and we all take our seats. He steeples his hands together as if in prayer. 'I apologise for not being able to take action yesterday as you requested. Mr Ireland,' he says, looking at me, 'I now understand your threat about consequences, and these will be serious for both me and the school.

'For the record, I've been in numerous meetings with Head Office since we last spoke. I can confirm that, as of this morning, Justin Heeps has been permanently excluded from our school. You saw the Heeps family leaving just now, I gather. There will be a number of others facing temporary and permanent exclusion today.'

He pauses, before continuing, 'I can only sincerely apologise for the dastardly behaviour you've had to put up with, Hoang. It is an absolute credit to you that you've maintained such high grades with this going on in the background. Being totally honest, this was one of the things that made me question your claims of bullying, as most studies show when a child is being bullied – either at home or at school – the first place this is reflected is in their grades. But you have proven to be the exception to the rule. Well done.

'Mr and Mrs Tran, the school and I want to do more than apologise for what you and your family have been put through. We would like to offer both Hoang and Margaret here full scholarships for the rest of their time here, this being backdated to the start of this year. If Hoang continues with his excellent grades, there's also the opportunity for a full scholarship to the Australian Catholic University in Brisbane when the time comes.'

This is met by gasps from Rosemary and Bao and excited looks from both Hoang and Maggie. All I can think is: *What's the catch?*

'Thank you, Mr Dean,' Bao says. 'It would be very much appreciated. However, I need to understand what conditions would apply to this offer.'

Dean again steeples his fingers before responding. 'Our legal team is still putting that together, but in essence, we'd be asking that this matter be kept confidential. We would also expect this would prevent you from taking any further legal or civil action against the school or me for our failings in this matter.'

Bao takes his time responding, and it's clear from the way he and Rosemary are looking at each other that some sort of message is being conveyed between them. Eventually, he replies, 'We, as a family, want to put this horrid matter behind us once and for all. We have no desire to take you to court. I will have to take legal advice, but if your offer is genuine and straightforward, we will accept it.'

In the silence that follows, Hoang holds up the new list. 'Mr Dean, I had a lot of other students contact me. Here's a list of some more things that have been said about other kids here.' He hands it to Dean.

'Thank you, Hoang. I will review this and amend our plans accordingly.'

On the way out of the office, I notice Joe and his parents, or so I gather, sitting silently. Their turn next, I guess.

In the car park, we shake hands all round. Bao asks if he can treat us to a full lunch, telling the kids they can have the day off and join in as well. Apparently, his brother owns the best Vietnamese restaurant in town, and the two cooking together is something to behold.

As we're breaking up, I hear a girl calling out to Hoang and see Holly hurrying over to him, her own family trailing along behind her. Before she says anything, she bursts into tears. No one goes to her aid, as we all wait for her to compose herself. Wiping her face with her sleeve, she approaches Hoang, saying, 'Hoang, some horrible things have been said about you. I want you to know I'm truly sorry for having anything to do with it. I took the easy way out and liked those comments so I would fit in. I'm sorry I didn't stand up for you.' And she starts sobbing again.

Hoang reaches out, puts his hand on her shoulder and says quietly, 'I know you didn't say any of those things, Holly. Thanks for apologising.'

With nods all round, we leave the school.

Maria and I leave the Tran family and decide to head up to Port Douglas for morning tea, having promised to be back for lunch at Bao's brother's restaurant. Once in the car, we high five and agree we did a good job.

'So, is this more of that Mortice Suzie's told me about?' Maria asks playfully as we head off.

I smile. 'Sometimes proper justice needs a hand, and I'm happy to do my part.'

A bit up myself, aren't I!

Port Douglas is an easy 45-minute drive north of Cairns. It's a thriving (well, in pre-COVID days, anyway!) tourist town, like Cairns, claiming to be a 'Gateway to the Great Barrier Reef'. It does have plenty of options when it comes to diving and snorkelling, as well as bus and 4 x 4 tours to the lovely Daintree

Rainforest an hour or so further north.

The road up is a delight, running for much of the journey along the coastline. It's not hard to find a café in the main street. Maria chooses an organic joint, and I warn her, 'The coffee better be good.' But it is, and we sit quietly and relax, more than happy with a job well done.

Maria has confirmed our flights home are leaving Cairns at 4:30 p.m. We'll be back in time for a late dinner, so I give Suzie a call to let her know she'll be cooking tonight. Alas, it goes to her voicemail. I leave a message, and a short while later get a smiley face and red heart as a reply. Maria sees this on my phone and gags, pretending to be put off by the 'lovestruck' couple, as she happily calls us!

A little later, Maggie from Paramount gives me a call. 'Mort, you continue to astound me with how you manage to get these difficult jobs done!'

'All part of the service, Maggie,' I say. Don't think I blushed, but it's always nice to receive positive praise.

Now back to Cairns for our promised lunch. And what a lunch it is. The brothers have outdone themselves, and not just for us – their extended families are all here for the feast.

As we head to the airport, I concede to Maria that I might have to tell Suzie not to bother cooking. It certainly was a meal to remember!

22

Next morning, back in the office, Pig and I sit down for a briefing. He's curious about Hoang's CatchEm app, so I show him how it works, accessing his Facebook page. I say, 'Now, if I put the word "sex" in, what would it come up with?'

He knows I'm teasing and merely smiles. I input 'George', his former partner's name, into the app instead, then limit the time period to the last three months. It only comes up with three short messages, one from George, the others from mutual friends. Pig is suitably impressed.

We discuss the best way to patent CatchEm, and how it could be commercialised. Pig agrees to get in touch with a patent lawyer we did work for a few months back. Should give Hoang a good rate, we reckon.

'What have you dug up on our new Giovani mates?' I ask.

He pulls up his notes on his laptop. 'Well, it appears Nico, despite being three years younger than Louie, is the brains of the outfit. They're reputed to do enforcement work for the gangs, but probably on a freelance basis, as they've been connected to three separate Melbourne mafias. Not to mention their ongoing membership of the Redskins bikie club.'

'So, it could be any of three or four gangs who wanted Chris worked over?'

'Yes.'

I purse my lips. 'Ah, well. Just means it'll take a little longer to get where we need to go.'

Pig nods. 'They live together in an old cottage-style house on Chomley Street, Prahran, which they jointly own.' He shows me a photo off the web, and there are two Harleys sitting in the driveway, as well as what looks like a Mercedes A45 – the AMG 'hot hatch'.

'I bet their neighbours love them, coming and going on their Harleys,' I say.

Pig confirms the bikes are both registered to a company the two brothers are the directors of, whilst the A45 is registered to a different company, this one with a director named Zoe Romano. Pig shows me her license and a couple of photos from her Facebook page, which show her and Nico together.

'Good way to avoid losing your license,' I comment. 'Just have the company pay the fines!'

We agree we need to 'get to know them a little better' before deciding on the best course of action. Over a freshly brewed coffee, Pig offers to go down to Melbourne. I say, 'I wonder what the attraction in Melbourne is?'

He ignores me. 'We need to carry out a bit of surveillance, hopefully get some mics somewhere handy.'

'Ideally on their phones.'

'If I can drop the bugging app onto one like I did with Warden Thomas, that would be the best outcome. Hope they have AirDrop on.'

Plan made.

*

Next morning, with Pig on his way to Melbourne, I head over to Marissa Polonsky's unit in Stones Corner. I get there before 8:00, so I can hopefully see her routine. Sure enough, just after 8:30, she backs out of the carport in a little Hyundai i30 and heads off down Regina Street, likely to drop her daughter off at Buranda State School. Yes, I've done my homework, having checked out the closest school and its direction. I don't follow her, anticipating she'll return to her apartment before heading off to work a little later for her 11:00 a.m. shift at the barbershop.

I'm right. She arrives back after only about twelve minutes and heads back up to her apartment. I sit tight until just after 9:15, when I make my move, striding up the stairs and knocking at her door. A female voice answers. 'Who is it?'

'Ms Polonsky, I'm a private investigator, and I would like to ask you a few questions.' Silence for a few moments, so I add, 'My investigation is not about you, but I'm hoping you can add some background for me.'

Silence. Eventually, she opens the door, leaving the chain on. It's only open a little, but that's enough. With the door open six inches or so, it's easy to hide my hand behind it, as I quickly reach up and slip a small mic and camera over its edge. They're fixed to a U-shaped bracket, so they fit over the door, sitting flush against its inside. Fortunately, they're a beige colour, the same as the door. Knowing it's a possibility Marissa will call someone once I explain why I want to talk to her, I'm keen to use a mic rather than go through all the phone users from the nearest tower.

Whilst doing this, I introduce myself, showing her a business card with a fictious name and company. Knowing how intimidating I can be, I suggest we meet down the road at Stones Throw, the closest local café. My homework is thorough!

Marissa is still hesitating, so I suggest I can reimburse her for her time. 'How much?' is her quick response.

'Depends how helpful you are.'

After a pause, she says, 'I need to know what this is about first.'

'Fair enough. I understand you were an acquaintance of Dillion Benson. It's Benson we need to chat about.'

I note she doesn't try to deny knowing Benson, and her response is predictable. 'But Dillion is dead. Killed in that big bikie war thing a few months ago.'

'Yes, I'm aware of that. Our investigation is about an accident he had some time before those events.'

Another pause as she contemplates this. I slip a $100 note out of my pocket, letting her see the distinctive green colour, before adding, 'I'm happy to reimburse you for your time, and you'll get a free coffee as well.'

'Okay. I'll see you there in ten minutes, but I start work at 11:00, so this can't take long.'

I reply, 'I know.' Just want her to be a little unsettled.

Back in the Camry, I engage the door mic, interested to see if she calls anyone, but the only sound is the radio in the background. She hadn't seemed nervous or anything, so I already suspect this will be a bust.

I continue to wait until I see her come down the stairs and jump into her i30. Once we've both parked at Stones Throw, I order our coffee and we take a seat.

'How well did you know Benson?' I ask, placing my phone on the table with the recorder going. She gives me an appraising look. I'm guessing she's trying to decide whether to be upfront or not, so I prompt her by saying, 'We've done a thorough investigation of Benson, so if you want to be reimbursed, you need to be honest from the get-go.'

She waits whilst our coffee is served before starting. 'I met Dillion a few years ago, when he could've arrested me but gave me a warning instead. We had a bit of a fling for a while, then once the passion died, he'd pop up every so often and we'd connect randomly. It was never going anywhere, but it seemed to work for both of us.' After a pause, she says, 'Yes, I knew he was married. He didn't try to hide it. I certainly wasn't interested in marrying him, so it didn't bother me.'

'So, more "friends with benefits" than a full-on relationship?' I ask.

'Yeah, Dillion once called it that too, although he also called us "fuck buddies", so take your pick.' This is said with a suggestive smile.

I let the conversation lapse as we both take a sip of coffee.

'Okay,' I say, 'do you recall him mentioning a car accident where he was driving and the other driver was killed?'

She immediately answers, 'Yes, he told me about it one night when he came round. It seemed to be on his mind. He mentioned it a couple of other times as well, come to think of it. He talked about the coroner's report. Seemed worried what it might say. I didn't take too much notice – it wasn't anything that affected me, and I had other things on my mind.' She flashes a smirk.

I pick up my phone and pretend to play with it, checking to see if her phone, also sitting on the table, is open for AirDrop. As it is, I send it the app Pig had shared, meaning we'll now be able to hear any conversations she has. Not that I'm expecting much – she doesn't seem to know anything of importance – but you never know.

Unable to think of anything else to ask, I say, 'Anything else you can remember about the accident that might help?'

Marissa shakes her head, then glances at her watch. 'I need to get going.' She looks back up, giving me the full-on appraisal. 'Now Dillion's gone, it does leave a hole in my life, so I'd be happy to continue our acquaintance.'

I smile. 'You have my card. If you do think of anything that might be useful, please let me know.' As I say this, I slide the $100 note across the table, keeping it hidden under my fingers. She puts her hand on top of mine, so I slip mine away, and she has the note. She nods in acknowledgement.

As we leave the café, she asks, 'How did you know about me and Dillion?'

I wave at her as I get into the Camry. No harm in leaving a little uncertainty in the air!

Back in the office, I log my interview summary, noting the mic and camera are in position on Marissa's entrance door. I then decide to pull up our local prison warden's recent conversations. There's a lot of rubbish in there, with chats to his wife, kids, and mates. Then I see a call received from 'Joe'. This seems innocuous enough, until Joe asks if there's been any further contact with 'the three coppers'. No is the answer, and they hang up.

But this gets me thinking.

I decide to get Robert at Section V to set up an official meeting for me at the prison with former DI Fleming, using a fictious name and government department. Of course, Robert doesn't know the backstory about our previous dealings with this lot, so he refers to MGC.

MGC gives me a call. As usual, he won't discuss much on the phone, even though ours are both encrypted. Rather, he tells me he'll be in Brisbane on another matter later in the week and will drop by for a chat.

'Good by me,' I tell him. 'I'll make the coffee.'

Knowing MGC likes his reports, I start compiling an account of the full story. I'm confident he'll agree with my plan once he has all the information to hand.

*

Two days later, at the agreed time, there's a knock on the front door. Even though we've been waiting for him, I'm in awe that MGC is visiting our little set-up, along with Robert.

I greet them, introducing Maria, and pour us all a coffee. We adjourn to my desk, the closest thing we have to a meeting table. As usual, there's little small talk – other than MGC briefly asking where Pig is – so I hand over a copy of my report and leave them to read and digest it, waiting patiently for the questions to come.

Once MGC is finished, he removes his glasses, looks at me and says, 'Very well, what do you hope to gain by this little subterfuge?'

'Well, sir, I certainly thought we'd cut the head off this thing back when Lancaster was killed and his cohorts imprisoned. However, it's looking more and more likely that another extension or associated group have taken up the reins. If it wasn't for Benson's stat dec, this would be buried by now.

'We only have two known access points to this group, one being Nico and Louie Giovani down in Melbourne, the other our friendly prison warden. My plan is to get a reaction from Warden Carl Thomas and follow that wherever it goes. If their reputation is true, we won't get anything out of the Giovanis, leaving Thomas as our best option. We know he has "Joe" on speed dial, and we know this number is coming from the dark web, so it's not some local thug, but someone with at least a semblance of sophistication.

'Therefore, by reaching out and making an official appointment with Fleming, we should grab someone's attention. Hopefully, we can then trace them by watching and monitoring Warden Thomas.'

MGC sits unmoving as he comes to his decision. After five minutes of silence, he says, 'Very well. Robert, set this meeting up for Mort. I agree there's little chance of getting anything out of Nico and Louie. But let's monitor them anyway – they may lead us to something or someone.'

He nods to me. I reply, 'They will get hurt, General. What they did to Chris isn't right.'

'Don't let emotion cloud your judgment, Mort.'

'No emotion, sir. Just fact.'

With this, MGC stands. 'Is Suzie here? I'd like to say hello if so.'

I reply, 'Yes, that's her office over there.'

He heads directly over to the door (we'd closed it to retain our confidentiality for a change). Suzie pops out to greet him, and they chat for a few minutes before he says goodbye and takes his leave.

Once he's gone, I say to Suzie, 'Wow, you must've made an impression.'

She smiles sweetly. 'You think!'

23

The following Monday, Robert advises me I have an interview with former DI Fleming on Wednesday at Palen Creek Correctional Centre. I thank him and let Pig and Maria know things are in motion.

Wednesday morning comes, and Maria and I head out to Palen Creek Prison. She precedes me out in the Camry, whilst I take the Prado. Neither vehicle's registration plates will show up in any video surveillance. Well, they'll show up, but they'll be illegible due to a special chemical coating we give all the vehicles we use.

Once Maria arrives, she gives me a call, telling me she's got a good spot directly facing the entrance of the car park. We want to see if anyone takes particular notice of my arrival or departure, so she'll wait with the dashcam running, recording all vehicles that come and go. The dashcam is higher tech than the run-of-the-mill models; it even has infrared for when we need vision at night.

She tells me it's pretty quiet in the car park – only one car so far. I describe Warden Thomas's Ford Courier for her, but she says there's nothing like it around. She then remembers she saw a 'staff parking' sign on the other side, so we figure it's likely there.

As I approach the prison, Maria again confirms there's no one around. I know nobody has followed me, as I did the 'slow down, speed up, then stop suddenly' routine. All a bit over the top, really, as no one knows it's me turning up for the interview, but it broke the monotony of the drive out!

I head over to the office and present my credentials – my false credentials, that is. Soon enough, I find there's only one pace in the prison system: slow. But hey, I'm a patient guy, so it doesn't faze me.

I'm eventually led inside, having passed through two separate scanners and left my phone and keys in a small locker. On my way to the interview room, where former Detective Inspector Jack Fleming is already sitting, I keep an eye open for Warden Thomas but see no sign of him.

Fleming does a double take when he sees me. Clearly, he remembers me from the night not so very long ago when I killed Benson.

Good. I need him rattled.

I take a seat and slide my (false) card across the table, not saying a word. I let the silence stretch, but the minutes tick by without Fleming showing any signs of cracking, and I remember he's a seasoned interviewer, having been a senior detective for many years. So, I try a different tactic.

'Flem, I can have you out of here in a minute.' I click my fingers. 'Not to set you free, but so I can interview you without the constraints they impose in prison. Not saying you'd survive our talk, mind you, but that wouldn't bother me. One less crim walking the earth, as far as I'm concerned.'

I try the silent treatment again. This time, I see he's getting a little anxious. I let it drag on until he can't resist. 'What do you want from me?' he asks.

'Who beat up DS Chris Morris?'

This is news to him – or he's a bloody good actor, but I doubt that. He stammers, 'What do you mean?'

'Three days after DS Morris interviewed you, she was beaten. Badly. She was in the ICU in a coma for three days. Coincidence?'

He shakes his head. 'I don't know. I didn't say anything to anyone, except Josh and Bryce, and I doubt they have those sorts of connections.'

After a pause, as I watch him intently, I say, 'You implied to Chris you knew more than you were letting on about Benson's accident. What can you tell me?'

Nothing. I again let the silence stretch, but Fleming doesn't budge.

'You won't last five minutes with me if I need to extract you from here to get to the truth,' I say.

He looks up at me, fear now evident in his eyes. The question is, is he more scared of me or of who he's protecting by staying silent? The attack on Chris was an indirect threat to him too, I realise.

I sit there, watching him silently, and let a full five minutes go by. He doesn't say or do anything. I guess you learn patience in prison too.

'Well, next time we meet, don't expect to be able to walk away afterward,' I tell him. I get up from the table and bang on the door to indicate the interview is over.

On my way back, this time I do see Warden Thomas, standing in a doorway watching as I walk past. Hopefully, he'll report to 'Joe' and we'll finally learn something. That's why I'm here performing this charade, after all.

I call Maria and let her know I'll be heading out shortly. She'll follow me, keeping an eye out for anyone who might be tailing me.

Silly, really, I think. *If anyone wanted to know where I was going,*

I'm sure they'd put a tracker on the car, just like we do.

I pull up at a rest area on the outskirts of Rathdowney and check the Prado for trackers. Nothing. I go on into town, order a coffee and a tea, and settle down to wait for Maria. She pulls the Camry in before long, coming over and taking a seat on the picnic table I'm perched on.

Raising the takeaway cup in silent thanks, she says, 'We're clear. Must've been ten minutes after you went past before another car came along, and that was likely just a local farmer – he had a couple of dogs on the back of his ute. How'd the interview go?'

I pull a face. 'Didn't get anything, really. The only thing it's confirmed is that he knows something but isn't willing to share it. I threatened to pull him out of prison so I could get the truth out of him, and whilst he was suitably scared, he wasn't scared enough to tell me what or who he knows. Which, of course, tells us we're up against a serious crime gang of some sort, clearly still with connections within Queensland Police.'

'There's no way you can get him out of prison anyway,' she says, then narrows her eyes. 'Or is there?'

I smile. 'Ways and means, Maria. Ways and means.' After finishing my coffee, I say, 'Let's head back to the office and see who our favourite warden has been talking to.'

'Race you,' she replies, as she jumps in the Camry.

On the journey back, I call Pig and bring him up to date on the interview, telling him I'll let him know what calls Thomas has made once I get to the office. I also say I'm thinking about 'extracting' Fleming from prison so we can give him a real interrogation. Of course, Pig asks how we'd do that, and I reply, 'Mate, the security is so lax you could walk him out. With what I suspect he knows, though, I'm sure MGC can organise a "transfer". If we dress you and Maria up in some uniforms, pop lanyards around your necks and load you up with a bunch of forms to be signed, Bob's your uncle. Although, as a carrot, we'd also likely have to be prepared to set him and his family up in witness protection.'

'What would the 'stick' be?' Pig asks.

'Dump his body in a ditch,' I reply.

Pig then gives me an update on his progress down in Melbourne. 'I've set up a CCTV camera on the streetlight across the road from their home, and I've been watching their routine – I want to get inside and set up a few mics in the next couple of days. None of the windows are ever open, so I'm not getting much from the raindrop mics. I haven't had a chance to AirDrop the bugging app to their phones, either, but I'm working on it. Should be finished in a day or two, but I might stay over for the next weekend. I promised to take Stace for a drive along the Great Ocean Road.'

I ask, 'How's married life?'

'Well, she hasn't kicked me out yet, so I can't be doing too bad!'

Of course, Maria gets back first. I get a smug smile from her as I enter, but it's Suzie who mutters 'Granddad' as she returns to her office. Nice, aren't they? Just because I drive to the legal limit (well, when I'm not in a hurry!).

Maria sits waiting at my desk. She's already accessed the audio from Warden Thomas's phone, and when I sit down, fresh coffee in hand, she patches Pig in on Zoom and presses play. She's set the start for the time I arrived at the prison, so there's a fair bit of idle chatter. Then I recognise Thomas's voice saying, 'Is that him?'

Another male voice says, 'Yeah, he's the one sent from some mob called the Domestic Terrorism Authority – never heard of them, but they're part of Border Force, apparently. Wonder what they want with Fleming?'

'Dunno,' is Thomas's reply. 'Pity we aren't allowed to listen in, ah!'

Hmm, I think, *I bet you would if someone made it worth your while.*

Some twenty minutes later, the second voice says, 'He's finished. He's coming out now.'

Thomas mutters, 'Okay.'

Silence from the recording, then a door is closed quietly. I say to Maria, 'Shutting the office door so he has privacy?'

Sure enough, we hear him dialling, and the number he rings comes up on the screen – it matches the one in his contacts for 'Joe'. The call is answered by a male voice, but it's heavily distorted; he's clearly using some sort of synthesiser, so there's no chance of the voice being recognised.

Bugger, this bloke's going to serious lengths to hide his identity!

Thomas tells Joe of my visit. Joe asks, 'Any idea what was discussed?'

'No. We aren't permitted to record prisoner interviews.'

'Next time, make sure you do. I'm paying you good money to provide *all* information you can on those three cops. Clear?'

'Yes, Joe. I'll try.'

'Make sure you succeed. For your own health, and that of your family.'

Maria stops the recording there. I look from her to Pig and say, 'Shit, we went to a fair bit of trouble setting this up, and it didn't even give us any new leads to follow. Thoughts?'

Maria shakes her head, whilst Pig looks pensive. 'Looks like we'll need to move to plan B and snatch Fleming then,' he says, watching Maria with a half smirk on his face.

'But how can we do that?' she asks.

I explain the half-baked plan Pig and I discussed on my way back to the office.

'Well, as long as it's official,' Maria says. 'I don't want to end up in prison for breaking an arsehole like Fleming out of one!'

I add, 'Whatever plan we come up with, it's going to have to wait until we get back from the Invictus Games. It's only four weeks until we head off. How's the training been going down there, Pig? Hope you're out pounding the track at 5:00 every morning!'

There's a slight pause before he replies. 'At 5:00 down here, it's still bloody dark and cold, so I've been training every day... at 6:00.'

'There's a side benefit for you being down there, Pig,' I say. Maria sniggers, likely thinking I mean Stacey, but I go on, 'Melbourne's cold, wet and miserable weather is more like Canada than Brisbane, so you should be becoming acclimatised!'

We sign off with a laugh.

Bugger. Not a total bust, but a bust all the same. I send the audio of Warden Thomas and his mystery friend to Midge, just in case he has new technology that can break down the synthesised voice. If anyone does, it'll be Midge.

24

The following week, Pig's back home. One late afternoon, he says, 'Listen to this,' and plays a recording of a phone call.

Maria stops to listen as well. 'Yeah?' is the first thing we hear.

Pig says, 'That's Nico answering his phone.'

'Mate, it's Dicky here,' says another voice. 'How you going?'

'What's happening?' Nico asks.

'Got a little job. Ten in it for you.'

'Each?'

'Total, but I can maybe push it up a bit. It's not a big job, not even a hard one. Skye – you know, Fredo's new chick – she wants her ex Brian given a beating. Apparently, he's taken up with one of her friends, Denise, and she doesn't like it. He's a sales rep or something, so an easy one for ya.'

'Okay, when?'

'This Friday. He's meant to be taking Denise out Friday night, and she doesn't want that happening.'

'Why? What's her beef with this Denise?'

'Dunno. She wants to scratch her eyes out, the way I heard it. Still, she can afford the ten, so who cares?'

'Make it fifteen and consider it done.'

'Deal. I'll text you his address.'

Nico hangs up and says, presumably to Louie, 'Sounds like we'll get an easy fifteen k on Friday night. This chick wants her old flame touched up.'

'Cool. Haven't needed to use these for a while,' is Louie's reply, as he audibly cracks his knuckles.

Pig stops the recording. 'What do you say we get to this bloke's house before they do and sort them out?'

'Done,' I say, then add in a playful tone, 'I suppose that means you want to stay the weekend down there?'

But Pig shakes his head. 'Nah, I don't want to drop my training. Besides, there'll be too many questions.'

Maria says, 'So, you just break into this Brian's place and beat up these two goons when they arrive?'

'They've well and truly earnt it,' I say.

'Shit,' says Maria. 'I hope I never get on your bad side.'

'Justice doesn't always come from the legal system,' I say. 'Sometimes it needs a hand. Remember, this is confidential, so not for gossip.' I tilt my head towards Suzie and Jenny's office. Maria nods.

Pig adds, 'Just another form of Mortice!'

*

The next day, it's a typical Wednesday afternoon, a little after 3:30, and Suzie and Jenny are making coffees in the little kitchen by the office, chatting away as always. Suzie turns around to head back to her desk, then suddenly bursts into tears!

Jenny stops mid-sentence (something I wouldn't have believed possible if I hadn't seen it myself!) and looks to see why Suzie is crying. There I am, in the middle of the office, down on one knee with a little box in my hand, which I've extended towards Suzie.

Smiling, Jenny nudges Suzie, who's still blubbering, towards me. She comes over hesitantly. I wait a minute in absolute silence whilst she regains her composure. Then I say, 'Suzie Dunn, I love you. Will you marry me?'

Suzie is outright crying again, but she still manages to wrap her arms around me, saying, 'Yes, *yes*, I'll marry you.' She holds her hand out and I slip on a lovely engagement ring. It fits.

We kiss. It lingers. Pig and Jenny start clapping, which, of course, makes us break apart, and I whisper, 'Thank you!'

I get another kiss, then Suzie dances over to Jenny. She grabs her hands, and they do a little circle jig, like young kids do. Suzie sings, 'I'm getting married, I'm getting married!' over and over again, stopping occasionally to admire the ring. She tells me more than once, 'I love the ring – and you!'

Pig comes over to me, a big smile on his face. He slaps me on the back and pulls me into a big hug. 'Congrats!' he says, and heads to the fridge. 'Let's have a toast.' I'd popped a decent bottle of champagne in there the night before, hoping there'd be something to celebrate today.

Suzie and Jenny stop dancing their jig to accept their glasses of champagne, and we toast. It's Jenny who says, 'So, how long have you been planning this?'

And I reply nonchalantly, 'Oh, the idea crossed my mind a couple hours ago, and I thought, *What the heck? She can only say no.*' This gets me a combination of snorts and giggles.

'I have to ring my parents,' Suzie says suddenly, grabbing her phone and putting it on speaker. When Caroline picks up, she exclaims, 'Mum, I'm getting married!'

'I know, dear. Isn't it wonderful?'

Suzie blinks. 'How did you know?'

Chuckling, Caroline says, 'Mort flew up yesterday and asked our permission. Wasn't that lovely, darling?'

Suzie bursts into tears again, coming over to land another kiss on me. Caroline asks, 'Suzie, are you there?'

Jenny grabs the phone. 'She's a little busy at the moment, Mrs Dunn!'

More giggling is heard before Suzie breaks the kiss and wipes the tears from her eyes, taking the phone back. 'So, Dad, if this bloke here,' she says, poking me in the ribs, 'asked to marry me, I hope you made him pay a big price.'

'No, dear,' comes the reply. 'He asked if we had a cooking model, so I offered him money to finally take you off our hands!'

This is, of course, met with laughter all round, then Suzie says goodbye, telling her parents she has to call her sister. She dials Nat, again on speaker. Somewhat surprisingly, Nat answers on the first ring, so Suzie starts all over again. 'Nat, I'm getting married!'

This time, there's a beat of silence before Nat says, 'Who to?'

Suzie gapes for a moment. Then, she clearly realises Nat is also teasing her, and they're quickly laughing and talking wedding stuff. Before ringing off, Nat says, 'I've just finished work, so I'm coming over.'

Pig says, 'I better restock the fridge.'

Unbeknown to anyone, he'd texted Maria. She rings Suzie to offer her condolences, telling her, 'Suzie, you can do much better than him. Look what he's done to you – had you kidnapped, covered in blood, and traumatised by seeing a man shot dead in front of you. Girl, I can't imagine what you see in the dude.'

Suzie is quick with the comeback, 'I love him!'

Good enough for me!

Maria says she's on her way, and it sounds like half their

netball team is heading over, as well as Suzie and Jenny's former workmates. When Nat arrives, she joins Suzie and Jenny in dancing their little jig, then asks to look at the ring. I see their three heads bowed in close inspection, before they come over to me.

'Mort,' Suzie says (I just hope she doesn't start calling me honey – I'm not the 'honey' type!), 'where was the ring designed? It's gorgeous.'

I smile. 'I designed it myself, and the gold in the band came from my mother's wedding and engagement rings.'

This gets a few oohs and ahs. Suzie says, 'And it's a perfect fit!'

'That was the easy bit. You're always leaving your rings lying around, so I just took one with me to the jeweller to make sure the size was right.'

Pig chimes in. 'So that's what all those squiggles on your jotter pad were. I thought you'd taken to doodling when you were on the phone.'

I just shake my head. Suzie slips her hand around my waist.

It turns into quite a celebration, extending long into the night. Later, much later, when everyone has gone home, Suzie takes my hand, leans in for another kiss and whispers, 'Come with me, mister!'

Who am I to object?

25

The next day is Thursday, and Pig and I fly down to Melbourne, using our fake names and driver's licenses in case someone tries to track us. As always, we travel separately, as two big guys travelling together get way more attention than one on his own.

We arrive early afternoon, rent a Camry at the airport, and head to Keilor Park, with a detour to the McCafé on Mickleham Road for coffee. With Pig in heavy training, I'm not going to eat a banana bread in front of him. Willpower – I do have some!

Before leaving the McCafé car park, Pig gives the number plates a little squirt of our special transparent chemical, so that whilst you can still see them clearly with the eye, on any camera they'll come up blurry. Handy when you don't want to be recognised! This chemical was a gift from our American friends a few years ago, after we did them a couple of favours.

We cruise past Brian's address on Flinders Street, Keilor Park, finding it a tidy single-storey bungalow in a row of similar homes. We cruise around the block and back up Williams Street to get a feel from the rear. These are old-fashioned places with larger back lawns than newer suburbs. Might be important to know if we need an emergency exit. It's the sort of street where we'd draw attention if we sat in the car to watch any comings and goings at his house, but Pig came fully prepared with Bernie, his little drone.

We stop at a park just around the corner, where we wander over to a picnic table. Pig unpacks Bernie and sends it skyward. Controlling it from his iPad, he brings it over the top of Brian's house, and we check the surrounds. His backyard is pretty tidy – no obvious obstacles if we need to leave that way. However, the house on Williams Street backing onto his has a dog, along with young kids, judging by the toys and little bikes lying around on the back lawn. One house over looks clear, though, as do both his immediate neighbours. So, our emergency exit is sorted: over the left-hand back fence, over the neighbours', and a quick stroll out onto the street behind. Looks easy – in daylight!

Once Pig's finished his reconnaissance, he brings Bernie down over the garage door and mounts a little camera on the gutter, looking straight down the drive to the road. No windows are open in the house, so Pig comments that Victorians mustn't like fresh air! We agree there's no sense in leaving a raindrop mic hanging over the windows, but we do drop one onto the gutter of the rear patio. You never know – they may come out there for a smoke. All we need is an understanding of who normally lives here so we aren't surprised whilst on the job.

We settle into our motel room and watch our cameras roll. Naturally, we used our false IDs and cash to get into the place, as we don't want to leave a trail. Of course, if anyone has sophisticated facial recognition software (like we do!), our anonymity won't last long.

We identify Brian from the image sent to Nico. He arrives home around 5:30, then another car pulls up into the driveway. A second guy gets out and uses a key to enter. Clearly a housemate or something.

Brian doesn't move all night, not even going outside, whereas the second arrival leaves a little after 7:00 with a travel bag in hand. Pig comments, 'I hope that means he won't be home tomorrow!'

*

As it turns out, all our preparation isn't needed. Nico's friend Dicky texts him Friday morning to say, 'Brian is scheduled to be home by 5:00. Planning on leaving at 6:30. His housemate is away for the weekend. No alarm in the house, either.'

Nico replies, 'On it.'

We listen as the two brothers decide to get to the house a little after 4:00, so they're safely inside and set up when the poor bastard walks in. I comment to Pig, 'That app of yours makes things easy.'

We've discussed a few of the other goings-on we've heard about from Nico's phone. At some point, after we've finished with the brothers, we'll pass on the full recording to MGC, and he can decide how to best use it. Seeing as it comes from an illegal phone tap, the data can only be used for information purposes such as backgrounding. Still, it's a handy by-product of the app's purpose.

At 3:30 p.m., we arrive at Brian's house on foot, having left the Camry at a local strip mall, where it won't gather attention. We walk straight up to the front door as if we own it. It's a simple lock, so a quick twist of Pig's picks and we're in. No fuss, no bother and no sign anyone has taken the slightest notice of our arrival. We quickly check to make sure there isn't an alarm and see that Dicky was correct.

The front door opens onto a short hallway, with a lounge room off to the left and a master bedroom to the right. We agree the best place for us to hide is the lounge, so when they open the front door and come into the hallway, we won't be seen. Of course, if they come in through the back door, this will mean a quick change of plans, but that's the beauty of the camera we have mounted at the front – we'll see them coming.

That is, unless they too have done their homework and come through the backyard. Ah, well. Can't cover all contingencies, can we? Also, they don't seem the type to do too much planning.

We settle in to wait. As waits go, it isn't a very long one. Just after 4:00 p.m., we see the brothers striding confidently up the drive, just like we did.

We pull down our balaclavas. We've had our gloves on since leaving the Camry.

It's Nico who bends down and uses his picks to open the door. He takes a bit longer than Pig did, so he needs to up his game.

We hear them whispering as they come in the front door. This is where our planning stops, as we simply have no idea where they'll go first. Master bedroom or lounge?

They separate. Louie goes into the master bedroom, Nico into the lounge. Nico doesn't look around. He's heading to the kitchen at the back – until Pig fells him from behind with one punch to the side of the head. This isn't just any punch, though; it's a well-aimed hit with knuckles extended so they hit on the nerves directly behind his ear. Down he goes in a heap. No grunt, but his collapse does make a noise.

Pig quickly goes past the motionless Nico to hide in the kitchen. I hear Louie coming before I see him, as I've stayed out of sight behind the door, waiting for him to come into the room to check what happened. Trouble is, he's now suspicious and has pulled a knife from somewhere, the action betrayed by the rasp of the blade against its sheath.

Hmm, I think, *that levels things up a bit.*

He creeps into the lounge in a crouch, knife extended. He swings around the door quickly and sees me standing in front of him. I smile. He lunges at me, knife raised, and brings it down in a slashing motion. I sidestep. As his momentum brings him across my front, I hit him in the side of the head, very similar to the way Pig felled his brother. Knuckles extended, full-on punch.

Same result. Down and out for the count.

Pig, who'd watched from the kitchen doorway, nods. Without having to say anything, we deliberately stomp on their right hands. We both wear steel-capped boots. They don't miss.

Then I remember Louie is left-handed, so I repeat the dose, breaking more bones in his left hand. He even stirs and moans a little at this second stomp.

With their hands immobile and useless, we don't have to restrain their wrists, but we do zip-tie their feet together and stuff masking tape in their mouths before taping it in. Don't want them enjoying the experience.

We wait. We know they'll only be out for the count for around five minutes, and we have a message for them.

Nico comes round first. Slowly, his eyes flutter open, and he shakes his head. He moves his right hand and howls in pain, not that we can hear much with the tape stuffed in his mouth. He kicks out and pulls his feet up to see they're tied together. Then he must realise he has company. He lies still, trying to look around without moving. We're standing at the top of his head, so it's very difficult for him to see us, but we've positioned Louie next to him. He unintentionally kicks Louie, which gets a groan. Louie lifts both hands and gives a muffled scream. I can even see tears in his eyes, which I'm sure are tears of pain. Both hands buggered, likely irreparable. Sniff, sniff.

I nod to Pig and kick Louie in the side of the head, whilst he does likewise to Nico. That gets their attention.

Leaning down, I rip the tape off Louie. He spits the ball out of his mouth and starts to say something. I kick him again, which shuts him up. When they're both quiet and attentive, I say, 'You two hurt a friend of ours. We don't like that. Do it again and we'll come back and make it permanent. Understood?'

No response. This time, without even looking at each other, Pig and I again kick their heads, and none too gently.

'Understood?'

Nico nods, but Louie spits out, 'You two are dead. Dead. You hear me? We will hunt you down and kill you slowly.'

I reply, 'Not going too well for you so far, is it, Louie? You'll be lucky if you can ever hold a beer again, let alone a knife, so good luck with that.'

He's swivelling his head around, trying to see us. Even in pain, it's clear he's a mean and vicious bastard. Nico tries putting a calming hand on his brother, but it's his right hand, and he winces big time when Louie moves and it falls on the floor.

I kneel down between their heads. It's still very difficult for them to see much of me, as intended. I let my close presence sink in. They stop and lie still.

'If you even *try* to find out who we are, or hurt anyone else we know, we will be back. You won't know when. You won't know where. We might be sitting in your lounge one night, or even in your bedroom. Or maybe we'll tamper with the brakes on your Harleys. When, one day, you need to stop and nothing happens, think of me. Or we might jam the throttles open. Same thing –

think of me. Or we might do the same thing to Zoe's little Merc. Maybe it'll be her who can't stop. She does like to speed, doesn't she, Nico? Understood?'

Silence. Another tap on the head with our boots.

'*Understood?*'

Nico nods. Louie starts a rant. 'You motherfuckers don't know who you're dealing with—'

I stuff the tape back in his mouth and tape it on, hard. As a farewell, I say, 'Tell Dicky I said hi.'

No harm in muddying the waters, maybe causing a bit of combustion within the ranks. The fallout should be obvious.

Once done, we kick them both in the head, this time aiming for the same pressure point behind the ear. They go limp as they lapse back into unconsciousness.

We look around. Other than the blood seeping from their broken hands, there's no damage, nothing out of place. We pull our beanies up onto our heads and fist bump as we head to the front door.

Whilst we walk back to the Camry, I pull out my prepaid phone and text Brian, saying, 'Don't go home alone.'

I get a reply asking, 'What? Who is this?'

I don't reply. Let it fall where it falls.

In the Camry, we again fist bump, and Pig says, 'Now that's more Mortice!'

After we deliver the car back to Hertz, we walk separately to the Qantas booking counter to ask if we can make an earlier flight. Yes, they have seats on the 7:30 p.m. flight, so with only hand luggage, we're good to go.

I text Suzie to say her late night has been cut short, and I'll be home earlier. The red heart comes as my reply.

Don't I love those, I think!

26

One afternoon early the next week, with nothing exciting to do, I pull up the video and audio files from the mic and camera I attached to Marissa's front door. I run this through at double speed, until suddenly I see the rear of a man's head. I stop the tape and rewind it to when the door opens and he enters the view. I also activate the audio.

It's obvious the man, who Marissa is calling Jeffy, is well-known to her, because they dive quickly into a long, passionate kiss. Marissa pulls away and says, 'Just as well my daughter isn't here. You're meant to call first.'

Jeffy replies, 'I know your routine.'

Clothing is being removed as they head away from the door. Where they're going is no surprise. The only problem is that all I'm seeing is the top of Jeffy's blonde head; you can imagine why his head is facing down!

I again fast forward until I see more action. Marissa, this time in a robe, heads to the front door with Jeffy tucked in tight behind her. *Bugger it*, I think, *still can't get a good sight of him.* Then I realise why he's walking so close behind her, as her robe suddenly falls off her shoulders and his hands are everywhere.

Marissa gives a little squeal and turns back into his arms.

Silence ensues for a few moments (well, it's not fully silent, but you get what I mean!), until she breaks away. 'You'll be late home if we start all over again.'

Jeffy mutters something, but I still can't get a view of his face. He straightens his clothing whilst Marissa resets her robe. Then, with the door open, Jeffy half outside it, she says, 'I almost forgot. I had some private investigator come by to see me a week or so back. Was asking about Benson and that accident he had.'

This has caught Jeffy's attention. He turns back to Marissa, and says, with real menace in his voice, 'Why didn't you call me and report it?'

Marissa has clearly also picked up on his tone. 'Sorry, Jeffy. I didn't tell him anything, just that Benson mentioned it a couple of times and seemed worried about the coroner's report.'

Jeffy barks, 'Describe him.'

Marissa shrugs. 'A real big bloke – like, I mean *big*. Short black hair, sort of military cut. Pretty good on the eyes, too.'

'Shit, him again. Get your phone.'

Marissa disappears into the bedroom and comes back with her phone, which she hands to him. I can't see what he does, but he gives it back quite quickly, saying, 'I've added a new phone number under my name. This guy comes back or calls you, I need to know immediately. Clear?'

'Yes,' she replies and reaches out to embrace him again, which doesn't last long.

I can't see them, since they're in the doorway now, below the camera, but I hear Jeffy say, 'I'm leaving. Make sure you call me if you hear from this bastard again.'

'Don't wait too long before coming by again.'

Marissa closes the door, turning the lights out, and everything goes black.

Well, well. Looks like I misjudged her. Something more is going on there. I need to get CCTV set up in the street so I can get more information on this Jeffy, and plant more equipment in her apartment, though I certainly don't want a camera in her bedroom – I might get embarrassed! I send the audio file to both Robert at Section V and Midge, asking if they can find the identity of the male voice, known at this stage only as 'Jeffy'.

Damn annoying that I didn't getting a picture of him at all. Almost like he knew the camera was there.

No, I think. *Not possible.*

27

The following Tuesday morning, we're just running a few database security audits when my phone rings from an unknown number. Unlike many these days, I like to answer unknown numbers – you never know where it might lead.

I answer as usual. 'Mort speaking.'

'Mort, my name is Don Thomson. I own DT Cooling, a specialist engine cooling manufacturer. Colonel Richards suggested you may be able to help me with a problem.'

'DT Cooling? You're down Yatala way somewhere, aren't you?'

'Yes,' he replies.

'So, what's the problem, Don?'

I hear him take a deep breath. 'We've been hacked. They stole our database, our financial records, our patented designs. Everything. Now we've received a ransom demand for four million dollars.'

'Do *not* say any more over the phone. We need to meet in person to discuss this.'

'But we only have forty-eight hours, or they'll release the design drawings on the net.' His voice is starting to break. A lifetime of work down the gurgler if we can't stop it, I suspect.

'We can meet you right now – well, in twenty minutes – at, say, Loganholme, halfway between our offices. Does that suit you?'

By now, both Pig and Maria are listening and clearly interested in what is going on.

Don replies, 'Yes, we can do that. Where would you like to meet?'

'Nikkalatte is a little café on Henry Street. Let's make it there. Please turn your phone off and remove the battery before leaving your office. If anyone else is coming with you, they need to do the same.'

'Why?'

'Not on the phone, Don.'

'Okay, thank you. We'll see you there.'

I hang up and say to Pig and Maria, 'A small mob called DT Cooling have been hacked. I've read about this company; their clients are all F1 teams – quite extraordinary how a little factory in Yatala services the F1 and supercar markets. Pig, grab a couple of our spare encrypted phones and come with me. Maria, dig up their address and go sit in their car park. Keep an eye out for anything odd or suspicious. If we take the job, I'll get you to go and ride shotgun in their office, so have your sleeves rolled up!'

Maria smiles. 'On my way, Boss.'

Pig comes out of our storeroom with a couple of phones in a bag, and we hit the road.

Nikkalatte is a local café renowned for good coffee and food. We've certainly been there before! We arrive first, so we take a table outside, and not long after our coffees are delivered, we see a Porsche Cayenne Turbo pull up. Geez, it has a lovely burble. Suzie would love the sound of it.

We watch the road to see if anyone seems to be following them, but it's clear. Two get out of the Cayenne. The driver is older, and I guess he's Don. The other, judging by his build and looks, is probably Don's son. He's looking at his phone as he walks, so he hasn't taken any notice of what I asked, clearly. We aren't off to a good start.

Being car fanatics, they can't help but stop and check out the café owner's rose gold (that's *rose* gold, not mere gold!) customised Holden Maloo ute. Seeing Pig and me sitting outside, they come directly over to us. I address the older of the two. 'Don?'

He nods. We shake as he introduces his son, Ryan, and I introduce Pig. I then say to Ryan, 'Was I not clear enough about leaving your phone, minus the battery, at your office?'

He looks a bit stunned. I continue, now addressing Don. 'I don't work with dickhead clients, so if you want us to retrieve your data and save you four million dollars, then you need to do as I say.'

I let my eyes swivel to lock back on Ryan. Without saying a word, he turns his phone off, removes the battery and hurries back to the Porsche to leave it there.

I ask Don, 'Coffee?'

'Yes, please. Skinny cappuccino – make that two, one with one sugar, the other without.'

I nod and head inside to order.

'Sorry,' Ryan says, when I return. 'I didn't see why we had to go phoneless to get here.'

'Well,' I say, 'someone just stole all your data, which is much more difficult than turning a phone into a tracking device or even a microphone.' I look at Pig. 'Either one of us could do that in five minutes. Give us twenty-four hours, and we'd have your full phone records. It really is simple if you know how to go about it.'

Having made my point, I turn to Don. 'Let's hear it from the beginning.'

'Before we get into the details, do you think you can help us?'

'Yes, I expect we can, but the timeframe will make it a challenge and it won't be cheap. Until I hear the full story and check out your security levels, though, I can't be sure.'

Don sighs. 'Well, yesterday, we all left the office as usual. Nothing seemed amiss, but this morning, the email wasn't working, and I couldn't connect to our server. Then, just before 8:00 a.m., I got this text.'

He shows me his phone. It reads:

'We have your data. If we receive four million in bitcoin by 8:00 a.m. Thursday, we will return it. If not, it will be uploaded onto the web for all to see. Free copies of all your patented designs!

Tick tock. We will be in touch. Await our bitcoin wallet details.'

I write down the phone number and share it with Pig, who immediately inputs it into his open laptop. Don's voice takes on a ragged edge as he continues, 'We have an automatic system that's supposed to back up our data every evening, but no one has checked it for weeks, maybe months, so we don't even know when it last worked correctly.'

'That part's easy. One of us can quickly identify the last backup update,' I say. 'Don, from what little I know about your business, I'm guessing your design drawings would be rather valuable?'

He nods. 'Couldn't put a value on them, but they're the backbone of the whole business. It would struggle to survive if a competent competitor got hold of them.'

'Talk me through your data security set-up then – or, better still, tell me your IP address, and we'll have a quick look for ourselves.'

This time, Ryan answers. 'What do you want to know?'

'Your IP address, for a start.'

He clearly isn't sure what this is. Pig, who hasn't said boo so far, says quietly, 'It's okay, I've got it. The phone is a Telstra prepaid, by the way.'

'I read about your financial results in the *Courier Mail* about a month ago,' I say to Don. 'It said you had forty million dollars in cash reserves if an acquisition opportunity came up.'

'Yes,' he replies, 'that's right.'

I take a moment to think through what we know.

'Don, I suspect you've had company for some time. Whilst it may seem sudden to you, it's likely that your hackers have been sitting invisible on your network for a few weeks, checking out what they can find. We'll be able to confirm that once we start investigating.'

'Can you track and identify the thieves?'

'Yes, most likely. Whilst cyber theft isn't our strong point, one of our global partners, a US-based entity, is at the forefront of tracking and tracing digital thieves. If you hire us, we'll engage them to assist us. The real challenge is the forty-eight-hour deadline. The first thing we'll have to do, if given the chance, is to try and increase this to four or five days – not an unreasonable timeline to pull together four million dollars.

'You also have to understand that a large percentage of these attacks come from within, or from "injured parties", so we'll need to discuss your staff in detail. Plus, we need to be made aware of any recently terminated staff who may be inclined to harm your business, or you personally.

'If we do come on board, as I said earlier, you and your staff will be expected to follow all requests from me or any of my team. As a matter of fact, one of my associates is already sitting in your car park, keeping an eye on who's coming and going.'

Don raises his eyebrows, whilst Ryan looks a bit shocked.

'She will enter your office, and *no one* will be able to leave without a full inspection of their cases and handbags. Remember, many of these ransom demands are inside jobs. You'll have to call your office and inform them of this. But first things first, this isn't going to be cheap.'

Here I pull out a blank contract form I always carry with me and fill in our usual payment rate, but go a little soft by making only twenty-five per cent payable up front, with the remainder due on successful completion and recovery of the data. Once it's completed, I flip it over for Don and Ryan, who leans over his father's shoulder. Don says, 'Ouch, that's a fair bit of money.'

'Yes, it is,' I respond. 'But not compared to four million dollars, or worse if your data and drawings are dumped on the internet.'

Ryan says, 'If we pay them, or you recover the data, how do we guarantee they won't release copies anyway?'

'Good point. You can't. But whether it's a good or bad thing, there is "honour amongst thieves" in the digital space. These hackers have a subculture, and they pride themselves on being honourable, strange as it may seem.'

Whilst Don is reading through the proposed agreement and no doubt debating whether to accept the cost of engaging us, I ask him, 'So, what did Colonel Richards have to say about us?'

Colonel Richards is Pig's and my former Army CO, and I know he must've said something positive to recommend us in the first place. Don replies, 'He said he's known you a long time, so he knows full well how you operate, and that you came through against all odds for another client of his.' He gives a slight grin. 'He also said to be sitting down when I saw your price!'

Pig snorts. Don and Ryan look at each other, and Ryan gives his dad a nod. Don turns to me and says, 'Very well. Assuming I sign now, what's the process from here?'

I give him a brief walk-through of the process, then ask, 'Do the staff all know of the theft?'

Don replies, 'Yes, it's not something you can keep quiet about, especially in a small office such as ours.'

'Okay. We've brought a couple of encrypted phones for you to use for the duration of the investigation. Copying your contacts across is easy, so it's just an enhanced handset as far as you're both concerned. But we'll hold onto your original phones for investigation as well.'

Pig pulls the two phones from his bag. I add, 'Is there anyone else in your office who needs an encrypted phone? Bear in mind, we'll be checking everyone's phones for ransomware and uploading their data for assessment.'

Don and Ryan shake their heads.

'For what it's worth, Don, I'm reasonably confident this is a local thief, simply because they've only asked for four million – ten per cent of what the press reported the other week as being your cash on hand. It's likely they'll have taken that literally, so they think you simply have to transfer the money. And this is where we can push back and point out the four million is all tied up in investments, and that it will take days, if not weeks, to free up.'

I pause here, thinking, then ask, 'How much do you have in ready cash? And will they know this from the data they've stolen?'

Don gives Ryan a sideways glance, making me think Ryan isn't privy to what he's about to tell us. 'We have less than two million in the bank. As you said, the rest is all in different interest-bearing investments. It's going to take a few days to free the money up, and we'll lose quite a bit because of the early withdrawal, though it's small change in the circumstances, I guess. But bitcoin – I don't know anything about this cybercurrency stuff. All seems a bit far-fetched to me.'

I reply, 'We can guide you there also. I'm not a fan, but I do know how it works.'

With no further prompting, Don signs the agreement with a flourish and hands the document to me. We shake hands all round. Deal done.

Now we start the hunt.

Before we leave, I ask Don, 'Have you advised your bank of the data breach?'

When he responds in the negative, I say, 'I'd strongly suggest you give them a call and request a daily copy of your transactions, emailed separately, so you can verify all of them. Who handles your accounts?'

'My wife, Mary.'

'A blunt question, but is she up to all the extra work, or is someone going to have to help her handle it?'

Quickly, Ryan responds, 'I'll give her a hand.'

We agree we'll follow their Porsche back to their office – but only after grabbing another coffee from the Nikkalatte girls!

28

On the way down to DT Cooling's office in Yatala, I call Maria and ask her to move into the reception area. 'Tell them you have instructions to not let anyone leave the premises until we turn up.'

Her response is, 'On it, Boss.' (She seems to think I like her calling me Boss – and I'm not saying I mind!)

Pig also sends an encrypted email with all pertinent information we have to date to Matteo, who Midge recommended to us a few months ago. He's more in the commercial field, and so far, he's come through for us as well. Unlike Midge, though, he does charge us, and to mimic Don, he's 'not cheap' – but the best never are. At my suggestion, Pig includes a query about whether Matteo can identify any bitcoin wallets established locally in the last few days. Particularly if there was more than one at the same time. These hacker types never seem to sleep, so we don't expect it'll be long before we get a response.

When Pig questions me on this, I say, 'It may be nothing, but the text says "we", so there's probably more than one. Plus, why not add in their wallet details if they already have them set up?'

'Fair enough,' Pig says.

Arriving at the office of DT Cooling, we enter behind Don and Ryan to an altercation. Maria is standing firm against a male employee who's demanding to leave. When he sees us – well, the size of us, I guess – he immediately backs off.

Our second greeting is with the office dog, a lovely ruby Cavalier, tail wagging furiously. His name is Scout, as introduced by Don. He loves a pat too!

Don calls the staff together so we can brief them all. It's only a small team of twelve, and they're quickly congregated in the reception area. Once the introductions are over, I take the floor.

'Good morning, everyone. As Don has told you, we've been retained to recover the stolen data. Most of these thefts are inside jobs, so I apologise in advance, but we will be requesting your full support and cooperation today and throughout our inquiries. I stress we will not be breaching your privacy, but we will be inspecting all personal luggage and effects. If we have any suspicions, we will investigate you further. Let's hope we don't need to take that step.'

Of course, Denis Smith, the man who'd been trying to get past Maria, speaks up. 'No bloody way I'm going to open my briefcase for any of you. I know my rights.'

Before I can reply, Maria says, 'It would be my pleasure to escort you to the local police station and have them do a personal search. You'd really enjoy being paraded around the station, wouldn't you?' She gives him the full glare and aggressive body language, causing him to step back, looking intimidated.

I let the room settle before I say, 'This is a criminal investigation, so whatever we find will be passed on to the police. Be assured, Denis, if we think you warrant a personal search, you will be getting one. Clear? Anyone else in any doubt about the seriousness of the situation?'

I'm met with a round of shaken heads. Satisfied, I continue.

'Whilst we've been talking, my colleague Julien' – we'd decided a few months ago to stop calling him Pig in a commercial environment, after frequent scoldings by Suzie, and, more lately, Stacey – 'has been doing a sweep of the office to check for any hidden surveillance equipment. Part of our inspection will involve an assessment of your phones, tablets, and laptops to ensure they haven't been compromised by trackers or microphones. Questions?'

'How long will this take?' asks Lucy, the receptionist.

'In most cases, five or ten minutes, max.' Nobody else speaks up, so I continue. 'Okay, let's get started. Denis, as you're in such a hurry to get away, I'll interview you first.'

Before heading to the boardroom for the interview, I take Don outside and ask for a brief run-down on all their staff. I take notes as he explains their roles and who has access to confidential files. It appears most of them do – being a small business, everyone helps each other out. Of course, I have to ask, 'So, why would Denis be in such a hurry to leave the office?'

Don pulls a face. 'He's a prickly one – a very good engineer, though. He's been here five years, I think, and has certainly participated in some of our more recent design innovations. Not sure where he'd be going this time of day. I run a pretty loose ship. As long as they do their hours, I let them come and go.'

'Do you think he may be feeling a little entitled or unappreciated, then?'

Don shrugs. 'He's paid well for what he does. I don't think he could get a better wage in the current market; he got a six-figure bonus last year on the back of his input.'

On re-entering the office, I go to the photocopier and make a few copies of my notes, then drop one off with Maria, who's started her own interview with Lucy. Pig pops his head out to let me know the office is all clear. When I raise an eyebrow, he gives a thumbs up. Whilst he was sweeping the office, he installed a few bugs of our own. He isn't conducting any interviews, but he'll be keeping an eye and ear on the staff's behaviour, having set himself up in Don's office.

I head into the boardroom. I'm looking forward to interviewing Denis, but it turns out to be an anticlimax. Instead of becoming all antsy whilst waiting for me, he's obviously reflected on his attitude and behaviour. Before I can say a word, he apologises, saying he hadn't appreciated the seriousness of the situation and wants to help in any way he can. Throughout the interview, he couldn't be more obliging or helpful, even though I test him by putting some pressure on him. A bit mean, I know!

In the end, I don't demand a personal search. I suggest he apologise to Maria, and he does, on his way out.

When we're finished with the interviews, Maria, Pig and I put our heads together to review what we found. Maria, like me, hasn't flagged anyone as suspicious or warranting further investigation. Pig confirms there was nothing suspicious from the staff whilst they waited to be interviewed. He adds that Matteo has replied, advising that the breach occurred three weeks earlier on a new admin PC that hadn't been installed with antivirus software, and that it looks to have been carried out by an organised hacker, not a local amateur who got lucky.

We ask Don and Ryan in to give them the news that so far, we've cleared their staff, although we have further checks to undertake. They also confirm they replaced an old computer three or four weeks ago. Don is devastated that he'd forgotten to load the antivirus software onto the new PC.

Our next priority is to try to gain an extension from the hackers, which would give my team more time and allow Don a chance to round up four million from his various investments.

Next morning, I'm back in their office. I acknowledge receipt of the twenty-five per cent deposit and advise we have no further updates. After discussing the wording of the text we want to send, we finally decide on:

'As you can see from the company bank accounts you have accessed, we do not have four million available to pay you within forty-eight hours.

We need these records back, so we are willing to pay you, but we need a further three days to free up the four million. Thank you.'

Don rereads it one last time, presses send, and comments, 'Well, there goes nothing.'

29

I don't know how long it'll take for the blackmailers to respond to Don's message, so I'm a little surprised when a reply comes in midafternoon the following day. Don's calls and texts are automatically copied to me, as we installed Pig's bugging app on the phone – with his consent, of course – so I can read it myself: 'We grant you a further forty-eight hours, but the price is now five million in bitcoin. Account details will follow.'

They're smart buggers, I think, as I dial Don. We discuss whether he can get the four million within the next forty-eight hours. He's started the process of freeing up assets by selling some of his share portfolio, and had a conversation with his bank manager about making a short-term overdraft whilst waiting for the sales to settle. Sadly, like all financial institutions these days, no one at the bank was authorised to make a decision quickly. Don was advised the extra two million needed was way over the manager's authority limit, and would therefore require a full application and review, which would likely take weeks rather than days. So, no help there.

Whilst I'm still talking to Don, Pig interrupts me, saying he has Matteo on the phone. I quickly put Don on hold, and Pig merges me onto the call, making it a three-way conversation.

After we get the greetings out of the way, Matteo says, 'I called you because your suggestion to check for any new bitcoin wallets was a good one. We have a double transaction going down now in St Lucia – and not in the Caribbean, but right there in Brisbane.'

Pig and I fist bump. Matteo continues, 'They're using a little local foreign exchange wholesaler, Kwik-X, whose system… well, let's just say isn't up to scratch! I've accessed their records and confirmed the identities of these two as Lei Chen and Jason Wang. They have the same address, which I'm emailing to you, along with copies of their passports. Apparently, they're Chinese nationals over there as students, but let's do a little deeper digging. Some of the IPs I'm getting indicate a possible connection to APT40, one of the larger and more successful Chinese hacker organisations.'

The speed at which this has all come to a head is stunning. I ask, 'Does APT40 stand for anything?'

'APT stands for Advanced Persistent Threat, and there are multiple groups under this umbrella, all designated by a number. In this case, Group 40 is based out of Hainan Province in China. APT3 operates out of Beijing, whilst APT10 operates out of Tianjin Province. APT40 has been particularly active in countries or regions where China's Belt and Road initiative is important. Many of these hackers are believed to moonlight – to line their own pockets, so to speak – as these two appear to be doing. This hack is highly unlikely to be part of an official APT40 attack.'

'Shit,' I say, 'the Belt and Road initiative is all over the news, with the Victoria State Government supposedly signing up.'

Pig confirms that he's received our two hackers' address – an apartment building on Sir Fred Schonell Drive, just off the University of Queensland's St Lucia campus. Thinking quickly, I ask Matteo, 'Do you have access to their bitcoin accounts?'

'Yes, I have them open now. They're meant to have a minimum of fifty thousand dollars, but Jason and Lei have only put in a hundred dollars each, so they've likely had to get special permission to open them.'

'Okay, I'm thinking we coordinate a trial run, which we tell these two is a test to confirm the transfer works. Once you tell us the funds are in their account, Pig and I will bust their door down. That way, we'll catch them red-handed before they've had a chance to transfer the funds onward, which I'm sure they're planning on doing.'

Pig gives me a big smile, so he clearly likes the plan. Matteo takes a little longer to reply. 'Yeah, man, sounds good. From what Midge has told me, you two are good at bumping heads, or worse. Let me know the when and where, and I'll be there when you bring the hammer down!'

We hang up, pretty pumped. We're in the middle of high fiving when Maria interrupts us, saying, 'Don has been holding this whole time, you know?'

I take the call and apologise to Don, saying we've identified the culprits and are now working on a plan to entrap them. Of course, this gets him excited as well. He wants to know all the details, but I only give him the overview and ask him, 'If it means saving the rest of the money, would you be willing to risk a hundred thousand dollars so we can catch these crooks in the act? There's every chance we can get it back for you within a day anyway.'

I get a raised eyebrow from Pig at this suggestion. I give him a thumbs up to let him know I have that covered (or so I hope, anyway). Don agrees, and once we've finished the call, Maria, Pig and I sit down to discuss these developments. First, we agree we need to update Robert at Section V of our discovery of two potential hackers here in Brisbane, along with their possible connection to APT40. After pulling their address up on Google Maps, we decide we need a firsthand look at their apartment building. Pig and I jump in the van and head over to St Lucia, leaving Maria back in the office, much to her disgust. We take Charlie, Pig's newest drone, with us – yes, Bernie has already been replaced!

On arrival, knowing we'll stand out in the student crowds around here, we don our hi-vis jackets and get a measurement wheel, so we have a visible reason to be walking slowly along Sir Fred Schell Drive. We identify their apartment building, a modern but typical student accommodation, three stories high and opposite a park, which is going to come in handy shortly.

Whilst pretending to take measurements of the footpath, we study the layout of the building. It's not flash enough to have security, and the foyers appear to be unmanned. When we can't see anyone around, I wander into the first foyer to get an idea of where their unit, number nine, is located. This foyer only goes up to Unit Six, so we move along to the next entrance.

Yes, this one goes from seven to twelve. The two units on the ground floor are marked seven and eight, so that means Unit Nine will be on the first floor on the left. With no one around still, I creep up the stairs and slip a little mic and movement sensor onto their entrance door, by the hinges. I choose a wood-coloured unit from my collection, so it blends in nicely. I take a close look at the lock. It seems standard, which means we can use our special 'door unlockers', another gift from our American friends.

I go back outside and rejoin Pig with the wheel. It's now getting towards dusk, so we decide to wander down to a café, grab an early dinner and wait for it to get darker, so we can put Charlie to work.

Whilst eating, we hear from our little mic. The door to Unit Nine opens and closes, followed by muffled voices from inside. Both boys seem to be home and speaking in their native tongue. A Google search confirms this is likely to be Mandarin if they're truly from Hainan Province.

Once it's dark enough, we head back to a picnic table out of sight of the road and the apartment building. Pig launches Charlie, which flies silently across towards Unit Nine, already loaded with two raindrop mics.

Pig's pretty good at placing these mics now. It takes a matter of minutes. Trouble is, all the windows are closed, so we're unsure if we'll learn anything much.

On the way back to the office, we discuss the idea of a little break-in to set up a camera and mic inside, but decide not to take the risk. These two are highly likely to be sophisticated hackers, who might well have little traps set up we may not notice, thus ruining our surprise.

30

The next morning, Pig comes in a little later than normal. Well, being honest, I only just beat him down, as we've been doing extended training in the lead-up to the Invictus Games (and, before that, the upcoming Gold Coast Marathon, which Pig, Suzie and I all entered). His yellow Australian uniform arrived earlier in the week, giving all of us a real buzz. Suzie, of course, took a photo of him in his outfit and sent it to Stacey, whilst Maria paid him out about 'canary yellow being the colour of cowards', preferring her black – the 'native' colour of all Kiwis, after their All Blacks, the world-famous rugby team.

Overnight, we received another email from Matteo, giving further background on Jason and Lei. They apparently arrived in Brisbane two years ago and are both studying Bachelors of Computer Science at UQ. Whilst their passports show they're both twenty-two, this is being questioned, as the identities are likely to be false. They receive money from home in China monthly, the source of which Matteo is still trying to trace. Then an email pops up from Midge, asking what we've found ourselves in the middle of, so clearly, he's involved in the background. Robert at Section V has also confirmed they hadn't come to the attention of the police at all.

Pig and I agree we need the takedown to be in the evening, which means we can't have the $100 thousand land in their account beforehand. Otherwise, they can transfer it out to wherever. However, banks don't transact after hours, causing us a dilemma.

We call Matteo to discuss the issue and he responds, 'No problem. I have access to their Kwik-X accounts, so I'll stop the deposits from hitting them until you tell me.'

'Okay, great,' I say. 'Let's plan on ten o'clock tonight, our time. We'll call you once we're in position.'

'Deal,' is Matteo's reply.

*

That night, Pig and I are again in our van, this time with Brisbane City Council contractor signs on the doors, so it looks different from yesterday. We park some 150 metres from the boys' apartment. Close enough for a quick getaway, if need be, but also far enough away to go unnoticed if they're being hypervigilant.

We've heard chatter from within their room, so we're confident both are home. As 9:30 p.m. approaches, we walk over to the park, this time with rubbish bags and pickers, collecting litter lying around on the lawns. Dedicated council workers, that's us!

At 9:45, we remove our hi-vis jackets in a dark corner of the park, leaving these and our rubbish collection gear out of sight for retrieval later. We separate and move in from opposite directions, since two large guys approaching together is far more noticeable than one wandering along on his own. But being the masters of our craft that we are, we arrive at the lobby simultaneously. I ring Matteo with my earpiece and throat mic in place whilst we're on the ground floor and say, 'Five minutes.' He acknowledges, and we keep the call live. We climb the stairs quietly and wait outside Unit Nine.

At a minute after 10:00, we hear loud excited voices coming from inside. It even sounds like they're high fiving. Matteo says, 'In,' confirming they can see the money in their Kwik-X accounts. Pig silently uses his door unlocker and pushes their door open. This is one of our riskier moments. If they have anything as simple as a chain door restraint, we'll have to force our way in, thus losing the element of surprise.

They don't.

Pig opens the door only wide enough for us both to slide through. They're just a few metres away from us, bent over two laptops on a desk in the small lounge space. At first, we go unnoticed in their excitement at becoming instant millionaires. Or so they think. Then one of them turns suddenly, saying something in high-pitched Mandarin. As Pig is closest, he quickly throws out a straight right jab. Having been on the receiving end of a few of these in our sparring sessions, I know they hurt. Number One goes down like a bag of cement. We have no idea who is who. Yet.

Number Two moves with surprising speed, launching an assault on me, feet flying at my head and midriff. I sidestep. Then, whilst he's slightly off-balance, I step in and give a quick one-two to his face, putting him too down and out for the count. Ouch, that even hurt my hand – but having heard bones crunch, I know Number Two is far worse off.

I secure them both with zip ties and duct tape (who says it only has 101 uses?). Pig, meanwhile, accesses their computers and starts copying everything off their hard drives and into our cloud. I confirm to Matteo all is under control, so he withdraws the recently deposited $100 thousand (fifty thousand from each of the newly opened bitcoin accounts), and this money simply disappears. We'd discussed crediting it back to DT Cooling, but decided if we did that, in effect, no crime would've taken place. So as an alternative, I had Robert at Section V supply me with a trust account managed by the Australian Cyber Security Centre. They can claim they recovered the money as part of their ongoing investigations.

I phone Robert and tell him all is done and dusted. As he's put his liaison at Queensland Police on notice, they're waiting on his call. I tell him he'd better contact the paramedics as well, to which he replies, 'I did that already, knowing where you're concerned, someone's always going to get hurt.'

I'm not sure whether to take that as a compliment or an insult!

We agree to wait for their arrival, as for a change, we're on official business. Matteo and Pig review the data we've captured, confirming we have Don's files, which, as far as either of them can see, haven't been copied or uploaded to any other location. Good to know.

A couple of minutes later, I'm not surprised to see DS Chris Harris and a colleague pull up outside. We've stayed in touch with Chris and know she's now in the police digital crime squad, still on 'light duties' since her beating. She's quickly followed by an ambulance.

I go to the door and greet Chris, and it's clear she already knew we were involved from the smile I get. Then it's all down to business, as we give them a summary of the events of the evening, whilst the paramedics clean up who we now know to be Jason's face. They comment that I'd done a good job on realigning his nose, which is going to require surgery.

We're headed home within an hour. On our way across the

park to collect our rubbish bags, we fist bump, and Pig comments, 'More Mortice, ah!'

We grin and head back to the van. I give Don a call, as promised, to tell him we've caught the culprits and he'll be getting his $100 thousand back, even if it might take a few weeks, as official channels move slowly.

Done and dusted. He asks to take us to lunch in appreciation of our good work. Seeing how it's a nice gesture and he included Maria in the invite as well, we agree to meet him, Ryan and Mary at the Fitzy's Tavern in Loganholme the following day. I also tell him I'm happy to wait until he's received the money back before settling the account.

I am getting soft, aren't I?

*

Three weeks after Jason and Lei's arrest, it's become big news. It's even gone a little political, with the Chinese ambassador claiming innocent students have been victimised by the nasty Australian police and media. Then the Vice-Chancellor of the University of Queensland enters the fray, reiterating the ambassador's message and calling for an investigation, and I decide enough is enough.

Early next morning finds me sitting in Colleen Hill's favourite café. When she walks in and sees me, she does a double take, so I raise the coffee I'd already ordered for her. She comes over, smiling. 'Well, I must say I'm excited to see you – I hope it means a good story.'

'That depends how well you write it!' I say. 'This is off the record, so you'll need to use your own connections to confirm what I tell you.'

I give her the background on Jason and Lei's arrest. They've now been connected to APT40, and the CIA and FBI are wanting to interview them both for possible attacks against US targets. There's even been talk about extraditing them to the US to face more serious espionage charges there. This is all unofficial, but it's great background for a seasoned journalist such as Colleen. I can see her excitement building as she digests what I'm telling her.

Once we're finished, Colleen puts her notebook away. She's a little old fashioned, still using pen, paper and her own version of shorthand ('No one can copy what I've written, then,' is her explanation when I ask). She tells me the UQ Vice-Chancellor is holding another press conference this afternoon, so she might ask some pointed questions.

I make sure I'm home in time to watch the 6:00 p.m. news to see how it went. Whilst Colleen has been edited out to make the TV reporter look good, the Vice-Chancellor certainly struggled to put a positive spin on his position in light of the new facts!

31

Before we head stateside for our holiday and the Invictus Games, I have a couple of issues I need to tidy up. One is to revisit Beth, Benson's wife, to chat further about his behaviour at the time of the accident. The other is to follow up with Marissa, Benson's mistress. It's sort of been bugging me (well, truth be told, pissing me off!) that I misread Marissa, as evidenced by her conversation with Jeffy.

A couple of days after listening to the recording, I went back to her place and planted more surveillance equipment. This morning, I run through the footage. No sign of Jeffy since that one night, and I know from the app on her phone she hasn't talked to him, either. I'm intrigued about what sort of relationship they have, since he said he had her routine but hasn't been to visit for a few weeks. She does seem to have a new man in her life, who stays over a couple of nights per week, so good on her.

That done, I quickly check Zarraffa's staff roster and see Beth is working this afternoon, so now's as good a time as any to go and have a chat. When I arrive, they're quite busy, so I order a large long black – yes, with toasted banana bread – and take a seat. Beth didn't serve me, but she did give me a smile when she saw me come in.

Once things quiet down, she makes herself a cappuccino and comes over. We do a mock salute with our coffees.

'Gee, am I glad you walked in here those few weeks ago!' she says. 'You certainly changed my life and that of my girls. And I don't know where you found that Suzie Dunn, but she was awesome.'

I let her prattle on a little before bringing her back to the point of my visit. 'Beth,' I say, 'last time I came, I asked you about Dillion at the time of the accident. Have you recalled anything else from around then?'

She takes a sip of her cappuccino. 'Yes. Not sure how important it is, but after you left amid all that excitement, I did remember that he had a phone call from DI Lancaster about 5:30 the next morning – and Lancaster rarely rang that early. I don't know what they talked about, but it seemed as if he was checking up to see how Dillion was, which I thought was odd. It was certainly out of character for him.'

'Okay, but nothing else? Did Dillion have any injuries at all?'

'No, nothing serious. No bruises – just a bit of a sore back, he told me.'

'Thanks, Beth. I hope the future stays bright for you and your two girls. If anything else comes to mind, or you need any help at all, keep my card close!'

We shake hands, and I head back to the office empty-handed. I do consider complimenting Suzie about how she helped Beth… but then again, maybe I'll let sleeping dogs lie.

32

It's a quiet Wednesday afternoon, and Maria, Pig and I are all tapping away on our laptops, working on separate digital audits. As our workload continues to grow, we're upskilling Maria to do some of the more rudimentary assessments, and she's loving it. I make Pig do most of her training, as they get on like brother and sister, always stirring each other up. I love watching their interactions – from the other side of the room!

The doorbell chimes. Jenny comes out, saying they're expecting a client named Angela. She opens the door, and there's Angela, with three young kids in tow. She's clearly upset, so Jenny settles the kids in the waiting room before taking her through to meet with Suzie.

It isn't long before we can hear Angela sobbing her eyes out. Really loud, heartbreaking stuff. The youngest of the kids, a boy around three, starts wailing, saying 'I want Mummy' over and over again. The eldest girl, who I'm guessing is around ten or eleven, hastens over to try to soothe him, but to no avail. The younger daughter has now also started bawling. Even over them, we can still hear Angela crying.

To my surprise, Pig gets down on the floor next to the little boy and gives him a big hug, soothing him and his sister. I'm not sure if it's thanks to his size or just his calm nature, but he quickly has them calmed down. Then, bugger me, he's reading them a story! Suzie keeps a toy box and children's books in the waiting room, as many of her clients have young kids who need distracting when they visit. The three kids all sit there quietly, with Pig in the middle (Piggy in the middle, heh heh!), absorbed in their story. When Angela and Suzie finally come out, they stop, staring open-mouthed at the scene in front of them.

Angela can't thank Pig enough for his kindness. Even Maria compliments him, saying, 'I didn't think you had that in you.' Of course, Pig doesn't rise to the bait, but merely smiles.

No doubt we have an empathetic Pig in our midst!

Once they're gone, Pig, Maria and I file into Suzie's office. It's obvious she and Jenny are both caught up in the atmosphere. I ask, 'What was that all about?'

Suzie wipes her eyes on a tissue. 'Angela's former husband, Mike Taylor, is months behind in his maintenance payments. Angela doesn't work, with the three kids, and is now weeks behind on her rent. The real estate agent has instigated eviction proceedings against her. What's more, her eldest daughter, Charlotte, needs glasses, and he's refusing to pay for them. Charlotte desperately needs them – she's falling further and further behind at school, simply because she can't see clearly. There's a long history of domestic violence as well, some of it pretty brutal. Angela's done well to get away from him. Then, yesterday, the bastard told Angela he's heading off overseas with his latest floosy for a month's holiday, saying she'll have to wait until he gets back before he'll "try to catch up". As you heard, she's beside herself.'

We sit in silence, absorbing what we've heard, until I ask, 'Isn't there some sort of authority you can report this prick to?'

'Yes, of course, the Child Support Agency, but they have an

arbitrary limit of eighteen thousand dollars and don't get too bothered if the amount owed is below it. Most of these arseholes know this and keep their arrears down around fifteen to sixteen thousand. But to a single mum with kids, that's a *lot* of money.'

Pig asks, 'So even though the authorities know he's way behind in his child support, he can still go off overseas?'

'Yes,' Suzie answers, 'unless we can get a court order to prevent him from going.'

'How can we make that happen?' I ask.

Suzie gives me a long, searching look. When I glance at Jenny, I see the same glimmer of hope in her eyes too. 'First, we'll have to prove he's withholding or hiding funds, as he has to declare his monthly and annual income to the CSA.' She pauses, before adding, 'Angela has mentioned how he's spending money on toys. He bought a jet ski a few months ago, and upgraded his work ute to a new Hilux SR5. He's also been to Bali and Fiji for holidays – never offering to take the kids, I might add. According to the income statements he's lodged, he shouldn't be able to afford any of that, let alone an around-the-world trip for two.'

'What does he do?' I ask.

Suzie already has Angela's files up on her screen, so she flicks to Mike's income statements. 'He works for a civil construction company – Bennett Building Company – as a contract carpenter. Apparently, he's paid forty-five dollars per hour, and he's been employed by them for five years now. Angela's said she can't understand why he can't pay up, as they were always comfortable when they were married. She hadn't needed to work once the kids came along. This suited her, since she always wanted to be a full-time mum.'

Silence descends. All eyes turn towards me as the cogs churn.

I say, 'What will you need and when to stop him from travelling and force him to pay up?'

Suzie has a little side discussion with Jenny before turning back to me. 'I'll need forty-eight hours to petition the family court for an urgent hearing. If we're going to stop him from travelling, the hearing will need to be at least two days before his scheduled departure, so realistically, I'll need to make the petition a week before his departure.'

'We don't know his exact departure date though, do we?' I reply.

'No.'

'Okay, then,' I say, as I get up, followed by Pig and Maria. 'We'll work up a plan and let you know.'

I smile at Suzie. She smiles back, making my heart flutter (ah, love!), and says, 'Angela can't afford your usual exorbitant fees, you realise!'

'She can afford a small fee on a success-only basis though, can't she?' I ask.

Back at my desk, I set out a task list. 'Maria, first up, get yourself accepted as a "friend" on Mike's Facebook and Instagram, and any other social media he uses. Then use Hoang's CatchEm app to go back through his posts and document any that show him splashing cash around. Get details of where he stayed in Bali and Fiji, find the registration of his new ute so we can verify the cost, and so forth. Most importantly, let me know if you find who his travel agent is, so we can check when he's departing, where he's going and what it costs.'

'On it, Boss.'

'Pig, you check out this Bennet Building Company. I suspect they're splitting his income somehow, so we need to know how they're doing it.'

Pig nods, and they both head back to their desks to begin their tasks, whilst I return to Suzie's office. As she's on the phone, I ask Jenny to dig out Mike's last three years of income statements to the CSA and details of his lawyer. Jenny responds quickly. 'That's easy. His lawyer is Phil Brownlow. He's as sleazy as any of them. Suzie comes up against him regularly – I truly can't stand him.'

'It'll be good to bring him down a peg or two, then, won't it?'

Jenny gives me a sticky note with his details on it. As I walk back past Maria, I ask her to note any likes or comments from Phil Brownlow. Jenny emails me the income statements a short time later. I already think $45 an hour for a contract carpenter seems quite low, especially if he works on any union sites – the rates can rise to well over $100 per hour. So, I go back through the statements and note he's never had a rate increase. Another unlikely event.

Pig breaks the silence. 'I'm in Bennett's system, checking out their accounts payable, and it looks like Mike's pay each fortnight is split between his personal bank account and a second one in the name of Adrian Taylor, who gets a further forty dollars per hour. Same CBA branch, but it definitely goes into a separate account.'

'Okay, great. We'll have to find out who that is – likely a relative, by the surname. Get copies of a few of his invoices and matching remittance advices, so we can document this.'

Maria pipes up, likely a little miffed that Pig had an update before her. 'Adrian Taylor's his father.'

Pig beats me to it, asking, 'Has he befriended you yet?'

'No, not yet.'

'Maybe your profile photo's scaring him off.'

Maria doesn't have a reply for him.

Then, a little later, she shouts out, 'I'm in! He's just accepted me as a friend on both Instagram and Facebook. Sent me a little message too, saying he can't resist a good-looking woman interested in him.' She accompanies this with an imitation of shoving her fingers down her throat.

After a few minutes, she emails me a copy of a 'Hello World' travel itinerary for Mike Taylor and Robyn Johnson, copied off his Facebook page. What a show-off!

I read this aloud, saying, 'Wow, quite a trip, and business class all the way. Flights between Brisbane, Los Angeles, Las Vegas, Denver, New York, Washington DC, and Orlando, and a ten-night Caribbean cruise out of Fort Lauderdale! Staying at some fancy hotels, too – a Four Seasons, and a couple of Ritz Carltons. No cost is shown, but my guess is it's way over a hundred thousand dollars. Shit, he must have some coin tucked away – and we're going to find it and bring this bastard to justice.'

Both Maria and Pig concur, Maria with a 'Damn right' and Pig with a more vehement 'Fucking oath!'

We are on a mission!

I then access Hello World's system. When I check how their invoice for Mike Taylor was paid, I see it came out of the Adrian Taylor bank account, and save copies of both to our cloud database. Another box ticked.

That night, Suzie once again surprises me by cooking… well, using the microwave to heat up prepared meals. 'It's really lovely you're trying to help Angela and her kids, so thanks,' she says, placing her hand on top of mine.

'No *trying* about it – we'll give you what you need to pull this prick into line.'

Suzie smiles. 'Don't forget, everything you give me has to be accepted as evidence by the court, so it can't be dodgy.'

I feign hurt, clutching at my heart. 'Me, dodgy? How can you even think of me like that!'

Of course, I'm grinning as I say it.

*

It takes a couple of days to collect the evidence we need, but it's obvious Mike has no idea how dumb he's been, on one hand flouting the law by not paying child support, on the other flaunting his toys and girlfriends for the world to see. Maria's done a thorough job of documenting his purchases, including the latest jet ski, the holidays to Bali and Fiji – these with some other woman, Trudy Jackson, who we assume to be Robyn Johnson's predecessor – a few long weekends away, and a skiing trip to Queenstown in New Zealand. He certainly is living the good life without caring for his own kids. Maria also comments how quick and easy it is to gather evidence once she has the hang of using Hoang's CatchEm app.

What an arsehole this Mike is turning out to be.

Now we have proof of what he's been spending his money on, Maria's tasked with building a cost estimate for each of these items. Pig, meanwhile, has been trying to get into CBA's system to see what these two bank accounts show. However, whilst we've had success in accessing other banks' account records previously, CBA seems to have tightened their systems up. Never mind – there's more than one way to skin a cat.

Now that we've opened up Mike's Facebook and Instagram, it's easy to access his email. I scroll through it until I find one from CBA with a statement attached. This is for his main account, so I keep looking until I find another email from CBA, this time with the Adrian Taylor account name. Further proof this is his money.

I check the balance and his main account only has approximately $1,500 in it (wouldn't want it too high – he may have to show it to the court at some time). But the Adrian Taylor account still has $26,777 in it, and the statement shows the withdrawal of $124,862.50 paid to Hello World Travel.

Boom and BOOM! Now we just have to find a way to make this information presentable in court.

The three of us decide to have a catch up, so after Pig and I have made fresh coffees, we assemble at my desk, which seems to be the convenient meeting point. Maria isn't addicted to coffee, preferring to drink tea, and nowhere near as much as we do. Pig tells her she can't have been a real soldier because all soldiers are heavily addicted to caffeine – it's the only way to survive the boredom!

What do we have that can be used as proof in court? We make a list in backwards date order, starting with the around-the-world trip. We can't show the actual invoice, as we'd gained it 'unethically' (Suzie's term, not mine!), so we did what we had with all the other toy purchases – we requested a quote from Hello World, and this came in at $127,300. Our list is:

- American holiday for two: $127,300.
- A used Sea-Doo jet ski: $18,500.
- Queenstown holiday for two: $10,000.
- New Hilux SR5 work ute with accessories: $68,500.
- Yamaha 450 Enduro dirt bike: $19,000.
- Fiji holiday for two: $8,000.
- New custom-built dual-axle work trailer: $24,000.

It's a nice round $275,500 spent against a stated income of $1,800 per week. I would like to see that! I'm keen to get to the heart of the issue – namely, how and why his employer is doing this – so Pig and I decide to pay them a visit. It's a bit of a risk, but having their statement about why they're splitting the arsehole's income will be the icing on the cake. Another coffee as we strategise!

*

Just after 9:00 a.m. the next morning, Pig and I enter the offices of the Bennett Building Company in Woolloongabba, not far from the famed cricket and AFL stadium, 'the Gabba'. We approach the twenty-something-year-old receptionist and I request a meeting with Fiona Williams – we did our homework, checking who was who at the Bennett Building, and found Fiona is their financial controller. A good place to start.

Of course, like all good receptionists, this one doesn't make it easy. She asks, 'Do you have an appointment?'

'No,' I reply, 'we're family court auditors, here on a rather sensitive and urgent matter.' I hold out the ID tag hanging around my neck. It's surprising how a lanyard somehow makes you look more official; we'd whipped these up in the office last night. Fortunately, no one ever checks them!

The receptionist doesn't have a name tag and hasn't introduced herself, but she picks up the phone. Whoever she's talking to asks her something, which she then relays to us. 'Can you tell me what it's about?'

I reply firmly. 'No. As I said, it's a sensitive matter, and consequently, it is confidential.'

After a lengthy silence, followed by a short comment, the receptionist hangs up. 'Fiona will be out in a minute.'

Not long after, a smartly dressed older lady comes out into the reception area, reading glasses twirling in her left hand. 'I'm Fiona Williams. How can I help you?'

As usual when trying to impress, we stand close together,

a doorway and a half of solid muscle. A rather daunting look, we've been told. I hand her my card, saying, 'We are investigating some anomalies on behalf of the family court. We need to discuss your payments to one of your contractors. Is there somewhere we can talk candidly?'

This blunt message, heard by the receptionist as well, is designed to put Fiona on the back foot. Hopefully, she won't request formal proof of our supposed positions. It works, as she quickly glances at the receptionist, saying, 'I'm sure all our records and payments are above board, but let's go into the boardroom so we can discuss it.'

We nod in unison and follow her in. She moves to the top of the table. Must be power hungry, I assume, needing to sit there. Pig and I split – I take a seat on the left, whilst Pig takes one midway up the right – exit covered.

I take my time pulling a couple of manilla folders out and placing them in front of me. These are really just props, as I only have two pages to show her and discuss.

But first, more distraction.

'Fiona, thank you for seeing us. We appreciate that you're a busy lady, but we're investigating what may be a case of fraud, possibly in addition to contempt of court. We need your absolute assurance that what we discuss here stays between the three of us. Is that acceptable? Under the rules which we follow, we are required to ask if you would like a witness to sit in on our discussion. We'll be recording it, and we can send you a copy once it has been filed, if you wish.'

Looking suitably intimidated and apprehensive, Fiona asks, 'Why do I need a witness?'

I reply, 'You don't. But if your responses don't match the facts as we know them, you could be in deep trouble. So, our mandate requires we give you that opportunity. If you're going to tell us the truth, you have nothing to worry about.'

She takes her time regaining her composure, then says, 'I'm comfortable for now without a witness. Depending on where this goes, I may change my mind later.'

I nod. Pig starts the recording app on his phone and pushes it into the centre of the table as I start. 'Can you please state your full name, address and occupation for the record?' (Yes, I've watched plenty of detective movies on TV!)

She dutifully responds. I ask how long she's worked for Bennett's (or BBC, as it's apparently known), and she replies that it's been eight years, though she was promoted to her senior role only two years ago.

Now down to tin tacks.

'There's a contract carpenter, Mike Taylor, who's worked with you for over five years. Do you know him or know of him?'

'I know the name. I may have met him at one of our Christmas parties or other functions, but I don't really recall him. Why?'

'Why? He is way behind on his child support payments.'

Fiona seems puzzled. 'But what has that got to do with me or BBC?'

I silently pass across two invoices, with matching remittance advice, showing payment going to two different bank accounts. She doesn't see it straight away, glancing back up at me before she reviews the documents more closely.

'Okay,' she says, 'I can see we're splitting each invoice and paying to two different accounts, but we often do that if there's a two-man team. They invoice us separately and we pay accordingly.'

'Mike Taylor is a one-man band. Never had another employee.'

I'm not sure of this, but it's highly probable. 'The situation gets worse, for you personally and for BBC – as well as for Mike Taylor, of course. He only submits the invoices you pay to his first account to the Child Support Agency. The question is, are you and BBC also complicit in his crimes? We suspect he hasn't declared his other income to the ATO, so he's been a really naughty boy. The remittance advice doesn't show you making any tax deductions, either.'

Silence. A lengthy one. But Pig and I are patient.

Eventually, Fiona sighs. 'Can you leave this with me? I need to check it out and see why we're doing this. It's not the way we're supposed to operate.'

'We aren't going anywhere, Fiona. This is a critical issue, and we need to leave with both our evidence and your assurance you won't divulge this conversation to anyone, not even your husband.' (I'd noted she's wearing a wedding ring, so this is an educated guess.) 'Can I suggest you pull your file on Mike Taylor and bring it back here so we can discuss it?'

'Okay. All our records are digitalised, so I'll go and grab my laptop.'

'Not a word, please,' I get in before she leaves the room. She quickly pops her head back in, asking if we would like coffee or water. I reply, 'No thanks, we're good.'

Don't want to dwell any longer than we have to!

She comes back a few minutes later, carrying her open laptop, and sits down. After tapping at it and rolling her mouse for a while, she says, 'Here it is. Apparently, this has been going on for nearly four years, so long before I was in charge. There's no way I would've authorised it.'

'Who did, then?' I ask.

'Our operations manager, Dick Bennett – he's the son of our owner and managing director. It was agreed way back to split Mike's bill fifty-fifty to "help him out". That's what it says here in the file.'

'Have you ever received a request from the Child Support Agency to verify his wages?'

'Yes, we have one on file from three years ago, signed by my predecessor, Ken Evans.'

'Did he confirm the incorrect information, then?'

She pauses, likely debating how to answer that, but really, her only option is to be honest. 'Yes.'

I let the silence lengthen, simply staring at her until she looks up from her screen. To her credit, she makes direct eye contact.

'I'm no lawyer,' I say, 'but I know it'll be a bad look when this comes out in public.'

Again, I let the silence linger. I glance at Pig, as if we're deciding something between us, and Pig nods. (He hasn't said a word since we arrived, so he's doing a good job of being the big, silent type!)

Turning back towards Fiona, I say, 'I will require a formal statement from you on behalf of Bennett Building Company detailing the total amount you've paid to both these separate accounts, year by year. If you also include an admission of guilt, stating that you've recently discovered this error and it is being rectified immediately, this may get you off the hook. No guarantees, but it'll look better than us having to report you.'

Fiona puts her head down, and I can hear keys clicking as she types something up. I'm hoping it's the statement I've requested, and she isn't accessing the family court to see if they even do audits on delinquent fathers!

Before long, she gets up, saying, 'I've printed out a draft, so I'll go and get it.' She heads out and comes back with three copies, handing two to Pig and me and keeping one for herself.

The statement is short and to the point. It details how BBC has split Mike Taylor's income between the two bank accounts for the last three years. I think it's perfect for what we have in mind, so I look to Pig to see if he's happy. He nods, and I say, 'Thank you, Fiona. If you can sign this, we'll submit it with our report. You may get some follow-up, but as long as you claim you identified the issue and rectified it yourselves, you should be good. I would check whether you're doing this for any of your other contractors or employees. If you are, please send me a list of them, along with the amounts. And not a word to anyone, particularly Mike Taylor. Understood?'

'Yes,' she says, as she hands me the signed statement.

We stand. I shake her hand, thanking her for her assistance, and exit their offices, nodding to the receptionist on the way out. Back in the Camry, Pig and I fist bump and acknowledge we've done well. A big bluff that worked out – we'll just have to hope she doesn't follow up with the family court anytime soon!

Back at the office, we ask Maria to join us, and we prepare a summary of what we can now officially prove: Mike Taylor has been understating his income, with the help of Bennett Building Company, by over $150,000 PA for the last three years. He has spent approximately $275,000 in the same time period. Adrian Taylor is his father and a retired chef. Maria has also documented that his lawyer, Phil Brownlow, 'liked' many of his toys when he showed them off on Facebook and Instagram. Mike hasn't paid tax on the understated income, so he's going to be in hot water there as well.

We agree it's time to put our findings to Suzie, so we troop into her office. Suzie and Jenny put aside whatever they're working on, and I table our report, including the supporting documents.

They silently read through it all. Suzie finishes first and looks up, with what looks like a hint of a tear in her eye, to smile at me. When Jenny's done, she beams at Suzie and they high five.

Jenny turns to us. 'Wow, this is dynamite. We can blow him up with this! He won't see it coming, either.' She asks Suzie, 'Will they give him jail time for this?'

Suzie shakes her head. 'It's highly unlikely, because the kids would only be hurt more if there was no income coming in – but Mort, Julien, Maria, this is so good and thorough. Thank you! You sure we can use it all in court?'

This last sentence is said whilst she's staring directly at me. Pig and I, almost in unison, mime a dagger to the heart, which makes all of us laugh.

Once we settle down again, Suzie says, 'This is more than enough to request an urgent court hearing. I'll get right on it, and I'll let Angela know there's been some developments that may require her attendance in court. Still, I don't want to get her hopes up too much, in case we don't get anywhere.'

I growl, 'If that doesn't get action by the court, I'll take matters into my own hands.'

The look of alarm on Suzie and Jenny's faces makes me laugh. 'I meant I would rent them a house, so they aren't homeless – I'm not sure what else you were thinking!' I say this with perfect innocence.

*

A few days later, Suzie comes out of her office, waits until Pig is off the phone, and says 'We just got our court hearing for Angela. It's next Tuesday, so just over a week before Mike's departure overseas.'

Pig, Maria, and I exchange fist bumps. I say, 'We might come along and watch.'

I get a surprised look from Suzie, but she smiles. 'Happy to entertain you after what you've done for Angela.'

Then she blushes, and I grin!

33

The next morning, out of the blue, an email arrives from Robert at Section V, advising they have a match for Marissa's 'Jeffy' – Commander Jeffrey Connors of the Australian Federal Police.

Commander? I think. *Shit, that's getting pretty high up the tree.*

To be honest, I'm a bit surprised the Australian Cyber Security Centre has come through. I'd expected Midge would be the one to come up with a nugget, if anyone, and with the time it's taken, I'd largely given up on either of them identifying our Jeffy.

I flick the email to Pig just as another comes through, this one an invite for a Pexip video conference (a platform similar to Zoom or Teams, but encrypted and totally secure) with Robert and Major General Charles Rutherford. I let Pig know, and he replies, 'Let me see what I can find about Jeffy first.'

'Good idea,' I reply. 'Maria, dig up what you can on a Jeffrey Connors, commander in the AFP, please.'

She'd looked up when Pig had mentioned Jeffy. 'On it, Boss!'

She hits social media, whilst Pig digs who knows where. I leave them to it, thinking of the ramifications of an AFP commander being bent and on our trail.

A couple of minutes later, I have my headphones on as our encrypted Pexip call comes through. I just had time to make Pig and me fresh coffees!

MGC takes the lead. 'The voice match only came through yesterday evening. Somehow, Jeffrey's voice hadn't been recorded until recently. I'm going to look into why it wasn't already on file, as protocol requires.'

He shakes his head. 'Whilst the voice match is nigh on a hundred per cent, I would still like visual confirmation as well. We don't yet have an ID to match to the back of his head, as the only photos we can find are those for his AFP security pass and Queensland driver's license. Apparently, he's based in their Brisbane office in Newstead.'

Suddenly, a photo of the back of a blond male head pops up onto our screens, quickly followed by the image of Jeffy's head taken from the secret camera on Marissa's front door.

Pig comments, 'Looks the same to me.'

'Where was that image taken?' MGC asks.

'From the CCTV cameras outside the AFP office.'

'How? No, never mind, that's what we pay you for. Nice and quick, Pig. Thank you.'

It's my turn to add my two bobs' worth: 'No doubt we need to double-check, but with the voice match, it's highly likely to be the same man. Clearly, we need to do some digging into Jeffy. What can you share with us, sir? When was his last internal AFP assessment carried out, and what did they find?'

Robert and MGC, who are in the same room, confer for a few moments. Eventually, MGC says, 'The last assessment was eighteen months ago. He was given the all clear, but there is a note saying he was recently separated from his wife, which consequently recommends his follow-up assessment take place in one year rather than the standard two. But there's no record of this follow-up having been completed.'

'Sir, how confidential have your inquiries been? Does anyone in the AFP know we've identified him as a possible criminal?' I ask.

'No. At Section V, we have full, confidential access to their internal records, so no one within the AFP would be aware of our search.'

'Good,' I say. 'At the conclusion of the Lancaster investigation, all files were sent to the AFP for further investigation. Would Jeffy have had access to these, or was he involved in any follow-up investigation?'

'It might take us a little time to search through their investigative files to find out. Can you remind me which companies were paying Lancaster's bookkeeping company?'

Pig nods. 'On it. I'll send through a list shortly.'

Just then, Maria hands me a few pages – screen shots from a Facebook account, by the look of it – and whispers, 'I've found something.'

I stop her and say to MGC and Robert, 'I'm going to add Maria, as she has something to share.'

I can tell Maria is thrilled at being included, as she quickly goes back to her desk and dons her headphones, which she usually only uses to listen to music, or to drown Pig and me out! When on the call, she starts again. 'Sir, Mort asked me a few minutes ago to look into Jeffy's social media accounts. His Facebook and Instagram are both petty bland and innocent, mainly about his kids, but one "friend" stood out – a young lady, and I use the term loosely, if you get my meaning. You wouldn't expect a top-level AFP officer to associate with her type. On her Instagram feed, there are a number of photos of the two of them, and some are quite risqué. Mind you, his name is never mentioned, but there is no doubt it's Jeffy. Her name is Yolanda Richardson.'

There's silence as we all contemplate this, until I say, 'Sir, seeing as we've already started, and have the background of the earlier Lancaster investigation, why don't we keep digging? It's off the books then.'

'Very well,' MGC says, 'please proceed. Maria, thank you for your report. And Mort, whilst your investigation will be off the books, you will assuredly be *on* the books.' He gives a slight smile. Well, well, MGC trying a little humour – it's his way of saying we can send him the bill!

After we all sign off, Pig and Maria wheel their chairs over to my desk to make a plan. It's agreed Pig will rummage back through the Lancaster files and find the names of the companies we proved were paying 'protection' to Lancaster by way of 'compulsory' use of his accounting firm (no old-fashioned brown paper bags these days!).

He adds, 'I'll access their Xero files as well, just to see if they're still making these sorts of payments.'

I raise my eyebrows, then see the sense of what he's saying – our friend Jeffy may have simply stepped into Lancaster's shoes and continued the same extortion racket. Bloody poor form on behalf of both the Queensland and federal police if this does prove to be the case.

Maria will continue to track through both Jeffy and Yolanda's social media to see what else comes to light, using Hoang's CatchEm app again. I ask her to add Marissa to her list of targets, knowing she'll get more on her than I would, and quicker too. Me, I'm going to dig into Jeffy a bit more.

We split up with a renewed focus on what we need to achieve.

34

Tuesday morning arrives and the three of us head to the family court in the city. The hearing is set for 11:00 a.m., but Suzie has warned us that the court rarely keeps to time, so it could be early or late. We get there before 10:30, just in case. As luck would have it, the court is running late, so it's near 11:30 before the case is called.

Angela and Suzie are already in position at the front of the court, as are Mike and his lawyer, Brownlow. After settling into his seat, the judge says, 'I have a petition in front of me requesting a review of child support payments that are several months in arrears. It also claims that the income reported may not be factual.'

Brownlow shoots up, saying, 'Your Honour, my client hasn't had time to review the claim and requests a delay for six weeks.'

The judge asks, 'Why such a lengthy delay, Mr Brownlow?'

'Your Honour, my client is off on an overseas holiday next week, so we will not have time to review these claims and dispute them prior to him leaving.'

Suzie jumps in before the judge can respond. 'Your Honour, that is exactly the point. Mike Taylor is some fifteen thousand dollars in arrears on his child support payments and claims he can't afford to catch up, but apparently, he *can* afford to fly off on a month-long holiday.'

The judge looks at Brownlow over the top of his glasses. 'She has a point. Care to clarify the situation for me?'

Slam dunk! Brownlow has dug himself – or, more correctly, his client – into a hole. He looks down at his folders, before saying, 'Your Honour, I have not asked my client how he is funding this trip; it's none of my business. I simply assumed a friend or family member was paying for it.'

'Very well. Mr Taylor, if you want to go on this holiday, we will proceed and take care of this matter now. Do you agree?'

A whispered conversation ensues between Mike and his lawyer, before Brownlow says, 'With the court's permission, I need to register my objection to the lack of time I have been given to prepare to refute the claims in this absurd application.'

The judge responds quickly and firmly. 'You had over forty-eight hours' notice. That should be plenty of time for a good lawyer. Proceed, Ms Dunn.'

Nice!

Suzie then lays out in all the gory detail how Mike has fraudulently understated his income since the separation, assisted by both his own father and his employer. She explains how he never once paid the agreed monthly sum, but always stayed just below the limit set by the CSA. Then she tables his spending on toys and holidays. It is a rather damning picture, and it appears Suzie hadn't told Angela the full story, as she gives a few gasps and even sheds tears when some of the amounts are mentioned.

Suzie finishes off by saying, 'Your Honour, as you can see, Mike Taylor has deliberately understated his income not only to the CSA but also the Australian Tax Office. He has spent huge amounts of money on himself, and yet his eldest daughter is denied reading glasses because he "can't afford them". This has directly resulted in Charlotte falling behind at school.'

Angela's quiet sobs add a real exclamation point to Suzie's closing statement. Suzie sits down, pulling her in for a comforting hug.

The judge lets the silence linger before responding. 'Mr Brownlow, I look forward to hearing your explanation of these claims. Proceed.'

Of course, Brownlow starts by again objecting to the matter of proceeding without adequate time to prepare. The judge interrupts him, saying, 'I'm happy for you to put Mr Taylor on the stand, and we can all question him, if you'd prefer.'

This settles Brownlow down. He carries on, not making a dent in the case against his client, but putting in a long and waffly effort anyway. On more than one occasion, he claims that he was 'unaware' of Mike's spending largesse.

Once he's finished and seated, Suzie rises, saying, 'Your Honour, can I refer you to pages five, seven, ten and fifteen of the documents in front of you? On each of these pages, you will find evidence of Mr Brownlow "liking" Mr Taylor's Facebook posts about the various toys he has bought.'

Brownlow is now glaring daggers at Suzie, raising my hackles. The judge looks at him, saying simply, 'Mr Brownlow?'

'Your Honour, I repeat I had no idea my client was spending this sort of money. I can only think my receptionist, who I encourage to show support and encouragement to our clients, has liked these posts on my behalf.'

Hmm, I think, *he's quick on his feet.*

The judge studies him sternly. 'If I find you have any other clients carrying out the same tricks, I will have you for contempt of court.'

Brownlow mumbles, 'Yes, Your Honour.'

'I will take this matter under advisement and will deliver my verdict next Tuesday at 11:00 a.m.,' the judge says. 'I will require both Mike and Adrian Taylor to be present.'

With a bang of the gavel, the proceedings come to a finish. There's a bit of whispered conversation from the few onlookers in the courtroom. Brownlow is giving Suzie the eye again, Suzie blithely ignoring him as she has an animated discussion with Angela and Jenny, who sits directly behind them.

Mike makes a half-hearted effort to say hello to Angela, but she brushes him off nicely. As he leaves the court, he seems to recognise Maria, saying just loud enough for us to hear, 'Bitch.'

She, of course, stands aggressively in front of him. 'What did you say, arsehole?' she asks loudly.

Before Mike can respond, Brownlow has pulled him out of harm's way. Likewise, I quietly tell Maria to let it go. We don't need local journos sniffing around.

Suzie, Angela and Jenny join us outside, all smiling happily. When Suzie re-introduces us three to Angela, she gives us all big hugs and heartfelt thank-yous.

'Come on,' I say, 'let's get a bite to eat and celebrate.' I lead the way into Linger Longer Café on nearby Tank Street.

Over lunch, Angela asks how much she owes us, and appears truly astonished when I say, 'Let's call it five hundred dollars, and you make sure those kids have a nice, safe home!'

Later, I ask Jenny and Suzie for a list of other clients they have whose ex-partners are represented by 'that sleazebag Brownlow', as we've all taken to calling him. When they ask why, I say, 'I didn't like the way he looked at Suzie, and he deserves to face a little justice.'

Jenny nods enthusiastically. 'I'm on it! There are a few.' Then she nudges Suzie, saying in a loud whisper, 'He's jealous!'

Next Tuesday, we're all once again sitting in court when the judge brings us to order. Mike is ordered to stand, but before the judge can say anything more, Brownlow gets up. 'Your Honour, my client has paid all arrears to the CSA on Friday, and now owes nothing in child support. In addition, he has paid for a year's worth of contact lenses for his daughter.'

The judge looks at Suzie, who nods. 'Very well,' he says. 'I will take that into account.' He fixes Mike with a hard stare. 'I find you guilty of contempt of court and sentence you to six months in prison. However, as you have paid full restitution, I will suspend your sentence for twelve months. If, in that time, any of your payments are so much as one day late, you will be locked up. I'm sure Ms Dunn here will be only too happy to keep me informed. Do you understand, Mr Taylor?'

Mike nods. 'Yes, Your Honour. Thank you.' He sits down again, head hanging.

'I have also noted the complicity of Bennett Building Company in this matter, but as they apparently identified the issue and rectified it themselves, I see no need for further punishment.' The judge glances at the documents before him, then continues, 'Mr Adrian Taylor, please stand.'

An older man sitting behind Mike gets up, whilst his wife or partner holds his hand. He appears very apprehensive.

The judge says, 'Mr Adrian Taylor?'

'Yes, Your Honour.'

'You, sir, have also come *very* close to being found in contempt. As I'm obliged to do, I have reported you two to the ATO, who I'm sure will be investigating you both. I'm sure you thought it was a harmless ploy to help your son, but did you ever think of your grandkids?' The judge holds Adrian's eye, and finishes by saying,

'From one grandfather to another, how could you?'

There isn't much of a spring in the Taylors' steps as they make their way out. Maria, being Maria, is standing large and tall at the exit, making sure Mike has to squeeze past her as he leaves. He doesn't give her the satisfaction of even looking at her.

We once again adjourn for lunch at Linger Longer, with Angela insisting it's her shout. She tells us she's taken Charlotte to the optician and is hoping they'll receive the contact lenses in the next day or so. Even using a pair of reading glasses the optician lent them has helped Charlotte markedly. Her confidence has soared, and she's suddenly excited to be going to school again. They're moving into a new house in a nicer neighbourhood, though it's still close enough for the kids to remain in their schools and kindergartens. It's nice to hear the enthusiasm in her voice, especially compared to the devastating wails we heard from Suzie's office only a short time ago.

Suzie seems to sense what I'm thinking, as she quietly slips her hand into mine and gives it a squeeze. It's all the thanks I need!

Before we all head back to the office, Maria lets Suzie know that of the five other clients of hers who have Brownlow as an opposing lawyer, three of their ex-partners appear to be carrying out the same rort. Maria's all over it, again stating how Hoang's CatchEm app made it easy to trace 'the dumb bastards', as she now calls them.

I tell Suzie I want to be in court when she brings the next case before the judge.

35

Pig, Maria and I have completed our digging into Jeffy, as we continue to call him. Before I send off an interim report to MGC, we decide to bring our findings together to see what the picture looks like.

Pig takes the lead. 'As far as I can tell, all eight businesses that were paying Lancaster's bookkeeping business, Allegro Accounting, are now paying another company called PHA Bookkeeping. PHA seems to have the same business model as Allegro. For example, the actual bookkeeping is done offshore in the Philippines – some of the staff's names are even the same.

'The prices seem to have gone up by ten per cent, though, and the payments all go to one of these new online-only banks, NetDeposit.com. I haven't had any luck accessing them, but I still have access to the companies' Xero files, so that's how I know where the money's going. These payments all started within three to four weeks after Lancaster went down.

'Second, PHA Bookkeeping is the trading name of a company called Roma Investments P/L as Trustee for Roma Trust. Its registered and trading address is the Brisbane office of the Big Four accounting firm PwC, so we can't get anywhere there, either. The sole director of Roma Investments is one Theodore

Smith, but I haven't been able to identify him. He doesn't have a current Australian license – in any state, the address given is again PwC's Brisbane office. It's quite a cleverly cut-out circle. The only connection I can find is that Jeffy was born and raised in Roma, a country town in western Queensland.

'I managed to get into PwC's system, and the only forwarding address they have for both Theodore Smith and Roma Investments is a box at Lutwyche Post Office. It's in the Lutwyche shopping centre, so it'll be difficult to identify anyone accessing it.

'Oh, another interesting fact is Roma Investments was incorporated only three weeks after we took Lancaster down, which is rather interesting timing.'

I nod to Pig – he's done a good job. Maria is keen to show what she's found too: 'I started with Yolanda and stalked a few of her friends on both Facebook and Instagram. The further I looked, the more unsavoury characters I found. So far, she seems to be in contact with a few members of the local Jackals bikie club and three fully patched members of the Melbourne-based Redskins bikie gang.'

Pig and I fist bump as I say, 'Boom!'

Maria's looking a bit perplexed, so I tell her, 'We identified the two thugs who beat up DI Chris Harris as members of the Redskins – now we have a connection! What are the names of the three Yolanda's in contact with?'

'One's simply known as Mo.' Maria shows us a photo of a big bald guy in typical bikie clothing with a massive handlebar moustache. Clearly his signature piece! 'In one message, Yolanda referred to him as "uncle", so they may be related. The other two are younger, around her age, which is thirty-two – fifteen years younger than Jeffy, I might add. They're Macca McKay and Sean

Jessop.' She shows us pictures of them.

I ask, 'Do we know their roles or statuses within the Redskins?'

'No, not yet. None of them are very prominent on social media, so it's hard to track any more down. But I must say, Hoang's CatchEm app has made this a lot easier. I just put in different phrases, and it comes up with anything related. Really cool!'

'Have you Googled their names to see what else pops up?'

'Yes,' Maria replies. 'Didn't get far with Mo, but both Macca and Sean have made the news for minor crimes.'

Pig says, 'Okay, I'll put all three into the facial and gait recognition programs, particularly Mo, so we can find out who he is. Also, do we know where Jeffy and Yolanda live?'

Maria nods. 'Jeffy has an apartment on Newton Street, Grange – not far from Lutwyche, I might add – whilst Yolanda shares a house on Little Street, Nundah, only about fifteen minutes away.'

'Who does she share with?' Pig asks.

Maria pulls a face, saying, 'Sorry, haven't got to that yet.'

I see Pig trying to hide a smirk. I let it slide, as he's really only trying to needle Maria, in their usual manner!

'Cars?' I ask.

'Yolanda drives an older Toyota Corolla. I haven't found a car registered to Jeffy, so I presume he uses his police one for personal travel as well.'

'Hmm, I wouldn't have thought that would be the case. Maybe check if there's a car registered to Roma Investments.'

'Will do,' she replies.

'So, what does Yolanda do officially?' I ask.

'She describes herself as an entertainer-slash-aspiring actress,' Maria says.

Looking at a couple of the images Maria has tabled, I admit

grudgingly, 'She does have the looks for it, I guess.'

Maria nods. 'Yes, my Ronnie would certainly notice her walking into a room!'

Of course, Pig can't resist that opening, and quickly says, 'Wandering eyes, wandering hands, ah!'

Maria flashes Pig a smile. 'No, my Ronnie does all right. Besides, I told him long ago what he'll lose if he ever cheats on me. I haven't borne him a brood of four kids to let him go off banging someone else.'

Again, Pig can't resist. 'So, what would he lose?'

Maria looks him in the eyes. 'His manhood.'

Ouch. Like Pig and me, Maria works hard on her fitness. Poor Ronnie wouldn't stand a chance!

After this little by-play, I offer my fist to Maria, and she happily bumps it – she likes being one of the boys! Pig muses, 'I wonder where Jeffy got the name PHA Bookkeeping?'

As we all contemplate this, Maria says, 'His kids' names are Parker, Henri and Aubrey.'

I smile. Not incriminating on its own, but another nail in Jeffy's coffin!

'Okay, my turn,' I say. I slip out four images, all of Jeffy entering or leaving different shopfronts, the store's name clearly showing in each photo. 'All four of these businesses, as confirmed by Pig, have switched from paying Allegro Accounting to PHA Bookkeeping. As you can see from the timestamps, all were taken from the stores' CCTV footage within two to four weeks after we took Lancaster out. Pig, do you know when these companies started paying PHA?'

Pig immediately starts digging through his file and comes back with dates that are within a few days of those shown on the photos. Another match!

I show a fifth picture. It's indistinct, but off to the side, you can see Jeffy talking to someone. 'This isn't a good image, so we'll need to ask Robert or MGC if their boffins can enhance it. Still, it's obvious this second person is very large – he's likely in the background in case any of their targets give Jeffy grief.'

Pausing to think, I tap my fingers on my desk. 'So far, we can't tie Jeffy to PHA Bookkeeping. We have to do that somehow. Pig, we might need to wander over to Lutwyche Post Office to see what we can set up. Let's also install CCTV outside his and Yolanda's homes.'

Pig nods, and I continue. 'MGC might be able to "lean" on PwC to see who within their set-up deals with Theodore Smith. They'd have to know if the name's bogus, and MGC seems to get on well with these corporate types. I'll also let him know we're keen to see how they've got on with digging into any AFP investigations of Lancaster.'

I turn to Pig. 'What say we head out to Lutwyche, Grange and Nundah now, knock off all three jobs in one go?'

'Deal,' he replies. 'You make the coffee whilst I put the goodies into the van.'

Good to know I'm useful, even if only to make coffee! I'm dutifully making our drinks – including a cup of tea for Maria, so she doesn't feel left out – when Jenny comes out of their office. Seeing me, she says, 'I hear there's been progress on the wedding day. Finally stopped dragging your heels, ah?'

I smile. She's teasing me, but yes, Suzie and I have finally settled on a date in the new year. Suzie, her mother, and her sister Nat have been scouring suitable wedding venues since the engagement (seems longer to me!), and they've apparently decided on The Loft in West End. I haven't seen it yet, but Suzie obviously likes it, so it's fine with me.

Early on, I told Suzie I'd pay for the wedding, as I didn't want her parents stressing over the cost now they were retired. However, they had refused, in their typically old-fashioned way, saying they'd always planned to pay for the wedding and were happy to do so. It'll only be a relatively small affair, anyway; I don't have many family or friends to invite, having essentially been cut off from society for my fifteen years in the army. Still, I know one thing for certain – Nat's two kids, Ollie and Amelie, are excited about being part of the wedding party!

36

We decide to head to Jeffy's place in Grange first. Pig has adorned the van with magnetic Energex signs – they're a major Queensland power company, so no one will be suspicious if we start climbing light poles and the like. He also checked the CCTV outside the federal police office and confirmed Jeffy is at work, so we should be good to go.

We find the house on Newton Street, a refurbished old Queenslander that's been split into two apartments. It's quite stylish! No cars parked outside, which hopefully means Yolanda isn't there.

The closest power pole is one neighbour away, so that'll have to do. I'm off up the ladder, with hi-vis, tool belt and safety harness on, whilst Pig puts safety barriers up around its base. We're both on the lookout for nosey neighbours but don't spot any. I attach a good wide-angle camera with zoom capability to the pole, and Pig checks the image on his iPad, confirming we're good to go.

Before coming down, I take the time to study Jeffy's apartment. I expect we're going to be back in a few days to set up a mic and camera inside.

After a quick pack-up, we're off to Nundah. It's a slightly

rougher suburb than Grange, but still pleasant enough, and the install is easy.

Finally, we head to Lutwyche Shopping Centre to check out the post office. When we get there, we realise we're a little lucky, as the post office boxes are in the underground car park. There are CCTV cameras everywhere, but we're always prepared. We grab a tape measure, measuring wheel and ladder and head over to the post box section.

Whilst I stand around fiddling with the ladder, Pig identifies that PO Box 685, Theodore Smith and Roma Investments' box, is down near the bottom right-hand corner. I quickly identify a suitable drainpipe affixed to the ceiling. After making sure I'm out of the traffic lanes, I head up the ladder and position one of our tiny fisheye cameras on the pipe with a zip tie, whilst hiding what I'm doing from the nearest camera with my body. Pig gives me a grunt to tell me the angle is spot on.

We decide to forgo a coffee, wanting to make a quick exit in case one of the security team becomes curious about what we're up to. Back at the office, I see Robert has emailed an invite for a progress report over Pexip next Monday. All three of us are invited, which gives Maria a buzz, and, of course, brings forth a bit of teasing from Pig, who suggests she's 'finally being invited to the big kids' table!'

37

The day has arrived – the day of the Gold Coast Marathon. Not that we're competing in the full race, but Suzie, Pig and I all entered the half-marathon. It'll be Pig's final hit out before we head over to Victoria, Canada, to compete in the Invictus Games. Just as important to me (well, not really) is that it'll be my chance to get even with Suzie.

You see, on all our training runs, she now stretches out, leaving me behind, and has become rather smug about it. Little does she know I've been letting her beat me and doing extra training in secret. The half-marathon will be my revenge! I can taste it.

On our current times, Pig should still beat us both, but we've closed the gap significantly, so it'll be interesting. They both assume I'll be dragging the chain, but that isn't how I'm planning it. Can't wait!

The Gold Coast Marathon is an iconic event that's been running for over forty years, which truly highlights the beautiful beaches, as the track follows the coastline. The half-marathon is an up-and-back course running beside the broadwater, a large lake-like waterway. Thus, the course is nice and flat.

Ah, I *really* can't wait. Vengeance will be sweet!

The race is at 6:00 a.m. on a Saturday, so the three of us knocked off early on Friday and booked ourselves into the JW Marriott for the weekend. (Don't worry – Pig has his own room!) The JW is within walking distance of the race precinct, so it avoids the hassle of buses back and forth.

It's 5:00 a.m., and Suzie and I are in the lobby waiting for Pig. When he arrives, his running blade looks nice and shiny, so I ask him if he's polished it. Surprisingly, he answers, 'Yes, I read that the more polished it is, the better it slices through the air.'

I laugh. 'That's not as important as how hard you're moving it!'

We set off from the hotel, and we're clearly not the only ones heading to the race. The full marathon is on Sunday morning, so everyone we can see is entered in the half. Other shorter races are later in the morning.

Disabled athletes still aren't common, so walking through the crowds with Pig gains quite a bit of attention. I even tell Suzie they're looking at Pig, not her. She pokes her tongue out at me, before reminding me it was the colourful top she wore in the Bridge to Brisbane last year that attracted me to her. (It wasn't, really – it was her bum, which I'd admitted to later!)

We arrive at the race precinct, and there's an awesome sense of anticipation. Everyone has no doubt been training for this day for months. The excitement is palpable.

As start time approaches, we split up. Pig's anticipating a time under one hour and fifty minutes and is in Zone A, whereas Suzie and I are in Zone B, with Suzie even having the audacity to question whether I should be in Zone C. Cheeky shit.

As I said, vengeance will be sweet!

The gun goes off. The front runners race away. Not that we can see this, lost back in the crowd of everyday runners. Suzie and I eventually get to the start line, from where our times are taken. As we both start our stopwatches, I say, 'See ya,' and I'm off.

If Suzie responds, I don't hear it. My goal is to get so far ahead of her that she can't use those long legs of hers to catch up. I'm committed!

Throughout the one-km, two-km and five-km marks, I'm holding my time, looking good. I'm on track for a sub one hour and forty-five-minute time. Have to keep my pace up, though. *Keep going*, I tell myself. *Hard!*

As I approach the halfway turning point, I keep an eye out for Pig. Whilst my primary goal is beating Suzie, I still wouldn't mind knocking Pig off as well. Ambitious, but you've got to have a goal or two.

I see him. He has turned and is heading back. I give a little fist pump as I hide behind a big pack of runners – don't want him seeing how close I am!

I make the turn, taking a drink refresher as I do. Now to check how far ahead of Suzie I am.

Bugger, I don't see her. Even in her nice colourful top. This makes me nervous, but I push on, still checking my times every kilometre. I'm on track.

With three kilometres to go, I spot Pig ahead of me, getting the occasional flash of sun off his blade. This comes just at the right time to give me a boost, helping me avoid 'hitting the wall'. I find a bit more energy and stretch out. When running long-distance, nothing happens quickly – if you're chasing someone down, it's stride by stride, minute by minute – but I am gaining.

Before long, he's only 100 metres in front of me. I resist the temptation to surge up and pass him, reminding myself I still have two kilometres to run. Need to stay the distance, and beating Suzie is the primary goal here!

One kilometre left. I'm twenty metres behind Pig, and I'm now comfortable I can take him. I try looking behind me, but don't get a chance to see any individual. Just need to push on. Hold my pace.

Five hundred metres, and the finishing chute is up ahead. I lengthen my stride, catch up to Pig and match his pace. He senses this and turns. Seeing me, he smiles and pumps his fist. I give him a nod of encouragement and we both stretch out.

Only three hundred metres now. Somehow, finishing with Pig seems better than defeating him, and it looks like I have Suzie beaten, so why not? (Then again, if he starts a sprint, I'm ready!)

A hundred metres to go. Suddenly, I sense someone next to me, a moment before fingers slip into mine. Yes, Suzie is right beside me, holding my hand and giving me the most beautiful smile.

Damn. Robbed of my vengeance. But I'll take that smile every day of the week! Pig has also realised Suzie's caught up, and the three of us cross the line together.

Bugger Pig, it's Suzie I'm hugging first. Revenge would've been sweet. But Suzie's smile — and her love — are much sweeter. (Ahh, I know, I know.) Still, she didn't beat me!

The three of us got a real buzz out of it. Well, Suzie and I did, although my well-laid plan came unstuck at the end. Suzie and I achieved personal best times, so we're happy. Whilst Pig also got a PB, he was a little disappointed by his time, and I remind him he's still in heavy training, so getting a PB was a great effort.

After collecting our finisher's medals, we don our race T-shirts. It isn't yet 9:00 a.m., so we'll be in time for a big breakfast back at the hotel. But first, Pig has media commitments!

Yes, Jenny wrote an article about Pig's upcoming trip to the Invictus Games, which was published in the *Gold Coast Bulletin*.

It mentioned how the half-marathon is his final outing, and even included a photo of him in his distinctive Australian Invictus Games uniform. A *Bulletin* reporter is there for a follow-up. They take a picture of him in his finisher's T-shirt, gleaming blade and all.

Quite the star is our Pig. Not that he's happy with all the fuss!

On the walk back to the hotel, we all recount episodes from our races, with Suzie telling us, 'I was nonplussed when Mort disappeared ahead of me, thinking *What the hell?* Then my competitive spirit kicked in and I told myself, *No bloody way is he going to beat me!*' She grins at me. 'I hid from you as I approached the turn so you wouldn't know how close I was – only about two hundred metres.'

I laugh. 'I did the exact same thing to Pig.'

Stacey rings as we're walking back to see how Pig did. When he tells her we all finished together, she says that was 'cool'. Maria, on the other hand, wants to know what Suzie was thinking, not kicking our butts when she had the chance – apparently, to use Maria's words, she 'let the sisterhood down'. All in good fun!

Back at the hotel, we agree to meet down for a buffet breakfast after showering. Once in our room, Suzie pulls me into an embrace. 'You know I could've beaten you, don't you?'

I give her a kiss. 'But could you have if I hadn't slowed to join Pig? Besides, I can think of a better way to use those long legs of yours!'

After another kiss, she responds rather hoarsely, 'And what would that be, mister?'

Suddenly, our showers don't seem so urgent.

We're late down to breakfast, where we're greeted by a smirking Pig. Picture it – a smirking Pig!

We now have the rest of the weekend at leisure. I've booked a table at Rick Shores, the renowned restaurant on the beach at Burleigh Heads, for dinner Saturday night. I was drawn there by seeing the receipt on Liz's visa. Suzie, on learning where we're eating, exclaims, 'How do you even know about Rick Shores? It's meant to be awesome – I can't believe you even know about it.'

I choose to ignore her. Seems my Suzie thinks I'm a cultural Neanderthal, doesn't she!

The view and meal are both as stunning as claimed, and the three of us have a lovely evening. We talk about the race, along with our pending trip to Canada for the games, then to the States for a two-week holiday, where we plan on visiting New York, Washington, San Francisco and Los Angeles. Of course, Suzie has to say, 'And shopping, don't forget the shopping! It's all on you, mister.' She gives me a smile and a dig in the ribs.

Plenty to look forward to. But Pig and I can't stop ourselves from talking about the pending disaster in Afghanistan, as the US has decided to withdraw their forces with little appropriate planning for a safe handover.

Pig says, 'I lost my bloody leg for the freedom of the Afghan people, and now these dickheads can't even organise a fucking safe transition. What about everyone who's suffered and died, all for bloody nothing?'

A sad note to end our lovely evening on.

38

Come Monday, we're all back in the office, having relived the buzz of our race with both Maria and Jenny. As 11:00 a.m. approaches, the three of us get ready for our Pexip video conference with MGC and Robert.

As usual, the meeting begins precisely on time, with MGC starting it off. First, he asks Pig and I how we did in the half-marathon. He's a little perplexed when we say we'd ended in a dead heat, particularly when I add that Suzie had finished with us as well!

Then he's quickly down to business and asking for an update from our end. However, I say, 'Before we begin, sir, we're keen to know what follow-up there's been from the AFP on the Lancaster investigation.'

A pause. Pig and I look at each other, instinctively knowing the answer before MGC confirms it.

'Unfortunately, it appears there has been absolutely no activity on these files since they were handed over to AFP. Which, of course, is appalling. The files are all tagged "pending arrival of further details", so they don't come up for review, and they're all signed out to Commander Jeffrey Connors. There's no warning in the AFP's system against Commander Connors or any of his team. So, they don't appear to have raised any suspicions internally. I haven't raised the matter with the AFP Commissioner, as I don't want to flag that we're investigating this just yet. I have, however, mentioned it at my weekly briefing with the prime minister, who I must say is equally appalled by this "disgraceful failure" – his words.'

We all shake our heads, before Pig leads off on our report. We keep it succinct, summarising the situation with PHA Bookkeeping and the possibly-fictitious Theodore Smith, as well as with Yolanda Richardson and her connections to both Jackal and Redskin bikies – which provide a direct link between Jeffy and the thugs who beat up Chris. I also suggest MGC has a little chat with PwC to find out more about Theodore Smith.

Once we finish our summary, silence lasts for several minutes, as both Robert and MGC make copious notes. Once he's finished, MGC says, 'Thank you, and well done. You've achieved a lot in a short time. Much more than we have, unfortunately.'

We agree to send the images of the three Redskin bikies and Yolanda through to Robert for further investigation, as well as the grainy CCTV picture of Jeffy with another man.

We sign off. Time for coffee!

After chatting for a little while over our drinks, Pig and I convene at my desk, whilst Maria remains at her own. She's busy doing a research job on another delinquent father for a solicitor friend of Suzie's. The word is spreading, which is good for business. Mind you, the rate has gone up since we helped Angela!

Pig and I recap our progress on what is now our major investigation and how it might be related to who killed Liz. We ponder if Jeffy and Lancaster are linked. The question is, did Jeffy have anything to do with Liz's death? His name hadn't come up anywhere. Then again, is he the mysterious 'Mr Jones' who accompanied Lancaster to the Rocklea International Motel on the night of the 'accident'? But why no other connection – no phone calls, no nothing?

Who killed Liz? We haven't made much progress. Yet.

Our conversation turns to Pig's training. With only a couple of weeks to go until the Invictus Games, he's taken some advice to fine-tune his training program. All three events he's entered in, the 400m, 1500m and 10,000m, will take place in the span of in four days. Fortunately, the 10,000m, which Pig considers his best event, is his also his last, so he won't need to run any further races after it.

*

The following afternoon, another email from Robert pops into my inbox, advising us that the following message has been intercepted by Australian Cyber Security Centre: 'Confirming meeting with Joe L at 2:00 a.m. Wednesday at the Newstead Gasworks.'

Shit. Who and what is this about? I wonder. The email also invites Pig and me to another Pexip meeting in a few minutes, so we don our headphones.

MGC takes the floor. 'I've kept "Joe Lancaster" as a key word, so when "Joe L" came up, the message was sent to me at Section V. However, whilst we captured the phone number the message came from, we have no record of it, and nor do any phone network carriers. We were also unable to identify the recipient phone number. I had my data analysts go back through the last seven days, using "Joe L" as a key word, but no other message has popped up. Because of the strong probability this is connected to the Lancaster and Connor inquiries, I want you two to take the lead on this. It may even be a trap.'

MGC steeples his hands. 'The message has also been forwarded to Queensland Police, but I'll have word sent through to Commissioner Black that you two are in the lead. They're to provide you with full and proper backup. I don't like where these inquiries are headed, so you'll be Operatives A and B, agreed?'

Pig says, 'Bear in mind, sir, some within Queensland Police are already aware of our identities.'

'I'll speak to Commissioner Black to ensure she and DI Harris don't refer to you by name. I'll also suggest that DI Harris is appointed as your liaison, as she already knows you.'

We formulate a plan, but with so many unknowns, it's really going to involve us acting on instinct as much as anything. It's agreed we'll wear our full bulletproof outfits, but we decide on handguns only. Don't want to be scaring the good citizens of Brisbane by being seen roaming around fully armed. Mind you, all good citizens are likely to be home tucked in their beds at 2:00 a.m. on a Wednesday!

*

The next morning, we meet Chris, again at MadCuppa, to discuss strategy. She greets us with her trademark smirk. 'So, who's A and who's B?'

Pig points to me, saying, 'He's always A – A for *alpha!*'

I ignore him. We get down to tin tacks, and Chris tells us that Kym Wright, newly appointed commander of the Special Emergency Response Team, has already been making her own plans. I quickly remind her that we're the lead, so SERT will be doing what we agree to. I suggest we have a face-to-face with this Commander Wright to ensure we're all on the same page.

Chris admits she does know Commander Wright, but not well. Apparently, she's one of a new wave of senior female officers promoted by Mel Black. 'Mind you,' Chris says, 'my own career has also benefited from the commissioner's fresh ideas and willingness to promote on merit, not on years of service.'

When Chris tries to call Commander Wright, she doesn't pick up, so Chris leaves her a message. Commander Wright sends a text a short time later, saying she's tied up working on strategy for tonight so doesn't have time to meet with us.

Not a good start, I think. Pig purses his lips, clearly having the same thought.

I ask for Commander Wright's number and give her a call myself. Again, she doesn't answer. I send her a text, copying in Mel, saying, 'Commander Wright, as we will be lead in tonight's activities, we need to discuss our joint plans. Otherwise, it may not end well. If unsure of our status, please check with the commissioner.' I sign off as Lead A.

I show Chris my message, so she's aware of what I've said. I don't show Pig – he knows me well enough to guess the gist of what I've said.

'Whilst Commander Wright may not know the background,' I say, 'and is likely to see this as little more than a training exercise, it's probably connected to an ongoing investigation. It may even be an ambush. That's why we'll be leading, and leading from the front.'

Chris asks, 'Connected to Lancaster?'

We don't answer, so she says, 'By the way, Commander Wright is new to SERT – she was inserted into the commander's role from outside the unit. She may be wanting to prove herself in front of her team.'

Another bad sign. As we're about to leave, I say to Chris, 'You don't need to worry about those two thugs that beat you up, either. They won't be doing it again in a hurry.'

She sits back down with a thump, staring at me open-mouthed. 'But they haven't been identified.'

'Not by the police, maybe.'

Now with her 'detective' face on, she looks from Pig to me and back again. We don't give anything away, so she says, 'Well, from me personally, thank you. But if our investigation couldn't track them down, how did you? The DNA from the skin under my fingernails didn't have a match.'

'In some respects, we have better resources than you do, Chris. We're also free of the restrictions you operate under.'

'I guess I'm pleased the bastards have been taught a lesson… or worse?'

I just smile, not letting on what we'd done.

'I've been meaning to ask,' Chris says, 'which of you came into ICU as my "partner?"'

I raise a hand. Chris nods. 'When the nurse said my partner was a hunk, after wondering what I'd missed out on, I determined it had to be one of you.' She smirks again. 'To be honest, I first thought of Pig, but on reflection, you would do as well!'

We all have a laugh, and Chris lays her hand on my arm, saying, 'I appreciated the flowers as well – thanks!'

As Pig and I walk back to the van, I can't help thinking about how all these women fancy Pig over yours truly. Go figure!

We're almost back to our office when I get a message from Commander Wright simply saying they're planning on assembling at Newstead Police Station at 11:00 p.m. and we're welcome to meet them there. I reply immediately (don't worry –

Pig is driving!): 'No. That is too close to the contact point. Please move your assembly to Zillmere Station, which is outside any likely area of reconnaissance. We, A and B, will meet you and DI Harris at 10:30 at the Coffee Club in Skygate Shopping Centre to finalise our plans.'

I again copy in Mel – I simply don't like the fact Commander Wright isn't accepting we have the lead on this. Our lives are most in danger, so I'm not taking any more risks than need be. I even text MGC, asking him to reconfirm with Commissioner Black that we have the lead and SERT are support.

Half an hour later, I get a reply from MGC: 'Done. She is in no doubt you have the lead.' Soon after, I get an acknowledgement from Commander Wright, confirming the 10:30 meeting.

Good. Hopefully, she's finally got the message.

I then decide we should know who we're dealing with, so I text Chris, asking her to call me when she can talk freely. She rings back an hour or so later. I ask her for background on Commander Wright, explaining that I'm trying to understand whether her attitude or her ego will be a bigger issue. Chris gives me a run-down on what she knows, having reached out first to a couple of colleagues who've worked with Commander Wright.

In the meantime, Pig has checked her out on social media. There's no doubt that she's pretty proud of her appointment as SERT Commander; however, some Facebook pages associated with Queensland Police personnel cast doubt on her abilities, questioning her appointment and her lack of suitable background and training.

Neither Pig nor I are very comfortable with what we've learnt. She clearly has an ego, and combine that with her inexperience… well, let's just say we don't want to be worrying about our backup if the fireworks start.

Then again, we can only control so much. Plan for the worst and hope for the best – wise words I live by!

39

A few hours later, Pig and I are sitting at the Coffee Club, only a ten-minute drive away from Newstead and tonight's 'playground', when we see Chris and Commander Wright pull up in the traditional SERT Land Cruiser 200. Commander Wright looks the goods in full SERT uniform, highly polished boots and all. Quite a contrast to Pig and me, dressed as we are in jeans, T-shirts and large (even on us!) hoodies. We'll strip down into our bulletproof outfits a little later.

We introduce ourselves by our respective letters to Commander Wright, who tells us to just call her Kym. *Good start,* I think.

Once coffees are ordered, along with a chicken salad for Kym and simple toasties for Pig and me, we get down to tin tacks. On my iPad, I pull up a map of Newstead with the Gasworks in the middle, laying out a cordon I want SERT to establish. Pig and I had worked the plan up earlier, so all I'm now doing is setting it in place. I don't allow any disagreement or questions, simply stating where Kim will position her teams:

1. Eastbound on Breakfast Creek Road, after the Skyring Terrace intersection.
2. Westbound on Ann Street after the Commercial Road intersection – I stress they are to be watching traffic coming

out of Skyring Terrace, Longlands Road and Commercial Road, so they'll need to pick their viewpoint well.
3. Northbound on Montpelier Road after the Ann Street intersection.
4. The fourth team is to be a 'roamer', cruising around the perimeter, ready to inject themselves if they need to. I suggest this should be their best team.

As Kym writes down the 'choke points' I nominated, Pig comments that the location doesn't provide good exits, making it relatively easy for us to choke the area with only three control points. I nod in agreement, whilst Kym and Chris look at us, a bit mystified, clearly not having thought of the location from that perspective.

I say, 'Kym, whilst I understand your disappointment at not leading this action, we suspect it's an escalation of a long-standing case we've been working on. That's why B here and I have been given the lead. We've been doing this for fifteen years with the army Special Forces. We're used to proactive situations and coming under fire, and believe me, if you aren't used to it, it can be very scary. Even if you are, it still can be terrifying, in fact. We also have the significant advantage of full bulletproof outfits – not just vests, but trousers, sleeves, helmets and face masks. They've been tried and tested a few times, I might add.'

She nods. 'Leo Jackson, one of my senior team members, speaks very highly of you both. He fought with you in Afghanistan.'

Pig and I look at each other. It's Pig who replies, 'You have a good man there.'

'Yes,' Kym says.

I reply, 'I understood our names weren't to be shared?'

Kym pulls a face. 'Sorry about that, but you already have a bit of a reputation with my team after your exploits in Darra last year, so it was too late to keep it as A and B.'

Bugger, I think. *More exposure risks!*

It's time for Kym to go and ready her team, whilst Pig and I need to change into our full kits. We do so in the van, double-checking each other, just as we always have when readying for battle. It's a similar practice to sky jumpers checking each other's harnesses and parachutes. (Yes, we've done quite a few parachute drops over the years, many behind enemy lines, but that's a story for another time!)

All set. After Robert and MGC touch base via our encrypted phones – not using the comms, where SERT and who knows who else will be listening – we head off. We cruise around the Gasworks, getting a feel for the area, on the lookout for anything unusual. We aren't expecting anything to pop up before 2:00 a.m., but we're ready if it does.

Twenty minutes later, we're out of the van, following a signal from the same phone that sent the message. The Australian Cyber Security Centre picked it up and patched it through to us via Robert.

We're following the phone on foot. The fact it hardly stops and just keeps moving at a brisk walk has raised our suspicions, and we're on full alert.

The signal turns right, through a shopping mall, past Noisetto, and away from the open spaces of the Gasworks. I immediately angle wider, slowing down, whilst Pig speeds up a little and stays close to the wall. This makes me more of a target if, as we now suspect, we're walking into an ambush. The attacker will have to show himself before he can see Pig.

As we approach the corner, Pig's tight on it, whereas I'm out in the open space, easier to see. Hopefully, Pig will get him before he gets me. If not – well, I'm in full bulletproof attire.

As we approach the corner, a figure jumps out from behind it and opens up on me with an automatic weapon. Shit, sounds like an AK-47 – dangerous in the right (or, rather, wrong) hands. I drop and roll. When I raise my head, I'm fully stretched on the ground, facing away from the attacker. I know Pig has that angle covered.

The attacker is down. He only got one burst away before Pig dropped him, and none of the shots even hit me.

In my ear, I hear Kym asking, 'Was that automatic weapon fire?'

Neither Pig nor I respond. We're waiting, focused, expecting a second assailant to appear. When nothing happens, I give Pig a grunt and slowly belly-crawl further into the open space, more in line with the alleyway the shooter had appeared from. Once I've moved far enough to have a good view, I see there's no one there.

Odd. You never send in only one assassin.

Then Pig warns me, 'Twelve o'clock!' I swivel round to face Skyring Terrace as a Land Cruiser 200 crawls along the road. It stops, and the streetlight flashes off something metallic hanging out the rear passenger window.

Brrrp. Bugger, here's our second assassin, also firing an AK-47. Every wannabe terrorist and gangster's favourite, from the sound of it. He isn't aiming at me – Pig's probably his target. I return fire. Two shots, and the gun drops out the window and onto the road.

The driver guns the engine and starts to move off at pace. I fire two more shots, one in the front tyre, one in the rear. I don't miss.

The Land Cruiser continues to speed up, even with two flat tyres. Up I jump, arms pumping, sprinting after it. I hear Pig in my earpiece. 'I've got your back.'

It's very difficult to drive any car with one flat, let alone two, and the Land Cruiser's a heavy vehicle, so they won't be getting anywhere quickly. And the SERT teams are still holding the cordon; the Cruiser shouldn't get too far.

Out onto Skyring Terrace. I stay in the left lane, the same as the Land Cruiser. The front passenger leans out, sending another burst of automatic fire in my direction. I'm not too worried. I know how hard it is to send accurate fire directly behind a moving vehicle – you simply can't get enough of an angle.

I'm in full stride now, legs and heart racing. I'm in the zone, and not to win a half-marathon, either. This is what I spent fifteen years training for. These occasions when you need total focus and application.

I'm actually gaining on the Land Cruiser as it lumbers along on its lopsided journey. The shooter's now half out the window, so to be on the safe side, I move over to my right, into the second traffic lane.

They're approaching Ann Street. I know if they turn there, I'll have to stop my pursuit, as it's a busy thoroughfare. There will be too many innocent people around.

I stop, dropping down into the shooter's stance. Knees bent, with a two-handed grip on my trusty H&K handgun, I take aim and draw in a deep, steadying breath. Suddenly, there's a squeal of brakes behind me.

Fuck!

I launch into a forward roll off to my left, out of the traffic lane. Too late.

Bang. Caught across the lower back by a car of some sort. *Shit, that hurt!*

The impact buggers up my roll and I end up flat on my face on the road. I look up. The Cruiser has turned left onto Ann Street, heading towards the city. I also notice a Toyota Prius taxi heading right onto Breakfast Creek Road.

Goddamn Prius, I think. *No wonder I didn't hear it coming. Electric bloody cars.*

I radio in a warning to the SERT teams that the wounded Cruiser is heading their way and wait for them to respond, but the impact seems to have buggered my comms. Gingerly getting to my feet, I head back onto the footpath. A couple of cars give me a wide berth.

I trudge back towards the Gasworks, feeling a little worse for wear. I suspect my ribs are broken. But I can still breathe okay, so hopefully they haven't punctured a lung. Fortunately, my bulletproof outfit prevented any further injury, and my visor has some healthy scratches, so it's easy to think what my face would've looked like without it.

One of the SERT teams rolls past in their Land Cruiser. It stops and backs up the one-way street, against the traffic, hazards flashing. As it comes alongside me, the front window winds down and Leo says, 'You okay?'

We nod a soldier's welcome to each other.

'Got hit by a bloody taxi,' I say.

'You got hit by a car and you're still walking?'

'It was only a Prius,' I say. 'Did you get my call that they turned up Ann Street?'

'We did, but got no reply, hence why we're out here looking for you.'

'Did you catch them, then?'

'No,' he replies. 'Haven't seen hide nor hair of them.'

I stare at him. 'Shit, they would've had to drive straight past you.

You couldn't miss them.'

'As soon as the shooting started, we were instructed to converge on the Gasworks.'

'Fuck!' I say. 'What's the goddamn use of a cordon if it's pulled at the first sign of action? Who pulled you in? No, don't answer that.'

Leo gives me a small, understanding smile as I shake my head, thinking, *Fucking amateurs.* They continue to back up alongside me, hazards on, until I return to the Gasworks, which is now a maze of police and emergency service vehicles, flashing lights everywhere. I head over towards what seems to be the main police contingent, seeing Chris, along with Kym.

Chris spots me and says, 'It appears they got away.'

I say loudly, 'Who pulled the cordon?'

Silence envelops the group. Kym answers, 'I did. Couldn't get any response from you or anyone, so I had no idea what was happening. I took the precaution of converging to ensure you and the surveillance team were safe.'

I respond, 'The whole bloody *point* of the cordon was to ensure they couldn't get away. We set this whole plan in play to capture them, and you went off it at the first sign of action.'

No doubt I'm a sight. When I'm in full bulletproof gear, I know I look huge, and my anger must be showing in my posture. Aggression personified.

I don't care. I'm bloody pissed this has gone wrong. I continue glaring at her, and at the group in general, until her phone rings and she heads away to answer it.

Fuck.

I see Pig sitting near the corner from which the first assassin appeared. That body, now covered in a tarp, is a few metres away from him. A large pool of blood emanates from it, dark red against the white concrete. *The concrete must've been recently washed to be so white*, I think randomly.

I head over and slide down the wall beside him. We fist bump. Leaning by his other side is a remote-controlled skateboard, a phone taped to its surface.

'You alright?' he asks.

'Nah. Got hit from behind by a bloody Prius. Didn't hear him coming – I was just about to shoot the bastards before they turned into Ann Street.'

Pig interrupts. 'Jesus, you sure you don't need an ambulance?'

'I'm a bit bloody sore, but I'm not going to die. The SERTS teams should've got the bastards, but they were pulled off station at the first sound of gunfire. Fucking amateurs.'

Pig shakes his head.

I point to the skateboard and say, 'So, we were following this?'

He nods.

'Shit, so it was definitely a setup.'

He nods again. Getting a lot of nods out of Pig, aren't I?

Just then, a grizzled older paramedic comes over. 'I hear one of you might need some attention?'

As he says this, he glances from Pig to me and back again. At the same time, I think he looks vaguely familiar. Pig jerks his chin towards me. 'He's the one you want.'

The paramedic gets on his knees beside me. 'Well, must be his turn – it was you I stitched up in Darra a few months back, so at least you alternate. You two will need your own personal paramedic if you keep this up. I'm Archie, by the way. I remember you were Julien, but sorry,' he says, looking at me, 'don't recall your name.'

'Mort,' I reply, and we shake hands.

'So, I don't see any blood. What am I looking for?'

Before I can reply, Pig says, 'He was hit by a car.'

Archie raises an eyebrow.

I add, 'It was only a Prius.'

'Still a bloody sight bigger and heavier than you, my friend. Let's have a look at you. Unfasten your top. Also, you might find it more comfortable if you lie down. Sitting like you are is likely adding to your pain.'

It is pretty sore, so I lie down. I unzip my bulletproof vest, then he pulls up my T-shirt so he can probe around my stomach and a bit lower with his gloved fingers. This makes me a little twitchy – us blokes don't like being prodded and poked down in that region!

He asks me to roll over, which I dutifully do. Once he's finished, he says, 'Looks like you have two or three broken ribs. You don't seem to have punctured a lung, so that's a plus. We need to get you to hospital, have them run some X-rays and scans to check you out thoroughly. How's the pain?'

'I've felt worse,' I reply.

'I can give you something for that, at least,' he says.

As he's readying his needle, I sense Pig becoming very alert, his hand reaching for his helmet.

I twist my head around. This is rather awkward, so I painfully scramble back up to a sitting position. Archie stops, keeping his hands well out of my way.

A Pajero SUV is slowly coming along Skyring Terrace, much as the Cruiser had not so many minutes ago. Pig's on his radio. 'Leo, two o'clock. Leo.'

I spot Leo, his hand reaching for his earpiece, which is out of his ear, sitting on his collar. Pig stands, pulling on his helmet.

'Archie, get down,' he says. 'Or better still, get around the corner, out of range.'

Before Pig can again try and raise Leo, not one but two AK-47s start firing, their distinctive rattle ominously loud in the evening air. One is in the rear window of the Pajero, the other way off to our left, out of sight.

Pig is off. I scramble to my feet, shoving my helmet on, zipping up my bulletproof vest and closing two of the clips on its front. These cover the zip to make sure it isn't a weak point. Members of the SERT team and general police are dropping like flies under the withering fire. I dash into the danger zone, taking a different trajectory from Pig. I'm running directly for the Pajero, whilst Pig is sprinting diagonally across its firing range, heading for the second shooter. We only have our handguns, so we have to close the distance before we can be effective. I'm running full steam, screaming like a banshee, wanting to get the attention of the gunmen. That way, hopefully a few of the police will get to cover.

I start taking hits. Two rounds in the chest, one to the left thigh and one to the helmet. Whilst they can't kill me, thanks to my bulletproof gear, I know from experience they'll leave a nice bruise for a few days after.

When I'm about eighty metres from the Pajero, I stop and drop into my shooting position. Bent knees, hunched forward, two-handed grip. One calming breath. Fire. I see Pig dive and roll, coming up in his favoured stance, gun raised, to take out the second attacker.

I'm focused on the gunman in the Pajero. One shot, two. I hear a muffled scream. Shift my aim forward as the Pajero starts to move off. Fire two more shots. Move my aim slightly higher and to the right, aiming for the driver.

No fucking way they're getting away a second time. Not on my watch.

The windscreen smashes. The Pajero comes to a stop. I'm off again, running directly towards its rear, as I see Leo, armed with his assault weapon, approaching it from the front.

The other AK-47 has fallen silent, so I know Pig has taken out that shooter. This doesn't divert my attention from the Pajero. When I reach it, with Leo covering me, I glance in the rear window. No doubt the shooter is dead – he doesn't have a face.

There's no one in the front passenger seat. The driver is slumped over the steering wheel, so I open the door, seeking a pulse in his neck. Nothing. Not surprising, considering the blood covering his face. Looks like another headshot.

As I've said, I don't miss.

Bugger, wouldn't have minded asking him a few questions back behind the shed, I think. But I note his blond hair, and do wonder…

As I don't have working comms, I'm not aware of what's being said and by whom. I now take the time to look around, absorbing what's happened and its bloody aftermath.

Pandemonium abounds. Dead and seriously injured policemen everywhere.

Leo joins me, asking, 'You okay?'

I nod, not yet acknowledging the excruciating pain in my ribs. We trot over to the nearest group of downed police – four SERT officers. As we approach, one slowly starts to move, then a second. I realise some of them have been hit hard in their bulletproof vests, knocking them down and out, but they're alive.

Leo and I immediately start checking them for wounds, applying field dressings as we go. It's not long before Pig joins us. We nod to each other – another good job done. We know the paramedics are right behind us, so we only look after the minor scratches and bruises, flagging any serious injuries for the pros.

There are more of these than I realised, too. Ambulances coming and going, sirens wailing.

After doing what we can, Pig and I head back over to our corner. As I sit down, I feel a stabbing pain in my chest, and not for the first time. Seeing me wince, Pig says, 'Better get Archie back to check on you.'

'Yeah,' I reply. 'It hurts like buggery, but he's got his hands full over there for now.' I nod in the direction of the groups of police, some still sitting, others milling around. 'Did you do a count?'

'There were five bodies covered in sheets, and I've seen at least six being taken away by ambulance, so it's a real bloodbath. A fucking disaster.'

I dig out my phone, saying, 'The shit's already going to be flying, so I'd better ring MGC and report in.' I dial. Engaged. 'Well, I'm sure it won't be long before he calls back.'

I'm not wrong. We've only been sitting for a few minutes when my phone rings.

'Sir,' I answer, 'I have you on speaker with Pig.'

'Sounds like a total disaster up there. Your report, please.'

Taking a deep breath (ouch, that hurts!), I say, 'Sir, you're right, it's a clusterfuck. I'm sure you have a more accurate body count, but we think at least five are dead.'

'Yes,' he says, 'five dead, eight taken to hospital, most with gunshot injuries. Two are in critical condition and being operated on now.'

Silence now as he waits for our summary. We run him through the situation, which is followed by another long pause, as MGC digests it and no doubt compares it to what he's already heard through official channels.

'Mort, you say you were hit by a car. Are you okay?'

'I have a couple of broken ribs, sir.'

Pig pipes up. 'He's been getting a lot worse, sir, so he likely has a punctured lung.'

I give Pig a look, implying, *Telltale!* He smiles back.

'Well, get yourself checked out, please,' MGC says. 'This isn't over by a long shot. There are going to be more bloody questions than answers, and I don't know when I might be needing you both again.' He sighs. 'As you say, this was a set-up, so someone wanted to flush you out.'

I add, 'The timing is likely to have been a response to my interview of Fleming, meaning we'll have to track down Joe, our prison warden's mysterious friend. Besides, Jeffy will certainly be a prime suspect.'

'Yes, that makes the most sense,' MGC says. 'I have to make a couple of calls, so I'll get back to you. Good job, boys. Goodness knows how many more lives would've been lost if you hadn't been there. Thank you.'

With that, he hangs up, as I think, *Wouldn't mind a decent coffee!* Pig has seen Archie and waved him over. Archie approaches, carrying his trusty instrument case. Pig greets him by saying, 'He's gotten worse.'

Archie looks at me, and I grimace. He says, 'No bloody wonder, charging off like that. Wouldn't be surprised if your broken ribs have punctured a lung. Especially carrying the weight of your armour. Down you get – strip the vest off this time, and lie down too.'

I start to do as I'm told, but hear a disturbance from behind me. I'm not sure what's going on, and frankly, it hurts too much to turn sideways, so I don't bother looking. Watching Pig's face for a reaction, I realise whatever is heading our way isn't going to be a happy occasion.

I'm not wrong.

Kym Wright comes striding up into my field of view, clearly beside herself. 'Look what you've done. Five dead, eight in hospital, just because you can't follow procedure. We had a good plan to cover this, but you and your mob had to do it your way. This is all on *you!*'

She breaks down sobbing. Before Pig or I can respond, Archie says, 'Not from what I saw. These two' – he indicates Pig and me – 'saw what was about to happen and ran straight into the gunfire, trying to draw attention to themselves, rather than the rest of you all standing around. Then they took both gunmen down. I couldn't think of a more courageous action they or anyone else could have taken, and they need to be decorated for their bravery. Heroes in anyone's language. Didn't see any of your men even fire a shot.'

Ouch, I think, *he could've left that last sentence off!*

Pig and I nod our thanks to Archie. Not every day someone calls you a hero – he clearly hadn't kept his head down as Pig had instructed.

Kym is still crying. I notice Chris is one of the other officers standing behind her, but it's Pig who puts his arm around her shoulders in comfort. Our empathetic Pig!

Archie resumes his inspection, pushing me down onto the ground, and Chris asks, 'Are you injured, Mort?'

Archie once again responds before I can. 'Yes, several broken ribs and likely a punctured lung now as well. That's what happens when you run full-tilt with broken ribs!' He glances at Kym.

'I suggest you get a sedative to help calm her down. This was a terrible tragedy, and it'll take us all a long time to adjust to what we've seen today.'

Chris replies, 'I will.' Then she guides Kym back over to where they'd all been standing.

Once the crowd has dispersed, Archie gets back to examining me, and I say, 'I might need you to make an official statement about what you saw. Not that I don't trust the cops, but there's going to be a helluva lot of arse-covering after this fuck-up.'

'Happy to,' he replies.

He draws his needle again. It seems like a lifetime ago when he was last poised to inject me. This time, he pushes the needle in. In no time at all, I feel my eyelids getting heavy, and away I go into la-la land.

40

SIX HOURS LATER

I sense a presence. A divine presence.

Then, a sniffle.

Bugger, that spoils it! But I know that sniffle. Suzie is my so-called divine presence – well, she is divine to me! I've heard her sniffle enough to know it's her. Mind you, it's normally whilst she's watching some girly flick on TV, not sitting beside my bed in hospital.

I haven't opened my eyes or moved yet, allowing my senses to reawaken slowly. Thanks to my years of training, I always instinctively wait to get my senses back before allowing anyone to know I'm awake. I don't expect a hostile reception from Suzie, but I suspect it'll be teary.

I open my eyes. Yes, I'm lying in a hospital bed, tubes running into my left arm and directly into my chest. Suzie sits to my right, her hand resting in mine. I squeeze her fingers, turning my head so she can see I'm awake.

Immediately, she bursts into tears, jumping up to give me a lovely hug with the words, 'Oh, Mort.'

Nothing more. Just plenty of sobbing. I hug her tightly, as much as the drips and my tightly bandaged midriff will allow. I'm not admitting to the tears in my eyes, either.

Finally, Suzie draws back. 'There are lots of people outside waiting for you to wake up. Even the general is out there. I insisted they all wait – they can take their turn, after me.' She takes a ragged breath. 'Mort, I love you with all my heart, and' – she gives a crooked smile – 'my body.'

I take the chance to give her a squeeze, as I still have my arm wrapped around her.

'A large part of that love relates to who you are, how you dislike injustices, and are willing to right these wrongs.' She takes another shaky inhale. I keep quiet, as it's clear she has been rehearsing this little speech. Frankly, I'm not sure where it's heading, so I have a small feeling of dread building in the pit of my stomach.

'I know you're immensely brave and very skilled in what you do. I also know you put yourself at risk in your fights against these injustices. That's why we're here in hospital, after all, but I want you to know…' She pauses to regain her composure. 'I don't want to change you, and I never will. I know every time you go out, you may be injured, or worse. But that's who you are, and I love you for it. Whilst I might say a silent prayer for you, I'll never ask you where or what you're doing, as I trust you implicitly. Truth be told, if I knew what you were planning, I would likely worry even more. So, there you go. I just wanted you to know I'm not going to try and pressure you to stop doing what you do. Please keep being you! And please keep yourself safe. I still have plans for you – for *us*.'

I take her hands in mine and look into her eyes, seeing the tears she's trying so hard to stop, then pull her in for a tight embrace. No need for words. But I still say a silent 'thank you' for having been blessed with finding Suzie.

This blissful moment doesn't last, as the door to my hospital room bangs open with a nurse pushing her cart in. Time for more meds and more tests.

As soon as the nurse leaves, Pig pops in. We have a nice man hug as best we can with all my tubes and strapping. A couple of minutes later, MGC and Robert join us.

Back to business. I'm not going to die. The world moves on.

After asking how I'm feeling, MGC says he's going to do a formal interview that Robert will record. He asks Pig and Suzie to leave. Pig acquiesces, but Suzie says, 'No, I'm staying. I am his lawyer as well as his partner and, as you know, I too have signed the Official Secrets Act.'

She spoke quite firmly, getting an appraising eye from MGC, before he nods. 'Fair enough.'

First, MGC brings me up to speed, telling me that Jeffy – that is, Commander Connors of the AFP – was the driver of the Pajero, who I'd killed. The three gunmen were all members of the Melbourne Redskins bikie gang, one of them being Sean Jessop, a friend of Yolanda's. Yolanda has been brought in for questioning and is facing charges as an accessory to murder. MGC also confirms that some colleagues of Jeffy's in the AFP had been concerned about his deteriorating behaviour for a couple of months, but bureaucracies move slowly, so nothing had actually been done about this. He adds that this, of course, will be a critical point in his report to the prime minister.

MGC's questioning lasts nearly an hour, taking more out of me than I care to admit. It's just a more detailed version of my brief report to him on the night. At the end, he confirms it is fully supported by my helmet cam and Pig's separate and independent statement.

'Robert will get this typed up quickly,' MGC says. 'Once we've all signed it, it'll be shared with Queensland Police. Their Ethical Standards Command will want to interview you, as they've naturally been tasked with a full review of the night's proceedings.' He doesn't say it, but it's obvious they'll be looking for a 'fall man' or two.

Suzie insists on seeing a copy of the interview questions, prior to them being given to me, so she can review them first. Like any good lawyer!

A few hours later, Chris slips through the door, carrying some Cadbury Favourites chocolates. On seeing Suzie sitting there, she hesitates, before smirking. 'I thought I should pop in, pretend to be your partner and sneak a kiss, like you did to me!'

Suzie smiles. 'Be my guest.'

So, Chris does, and I add to the moment by commenting, 'Wow, kissed by two hot ladies in the same morning!' bringing laughter all round.

Handing me the chocolates, Chris says, 'I didn't think you were the flowery type, so I brought you these instead. Feel free to open them now – I'm rather partial to them too!'

Of course, being the sweet tooth I am, I start ripping the cellophane off the box. We all help ourselves, whilst Chris brings me up to date with gossip from the police force. Kym Wright has been stood down from her role as SERT Commander whilst the investigations are carried out. Kym has apparently, and not surprisingly, taken the deaths of her team very hard, and is under medical treatment.

They keep me in hospital overnight for observation. My injuries are severe bruising to my lower back and lumbar region, three broken ribs and a punctured lung, so nothing serious or life-threatening. They'd inserted a chest tube to drain air from around the lung, but mainly I just need time to heal. I'm warned to minimise exercise and any unnecessary activity – and that a fifteen-hour flight is likely to become uncomfortable! *At least we're going to be up in the pointy end with lay-flat beds,* I think.

The following morning, two Ethical Standards Command officers have their turn, with Suzie sitting in, of course. Whilst they try to put a different spin on my statement a couple of times, they don't get far. I've had to give enough formal army reports to know to stick to my story, which Suzie had also reinforced a couple of times. It's reassuring seeing her at work. She certainly doesn't take a backward step (like someone I know well!). I also make the point that we have our own copies of the feeds from our helmet cams, implying that attempting to doctor the story wouldn't end well.

Then it's home to Suzie's care. That first night, as she tucks me into bed (I am a patient, remember!), I give her a little present, neatly wrapped with a bow and all. She squeals a little, so I say, 'Come on then, open it!'

She does, and tucked away inside a nice box is a new Amex Platinum Card in her name. I got another squeal. 'Thank you! I hear Amex cards don't have a limit.'

I growl, 'That one does,' but my smile probably gives my lie away.

After a lingering goodnight kiss, Suzie whispers, 'You make sure to follow your medical advice. Otherwise, the sexy nightie I bought for our holiday might be wasted!'

With that thought swirling in my head, I immediately decide to follow the doctor's instructions. To the letter. I reach for the painkillers on the bedside table, ready to do as instructed, instead of trying to tough it out in the usual blokey fashion!

41

FOUR DAYS LATER

Suzie, Pig and I are sitting in the Coffee Club in Brisbane International Airport. Time for a big breath whilst we wait to board our Qantas flight to LA and onward to Vancouver, Canada. We're enjoying one last coffee in Australia before we head off.

Suzie and Pig decide to take a stroll, and I stay to look after the hand luggage. Left to my own devices, my mind wanders back over the last few days.

When I was discharged into Suzie's care, after a couple of days at home, I got a little bored. I wandered down the stairs (slowly!) to see how everyone was doing in the office. Pig, who was on the phone, gave me a wave, whilst Maria came over and hugged me gently.

I headed into the kitchen to make us all a coffee – well, coffee for Pig and me, and a cup of tea for Maria. When I turned around, there was Suzie standing in the kitchen doorway, hands on hips. 'I thought I heard your voice,' she said, and pointed to the stairs. 'Back you go, you know the rules. Come on, off.'

After some (pretend) pleading, she agreed I could sit and enjoy my coffee, though she instructed Maria to ensure I headed back up as soon as I finished it. Jenny also came out of their office to watch. Behind Suzie's back, she gave me a thumbs up with a big smile.

Good to be surrounded by friends!

The next day, MGC had another Pexip call scheduled, so this time I had a legitimate reason for going down to the office. It turned out to be an update on the continuing fallout within the federal police. The AFP Commissioner had tendered his resignation, though MGC implied he hadn't been given an option, and there'd apparently been plenty of scrambling to bring the old Lancaster investigation up to speed as well.

After the call, over coffee, Pig and I discussed the outcome of our inquiries. 'I don't believe Jeffy was party to Liz's death,' I said. 'We haven't found any real connection between him and Lancaster and his crew. I think he just saw the opportunity drop in his lap and jumped in feet first.'

Pig nodded. 'That means we're no closer to knowing why Liz was murdered, or who did it.' He pulled his laptop over, and we made a list of what we do and don't know about Liz's murder.

Benson's statutory declaration, which we believe to be legitimate, implies that he didn't kill Liz. However, car tracking records clearly show Benson's car was used in a deliberate move to ram hers. The only logical reason for this was to kill her. Therefore, *someone* should be facing a murder rap.

Clearly, Lancaster set it up, paying Benson to take the heat. But why would Lancaster do that without being paid? That's the 64-million-dollar question. *Why* did they target Liz?

Why aren't there any photos on her phone? The tech told us there's no way of knowing how they were deleted. It's not hard to do; anyone could've done it if they got hold of her phone.

Someone was monitoring Fleming and the other two bent coppers in Palen Creek Prison – we just don't know who. Yet.

Benson's wife doesn't know anything. We're both a little pleased with how we'd helped her, even if it did cause me some grief with Suzie through my mindless act. No reason Beth should suffer because she was married to an arsehole! His 'fuck buddy' Marissa may know more, though.

Lancaster's old backyard may have something buried in it. Pig was keen to dig it up, but we'd have to wait for the right moment. We also never got a chance to interview his wife. In the days after we killed him, she left the country using a false passport, and withdrew money from one of his Cayman Island accounts before the federal police got around to freezing it. Sloppy buggers!

Knowing Jeffy sabotaged the AFP investigation, we decided we should double-check that the accounts were still frozen. Pig sent Midge an email asking if he could find any information on the accounts, or about where Lancaster's wife is living now.

Louie and Nico are likely out of the picture for a while after the beating we gave them, but we'll continue to monitor their phones. Something might break. Likewise, their mate Dicky is worthy of more attention once we get back from the States. Maybe a lot more, seeing as we can't track him.

Prison Warden Thomas is another open lead. All we can do is keep an eye on him, but with his Joe using a voice synthesiser and a dark web phone, we aren't confident we'll make much progress. Unless we catch a break. Plenty of work to get our teeth into when we get back.

I hear our flight being announced, and see Suzie and Pig heading my way. We're off! Pig will be competing in his first event at the Invictus Games in less than a week. Once these are over, it's off on our Canadian and American trip.

It's a holiday, a well-earnt one at that, so no adventures are planned... but they do seem to just follow us!

If you want to know more, you'll have to wait for the next instalment in Mort's adventures, coming soon. More mayhem and violence from Mort and Pig, this time joined by Suzie, as they pursue their own version of justice in America.

Call it Mortice, American Style – where everything is just BIGGER!

Shawline Publishing Group Pty Ltd
www.shawlinepublishing.com.au

SHAWLINE PUBLISHING GROUP

More great Shawline titles can be found by scanning the QR code below.
New titles also available through Books@Home Pty Ltd.
Subscribe today at www.booksathome.com.au or scan the QR code below.